ARMY GIRLS: OPERATION WINTER WEDDING

FENELLA J. MILLER

B

Boldwood

First published in Great Britain in 2024 by Boldwood Books Ltd.

Copyright © Fenella J. Miller, 2024

Cover Design by Colin Thomas

Cover Photography: Colin Thomas

A CIP catalogue record for this book is available from the British Library.

Paperback ISBN 978-1-80549-280-1

Large Print ISBN 978-1-80549-281-8

Hardback ISBN 978-1-80549-279-5

Ebook ISBN 978-1-80549-282-5

Kindle ISBN 978-1-80549-283-2

Audio CD ISBN 978-1-80549-274-0

MP3 CD ISBN 978-1-80549-275-7

Digital audio download ISBN 978-1-80549-276-4

Boldwood Books Ltd
23 Bowerdean Street
London SW6 3TN
www.boldwoodbooks.com

For my dearest brother, Tony — he doesn't read my books but is an invaluable sounding board and has saved me from several plot disasters.

1

CAMBERLEY BARRACKS, MAY 1942

Clara Felgate was sad to say goodbye to the chums she'd made at basic training but eager to get to Camberley barracks and begin the next step in her ATS career. She was going to train to be a driver in the Auxiliary Territorial Army – the women's army – and eventually become a dispatch rider and would then be using a motorbike. She was thrilled to have this opportunity.

Waterloo Station was noisy with clanking, hissing engines, guards, and porters yelling. Passengers – most of them in uniform – were weaving in and out of the chaos, the servicemen and women carrying heavy canvas kitbags over their shoulders.

Clara headed for the platform where her train

should be waiting, although nowadays trains were late as they had to shunt into sidings to allow troop trains past or wait at signals whilst crucial goods trains took precedence. She was hoping this was the case today, as if her train had left on time then she'd already have missed it.

Someone bumped into her and the ATS girl called out an apology as she ran past. 'Sorry, I'm desperate to catch the Camberley train.'

Clara increased her pace and followed. 'So am I, I'm hoping it's running late.'

Together they tore past the guard, not even pausing to wave their travel warrants.

'In here, ladies, you'll just make it,' an RAF chap yelled from the last remaining open door. 'I'll hold the door for you.'

Clara and her fellow runner threw themselves onto the train seconds before the guard waved his flag and blew his whistle.

'Shut that bloody door, you lot, why don't you?' the irate man yelled.

Clara tumbled through the door on top of her bag, just managing to drag her legs in safely as the helpful pilot slammed it shut behind her.

It took her a few moments to recover her breath and untangle her legs from the handles of her kitbag.

She pushed herself onto her knees and smiled up at the grinning Brylcreem boy. He had the distinctive gold wings over his breast pocket; she'd noticed them as she'd fallen into the train.

'Thanks for that, much appreciated.'

'My pleasure. Derek Goody, flying officer, at your service. Cutting it a bit fine, weren't you?'

'We both thought it would leave twenty minutes late, more fool us. I'm Emma Denny, pleased to meet you, Derek.'

Clara was now upright. 'I'm Clara Felgate. Are you stationed in Surrey?'

The handsome, dark-haired young man shook his head. 'No, a week's crash leave, so visiting the olds.'

She wasn't quite sure to whom he was referring as 'olds' but guessed he meant his parents or possibly his grandparents.

'Crash leave? You don't look injured,' Emma said as she looked him up and down.

'No, all tickety-boo. Pranged the old Hurry, though, and in rather bad odour with the skip, you know.'

Clara smiled and nodded but was actually unclear what he'd been telling them. Pranged must be an RAF term for crashed, a Hurry a Hurricane, and the skip his squadron leader, perhaps.

There were no seats on the train, which wasn't unusual, but the strong canvas kitbags when turned on end made excellent seats. The pilot shuffled up a bit and made room for the two of them and once they were settled, they began chatting.

'Are you off to Camberley barracks where the driving school is? My mother's always talking about you girls learning to drive and making a darned good job of it. So much so, I might add, that she's now insisting my father let her drive the family car as soon there's petrol to go in it.'

'Good for her,' Emma said and slightly turned her back on Clara, leaving her out of the conversation. 'I'm certainly going to learn to be a driver, but I don't know about Clara.'

'I am going on the course but as I can already drive a car, I'm hoping that learning to drive will be a piece of cake,' Clara said. She'd deliberately used this RAF slang term as it was one she'd heard a few times.

Derek moved his kitbag so they were sitting facing each other and she was no longer excluded. His little act of kindness pleased her but it made her a little wary of Emma. Maybe she wasn't going to make a friend of her.

'My family live a mile from the barracks – I hope that means I can toddle over and see both of you?

They've got an excellent NAAFI there and last time I was home, I was allowed to use it.'

Emma spoke first, not allowing Clara to answer. 'I was told they have regular dances, shows and so on at the weekends. I hope you can wangle an invite to one of them.'

'There's already a surplus of men on the base, Emma, so I hardly think a pilot will be welcome,' Clara said smoothly. She smiled at Derek. 'I expect they have socials in the village hall once a month – I used to love playing the party games and then dancing afterwards.'

He took her cue. 'They certainly do, although they hold them in the afternoon now because of the blackout. Mum said there's one this Saturday – I don't suppose you'll get the time off but if you do, Clara, I'll see you there.'

Emma looked peeved that the handsome pilot had invited Clara by name. 'Those sorts of occasions are more for old folk and children, not for someone like me.'

Derek raised his eyebrows and Clara hid her smile. 'Fair enough. Only tea and biscuits served, we have to nip across to the local hostelry for a quick bevy if we want any alcohol.'

'That suits me; I don't really drink. Mind you,

that's not really true as I do enjoy a glass of wine or champagne – not that there's any of that about at the moment,' Clara said.

'Hoity-toity! Gin and it for me, or a nice glass of sweet sherry. I've been known to drink a shandy if nothing else is available,' Emma said, but she was laughing as she spoke. 'I've never been to a social, I've heard about them and they don't sound too bad. It's the kiddies I don't like – for some reason, I just don't get on with them.'

Derek grinned. 'What about the old folk? Don't you get on with them either?'

'No – I mean yes – I like old people. I grew up with my gran and grandad and they're the best.'

Clara thought that Emma might be okay after all. 'My family disowned me when I joined the ATS. I doubt I'll ever see them again.' She wasn't sure why she'd blurted this information out as it wasn't something she usually talked about. Derek was easy to chat to.

'Crikey, that's rough,' Derek said. 'I suppose you were sent away to boarding school when you were very young. There are several chaps in my squadron who had upbringings like that. I went to the local grammar school and thank God I did.'

Emma was looking at Clara strangely. 'My dad

was gassed in the first war, never really recovered and died when I was a nipper. My mum remarried and I wasn't wanted. I was lucky – I was better off where I was,' Emma said.

They continued to chat about the war, the blackout and other less personal topics and by the time the train steamed into Camberley station, they were getting on well. The most important piece of information Clara had gleaned from the pilot was that the barracks were only a mile away.

Emma was actually quite funny, Derek was rather charming, and Clara rather thought the two of them might be interested in each other despite the somewhat tricky start to their acquaintance.

The journey was short – Camberley was only an hour away from London – and the train had clanked into the station still on time. The platform was crowded but Clara, being tall for a girl, was able to see over a lot of the heads.

'There are lots of other ATS girls carrying their full kit. I assume that means there'll be transport for us.'

'I'll say toodle pip, ladies, and hope to see you both at the social if you can get the evening free,' Derek said. Then, with a casual flip of his hand, he strode off swinging his leather suitcase in one hand, leaving them to find their own way.

Emma wasn't impressed. 'Well, that was rather rude, don't you think? I thought we were getting on famously but was obviously wrong otherwise he'd not have sauntered off like that.'

'He was friendly, but not my type. I thought that you two might have a connection, though.'

Emma hefted her kitbag onto her shoulder. 'I did like him, but impossible to make a real attachment if you're in different services.'

As they'd got on the train at the last minute, they had the furthest to walk to the exit. 'We better get a move on. We don't want to be left behind,' Clara said and increased her pace.

They emerged into the forecourt to find a milling crowd of ATS but no transport waiting. Clara appeared to be the only NCO amongst the girls and decided to restore some sort of order.

'Right, ladies, we're ATS, not housewives at a jumble sale. In a column, two abreast, if you please.'

She'd pitched her voice loud enough for them all to hear and they were so used to following orders that they did what she asked without argument. Once they were lined up to her satisfaction, she told them what she had in mind.

'We'll wait for fifteen minutes and if no transport has arrived by then, we'll march to the barracks. We need to be out of the way so we'll assemble over there.' Clara gestured towards a convenient hip-height brick wall which would be perfect for perching on.

Emma had paired up with a jolly woman who was old enough to be any of their mothers. She must be forty at least – but that didn't mean she couldn't be a perfectly competent driver.

Clara propped her bag against the wall and then walked up and down the line of girls introducing herself. Was fifteen minutes long enough to wait? Trains often ran late so the transport might well have factored that information into their arrival.

'We'll give it another ten minutes, ladies. There's a public WC over there so if anyone needs to use the facilities, now would be a good time.'

A handful of khaki-uniformed girls took her advice and rushed across the forecourt. Clara got the rest organised so they were standing side by side. They couldn't march in threes as they would take up too much room on the pavement or the road.

She glanced at her wristwatch. They'd been waiting twenty-five minutes – long enough. Those that had used the loo were now back and ready to march.

They were just exiting the station forecourt when a dilapidated three-tonne lorry turned in. The driver, a grumpy-looking male private, scowled out of his window.

'What the bleeding hell do you think you lot are doing? I ain't driven here in me lunchbreak just to find you lot had buggered off.'

Clara strode up to the lorry. 'Watch your language, private. You don't speak to an NCO like that. You're late. I'll be writing you up for your insolence and tardiness.'

The man opened and shut his mouth like a goldfish. She held her breath, waiting for his angry retort.

'Right, Lance Corporal, begging your pardon. If you care to hop in the back, I'll take you to the barracks.'

'The lazy sod should have got out and opened it for us. That's what drivers do,' Maud – the older lady – said sharply.

'It'll be quicker to do it ourselves. It'll go on his chargesheet, don't worry,' Clara replied.

There was no need for her to issue orders as two of the girls had already unhooked the tailgate, rattled back the canvas that covered the entrance and without waiting for her permission, threw their bags in and jumped up after them.

Five minutes after the lorry had arrived, the bags were safely in the centre space and the girls were sitting on either side on the slippery wooden benches.

Clara had chosen to sit by the exit and called to the girls sitting closest to the front of the vehicle. 'Reach through the canvas and bang on the cab, let him know we're ready to leave.'

The lorry lurched off. 'Brace your feet against the bags, girls; I think he's likely to try and dislodge us at every opportunity. He obviously doesn't like the ATS.'

Her prediction was correct but nobody ended up in a tangle of arms and legs and kitbags in the centre of the vehicle. It was only a little over a mile from the station so they should have arrived in less than fifteen minutes; it was over half an hour and they were still travelling. Clara picked her way through the bags, pushed aside the canvas at the rear of the lorry and then stretched over to thump forcefully on the cracked glass that separated them from the driver. Her fist hit the partition directly behind the driver's head.

Her signal to stop was ignored, although she knew he'd heard her. Unless she'd been misinformed, and they weren't actually going to the driving school at Camberley, their driver was taking them on a very circuitous route.

The girl whose feet she'd just stepped on tugged at the back of her uniform jacket. 'Here, what's going on? We should have been there ages ago.'

'I know, that's why I'm trying to get the wretched man to stop. I know he heard me banging.' Clara looked round to see to whom she was speaking. The private introduced herself as Gladys, a tough-looking girl from the East End of London.

'Give over, I'll stop the bugger.'

Not waiting for permission to do so, Gladys produced what looked suspiciously like a something a burglar would carry in order to break into a house. Assisted by her friend, she leaned across the gap and put the end of the metal tool into the edge of the glass and levered it out.

Clara was impressed and concerned in equal measures by Gladys and her friend. She nodded her thanks and took a firm grip on the shuddering chassis.

'You will halt this vehicle now, driver, that's an order,' she yelled into his ear.

If Gladys hadn't been hanging onto the back of her jacket, Clara would have ended up in the cab on top of him. He slammed on the brakes, throwing everybody from the benches. The rear of the vehicle was in chaos.

'Is anybody hurt? If you think you've broken a limb, remain where you are. Everyone else carefully get back on the benches.'

It took several minutes to sort things out but fortunately, nobody had been seriously hurt. The driver should have come around to the rear of the vehicle to check for himself, to investigate why he'd been told to do an emergency stop. He hadn't done so.

The girls sitting at the other end already had the pins out of the tailgate and it was dangling down. Clara scrambled over the kitbags and dropped to the ground. If she hadn't been leaning against the lorry, she thought she might have slid to the floor.

Where on earth were they? They certainly weren't where they were supposed to be. There were fields and trees in every direction and absolutely no sign of Camberley barracks.

She was joined on the ground by the first of the girls. 'Bleeding hell, I ain't seen nothing like this before. Where are all the bleeding houses?' Gladys said in disgust.

'I've no idea. I'm going to talk to the driver and see what on earth he's playing at.'

Emma appeared beside her. 'I just had a look,

Clara, silly sod has knocked himself out on the steering wheel so you can't ask him.'

* * *

By the time Clara had organised a stretcher party and moved the unconscious driver with a nasty-looking lump on his forehead to the rear of the lorry, she had some idea where they were but not why they were there.

One of the girls had clambered on top of the cab and had been able to see what looked like the barracks a few miles away across the fields.

'Right, everybody back inside. I've never driven a lorry, but I've driven a tractor and a car so I'm pretty sure driving this won't be too complicated. Emma, I need you to navigate. If you hang out of the window, you should be able to keep directing me towards the barracks.'

Nobody argued and, showing more confidence than she actually felt, Clara took her place behind the steering wheel. They left the canvas at the rear of the vehicle open so the girls sitting there could also help with the navigation.

Her finger was shaking as she pressed the button that started the engine. It spluttered into life immediately. She stalled twice before getting the hang of the clutch but once they were moving, it was easier.

An hour after taking the driver's place, she pulled up beside the guards at the gate to the barracks. Clara had already rehearsed how she was going to explain why she was driving but to her astonishment, the guard just nodded and waved them through.

She almost refused as she'd no idea where she was supposed to be going but thought it would be easier to explain what had happened when they were safely inside the perimeter.

'That looks like that could be the admin building, Clara,' Emma said, pointing to a substantial brick-built building a hundred yards ahead.

There were dozens of male soldiers marching about but their arrival was being ignored.

'Where are the ATS? I've a horrible feeling we've come in the wrong gate,' Clara said.

'Crikey, I think you're right. Shall I ask one of the NCSs over there?' Emma suggested.

Clara edged the lorry forward and Emma leaned out of the window.

'Excuse me, Corp, we need the medical centre, and also directions to the ATS admin building.'

The soldier nodded. 'Turn left just ahead and the hospital is on your right. Then turn left at the end of the road and keep going. Your lot are down there somewhere. We aren't allowed anywhere near.' The man grinned. 'You've come in the main gates; ATS vehicles have their own gate at the rear of the barracks.'

'Thanks, Corp. We weren't stopped at the gate so came in.'

'We have ATS drivers working here because of the driving school.'

Clara nodded her thanks and drove smoothly to the small hospital. Emma had the door open before they were quite stationary.

'I'll fetch the medics,' she said as she jumped down.

The semiconscious driver was rushed inside and as soon as Emma was safely beside her, Clara drove away. She'd make her report to her own officers. She wanted to deliver the girls immediately. They must be horribly late.

With some trepidation, Clara followed the corporal's instructions and on turning into the ATS section, she immediately saw the only brick-built buildings. This would be where the officers would be found. Now to face the music.

2

Clara drove the lorry across the swept gravel square
and down a narrow lane on the far side. From her
vantage point, she'd seen the tops of other vehicles as
well as a large, open-fronted building that she
thought was probably where they learnt how to
maintain an engine.

'I want to march the girls in a column when we
report at the admin building,' she told Emma, who
was looking somewhat surprised they hadn't stopped.

'Makes sense to appear in an orderly fashion.'
She was craning out of the window and sat back with
a sigh. 'I think I've just seen where we're going to be
billeted. There's a huddle of huts and what's obvi-

ously the latrines and ablutions just behind the admin block.'

'I'm sure it won't be any worse than places we've already lived in. At least we won't have to deal with scorpions in our shoes.'

Emma laughed. 'My brother's in Egypt and he's told us all about having to check their boots every morning.'

A sergeant was gawping at the lorry as Clara, with more luck than judgement, parked it neatly in front of him.

'I'll go and speak to him; would you get the girls out whilst I'm doing so?'

'Good luck with that; he looks a miserable old bloke and not impressed by your driving either.'

Clara made sure the handbrake was on, the lorry in first gear and then jumped nimbly to the ground.

'Sergeant, Lance Corporal Felgate reporting with...'

He waved a hand, indicating that she was to stop talking, and then, shaking his head, he actually walked over and peered into the cab as if expecting to find the missing male driver there.

Whilst he was recovering from the shock of having his precious lorry arrive driven by an un-trained female, Clara was pleased to see the girls were tumbling out of the back of the lorry and shuffling into a neat column.

'Where's the driver?'

'I was about to explain, Sergeant, that the driver knocked himself out on the steering wheel in the middle of nowhere and as I can already drive a car and a tractor, it made sense for me to take over.'

The sergeant shook his head, puffed out his cheeks and then roared with laughter. 'Well, bugger me, this is a turn-up for the books. Seems like you don't need any training, Lance Corporal Felgate, if you managed to get this old girl back here in one piece.'

He pointed to the path, neatly lined by white-painted stones, that led between two of the brick-built administrative buildings. 'Take your girls through there, Felgate. I warn you, there'll be a reception committee. I'm not sure if you'll be congratulated or put on a charge.'

Clara could hear him chuckling to himself as he wandered back into the garage and yelled for someone to park the lorry in the correct place.

'Okay, ladies, none of this was your fault. Heads high, shoulders back, let's show them we're the best intake they've ever had.'

Whatever the outcome of this adventure, it had

welded this group of disparate women into a solid team. She marched at the head of the column and didn't need to glance over her shoulder to know they were following her lead perfectly. One thing every trainee had to master fast was the ability to drill, to march correctly and to follow orders.

It was just good luck that this group was an uneven number so her being in front didn't leave one girl marching alone. She halted them directly outside the entrance to the block.

'At ease, girls, I'll let them know we're here.' Clara marched into the building and was met by an unsmiling officer – a senior commander. She saluted smartly.

'Lance Corporal Felgate, ma'am, and fourteen privates reporting for driver training.'

'Not only are you two hours late; your driver brought you through the wrong entrance. Exactly what is going on?'

'I beg your pardon, ma'am, but would it be possible for somebody to take the girls to their billets so they can get settled? I will remain here, of course, and give you a full report.'

Something flickered in the woman's expression and she looked slightly less formidable. She must be able to see the girls lined up outside and know that it was hours since they'd eaten or, more importantly, had access to a WC.

'Yes, Felgate. That makes sense.'

The senior commander sent a corporal out to take care of this and then pointed to the open door of what was presumably her office.

'There's a WC just behind you. Join me when you're ready.'

With considerable relief, Clara used the facilities, washed her face and hands and straightened her cap. Then she checked her stocking seams were straight and her shoes still highly polished. Satisfied she looked as she should, she marched into the office.

'Excellent, Felgate. Sit down and tell me exactly what happened.'

Halfway through her explanation of this extraordinary set of circumstances, an orderly came in carrying a tray with a very welcome pot of tea, sandwiches and cakes.

To her surprise, the senior commander poured out the tea, piled a plate with food and placed it in front of Clara.

'Whilst you help yourself, my dear, I'm going to enquire how the driver's doing.' After a few minutes on the telephone, she smiled and replaced the receiver. 'He has a slight concussion, nothing worse, thank goodness. However, once he's recovered from that, he's going to be in for a rather unpleasant few weeks after his disgraceful behaviour.'

The remainder of the interview was informal. Clara left the office relieved she wasn't going to be put on a charge and went in search of her cohort.

* * *

The accommodation for them was a wooden hut but to her dismay, when she arrived, Clara discovered there was no spare bed for her. The building was large enough for an extra one to be brought in. There was a big table with chairs around it at one end, a cast-iron, pot-bellied stove in the centre and the beds were arranged head to toe alternately down each side. There was a small locker positioned at the head end of each which didn't leave a lot of room to get in and out. There was also a row of metal wardrobes against the walls. She frowned. Perhaps another bed in here just wouldn't work.

'We're lucky, this building has only just been fitted out. The girls just finishing their course are bil-leted off camp,' Emma told her. 'Not sure why we're a bed short.'

'Never mind, I'll find one somewhere. They knew

how many of us were coming so there must be one for me in another hut,' Clara told them.

'It ain't right; you should be in with us,' Gladys said and the others echoed her disapproval.

It was Emma who came up with an explanation, one Clara should have thought of for herself. 'You're a junior NCO; I reckon you sleep with them, not in here with us.'

'That could be the explanation. Everything in here is tickety-boo so go in search of your tea. I take it you were told where the mess is?'

'It's the long, wooden building opposite the admin block. There's a nice rec room too, even got ping-pong,' Emma said happily.

'Where are the lecture rooms?' Clara asked.

'Buggered if I know,' Gladys said. 'They never told us that. I expect we'll find out soon enough.'

Clara followed them but continued to the main block, leaving them to join the other platoon of ATS learner drivers just completing their course. It was a gruelling twelve weeks and she was aware that a substantial proportion of the candidates were likely to fail and be returned to basic training or to be posted somewhere else.

She was hailed by a willowy, fair-haired corporal as she approached the building.

'Good show, I was just coming to see you. Senior Commander Reynolds has promoted you to corporal with immediate effect. I'm to take you to the stores to collect your stripes and then you're going to share with me. Not much, but better than the horrible hut your girls have to live in.' She smiled. 'I'm permanently based here in the stores.'

Clara barely took in what she'd been told. 'Golly, I didn't expect stripes. I'm Clara, by the way. I suppose you've heard about what happened to us.'

'I did; it's the talk of the barracks. That driver you had shouldn't have been on duty. He's a bit unstable and was about to be invalided out.'

'I did think his behaviour was peculiar. I suppose we'll never know what he intended to do with us out in the countryside.'

'If you hadn't known how to drive, you'd probably still be out there waiting to be found. I'm Ellen, pleased to meet you.' She grinned. 'I'm not surprised you got an extra stripe; I think you deserve a medal.'

Ellen led Clara though the maze of paths and across the main barrack square to the huge building that housed the general stores. She handed over the slip of paper Ellen had given her and was given a small packet in return. She had her sewing kit, her hussif, and would attach the stripes as soon as she could.

'I expect they'll want to send you off to OCTU when you leave here,' Ellen said.

'I don't want to be an officer. I want to be a dispatch rider and go abroad with the invasion force.'

'If you want to go abroad then you should ask to drive an ambulance. The FANY lot are the ones who drive them.'

'Aren't they now part of the ATS?' Clara asked.

'They are but a lot of them still think they're a cut above us. Do you speak French?'

'I do; I'm not fluent but I can get by. Why?'

'They'll snap you up when they know that. Why don't you learn to drive an ambulance, do the St John's course, and then do the dispatch rider training?'

'I'll think about it.' This was definitely something she would investigate.

Ellen stopped in front of a small huddle of huts, little more than sheds really. 'This is where the NCOs are billeted. Officers are in the main block.' She pushed open the door of the one she was standing in front of. 'Home sweet home.'

Clara stepped in. There were two iron bedsteads but both with real mattresses and, unlike the beds the privates used, they were made up ready to sleep in. There were a dozen hooks on the wall, half already in use, a shared chest of drawers and that was it. There was just enough room to open and close the door.

'Someone's already brought my kitbag over for me,' she pointed out, touched at this gesture from one of her troop.

'I've got the top two drawers; the bottom two are yours. The unused hooks are yours as well,' Ellen said. 'I'm going to run; I might just be in time for tea if I hurry.'

Clara was just hanging her greatcoat and cape up when there was a knock on the door. 'Come in,' she called.

The door flew open and Emma burst in. 'Blimey, this is a bit pokey. We've got more room in our hut.' She waved a similar packet to the one Clara had just collected. 'Thanks to you getting me to help, I've been made up to lance corp.'

Clara beamed and stepped forward to hug her new friend. 'You deserve it. Isn't this fun? If we'd marched to the base, we'd have missed all the excitement and neither of us would have been promoted.'

* * *

The next day, Clara escorted her group to the stores before they went to the mess for breakfast where they were given the necessary items needed to become a driver. She was now the proud owner of battledress trousers, shirt and battledress blouse. On top of that, she had a sweater, scarf and a balaclava helmet. These extras augmented the kit she already had.

She was keen to join her charges for breakfast suitably dressed. She'd already spent an hour with a sergeant being told what her duties would be and realised she was going to be spending most of her free time learning everything involved with being an NCO. Usually, a private was sent off to do a course, a cadre, before being given their stripes.

She greeted each girl by name as she walked past them and only got it wrong once. 'Everyone looks well rested and immaculately turned out. It's not my job to check your billet every day but I'm sure I'd find it as it should be.'

Gladys tugged at her sleeve as she walked past. 'Are we in competition with the other lot, Corp? I like a bit of competition.'

'Not directly, it's not like in basic training. However, I'm sure they'll be as keen as us to be the best group here.'

Clara moved on, chatting and smiling, and was

satisfied nobody was unhappy and all seemed to have settled in well. The ATS obviously had their own facilities and there must be around fifty of them. Thirty or so trainees and at least twenty general duties girls no doubt permanently based at Camberley – probably clerks, orderlies and cooks.

She finished her porridge and a slice of toast before standing up and waving the list she'd been given by the sergeant at the girls around the table.

'I've got this week's itinerary; do you want me to read it out or shall I just hand it round?' Clara called down the noisy table.

The consensus was to pass it round so they could read it themselves whilst they ate. Emma was sitting next to her at the end of the table.

'After you've all seen it, I'm going to pin it up in the rec room. We've got an introductory lecture which explains what we're going to be doing and then straight to the garage.'

Emma read it first and then passed it on. Clara needed some information from her. 'I've got to divide the girls into groups of three – I'm hoping you can at least give me an idea of whom not to put together as you know them better than I do.'

'Not alphabetically? That makes a change. There

are a couple of girls who don't get on so better to keep them apart.'

Clara made a note of their names in the little black notebook she'd been given.

'Which group are you going to put yourself in?'

'Actually, after the lecture, I've got a preliminary driving test. If I can pass that then I don't have to do the basic training.'

Instead of being annoyed, Emma nodded. 'That makes perfect sense; no point in you doing something you already know. What will you do instead?'

'I have to prove proficient at driving all the vehicles here – I know I'll be fine with any car or van but I do need a lot more practice with a lorry. I doubt very much I could reverse that safely at the moment.'

An orderly came round with a large, enamel teapot and topped their mugs up. 'We've got PT once a week, no regular drill and a remarkable amount of free time. There's the usual one night a week doing repairs and renovations to our kit and bath night but apart from that, we have the evenings off to study,' Clara said.

'I noticed there's a dance at the NAAFI on Friday night, church parade on Sunday morning, but it appears we can leave the base on Saturday if we want,'

Emma said, a little embarrassed. 'You seemed keen to go to the social. Can I come with you?'

'I expect most of the girls will go. I'm not sure that I will – I've got a lot of pamphlets and so on to read and digest. I've been promoted suddenly so I've got to learn it all in my spare time.'

'You will come to the dance, though?'

Clara shrugged. She didn't want to seem stand-offish and was well aware that if she wanted to fit in, she needed to at least join in some of the recreational activities. She did like to dance but this would be an event for other ranks only and she'd a good idea how some of the men would behave.

'Probably not this one, but I'll certainly come to the next. I won't be content until I'm sure I know everything I should. There are things you need to know about your new position, too. I'd be happy to talk you through them. In fact, I think it's probably my job to do so.'

'I tell you what, when you're up to speed, you can fill me in. Not everybody's like you, Clara; some of us want to have a bit of fun in our lives.'

Maybe Emma's promotion was premature as she didn't seem to have the right attitude for somebody with extra responsibilities. It was too soon to make such a judgement, Clara thought, and decided she would be better off sorting the lists rather than finding fault with Emma. Possibly Emma was right; life shouldn't be all work even if there was a war on.

'Excuse me, Emma, but I need to get these lists done as I've got to put everyone in their groups at the end of the lecture. Thank you for the heads up about the two that don't get on.'

Clara collected her irons and rinsed them in the bucket of tepid water by the door and then hurried to the ablutions block where she could give them a proper wash and dry them. Officers didn't have to carry their own cutlery and mug around with them and had an orderly to take care of their quarters and sort out their laundry but this didn't appeal to her.

She was determined to get herself attached to an infantry brigade and go abroad with them when the time came to take Europe back from the Nazis. Hopefully as a dispatch rider but if not, as an ambulance driver if that was what it would take. This had been her intention ever since she'd joined up. It was why she hadn't gone for a higher status technical trade like her friends but had opted for driving.

* * *

The lecture was more an information session, making sure that all the girls knew what was expected of them, how much free time they had, and what recreational facilities there were on the base and in Camberley itself.

The other squad didn't have their own NCOs so an ATS sergeant was looking after them. Clara told her squad which group they were in and that they now had to report to the garage.

'At the moment, there aren't enough instructors, which is why you're in groups of three. You'll have to take it in turns to learn to drive. In the morning, you'll go out in the car and in the afternoon, you're in the workshop.'

'What about the PT and lectures?' Gladys asked.

'That starts next week. This week is about getting to grips, literally, with driving and what's under the bonnet.'

Emma pointed out what no doubt the others were thinking. 'When do you get to learn mechanics, Corp? You have to be able to fix your vehicle as well as drive it.'

'I'm only involved with the tests today and then I'll be spending all my time learning how things work.'

Once a driver was trained and posted, she'd be expected to service the vehicle she drove and this was an aspect of the job that Clara was eager to learn.

3

Clara left the lecture and went in search of the driving instructor who was going to assess her abilities. This was more complicated than she'd expected as none of those she asked knew anything about this arrangement. Eventually, she got into conversation with a junior subaltern, the ATS equivalent of a first lieutenant, who seemed only too happy to talk.

'I'm afraid I can't help you find the instructor, Corporal, but I'd be happy to give you a tour of the camp and help you look. Do you know if it's an ATS or regular army person that you're looking for?'

'I've no idea, ma'am, but I'll be happy to explore this huge camp. I don't want my girls getting lost and getting into difficulties with inebriated soldiers.'

The officer smiled and nodded and didn't deny this could happen, which was a concern. 'Although there are probably a hundred or more ATS working here, most of them are billeted off base for that very reason. Only one squad of girls being trained as drivers are billeted here and the other squad are living in a private house.'

'Good heavens, I'm surprised that as they were here first, they aren't the ones living in the hut. Mind you, it's quite possible their billet is a lot more luxurious than what's available here.'

The young officer, who still remained anonymous as she'd not volunteered her name, pulled a face. 'Regrettably, the girls billeted off camp are obliged to walk across the golf course in order to get here and they have no hot water and no heating. That doesn't matter at the moment but I imagine it's really unpleasant in the winter.'

Clara smiled at the thought of those poor girls falling headfirst into bunkers and walking in their heavy shoes across the greens. They certainly wouldn't be popular with those that could still afford to play golf.

'I wonder why the golf course hasn't been ploughed up like other green areas,' she said to the officer.

'It takes years to get the links fit to play on so I expect someone wealthy and important has insisted that the links be left intact. I don't know about you, Corporal, but I hope the girls are making it impossible for them to play a satisfactory round.'

This comment surprised Clara as in her limited experience, officers didn't express opinions of a political nature, but she wholeheartedly agreed with this sentiment. She really wanted to know this officer's name.

'I'm Clara Felgate and I agree with you.'

'Actually, I know who you were; word has travelled about your rather unusual arrival yesterday and of your immediate promotion. I'm Sylvia Prescott.'

They nodded and smiled at each other. If all officers were like Sylvia then Clara might reconsider her decision not to join their ranks.

They marched around the enormous camp, not in the areas where the soldiers resided, but at the end of this tour, Clara knew where the cinema was and the gym and other places she and her troop would have to visit. They finished the long walk in the excellent NAAFI.

'I've got to leave you here, Corporal; it wouldn't do for us to be seen socialising.'

Clara promptly saluted and the action was returned, then she was left to either find her way back to the workshop or treat herself to a much-needed mug of tea. Unfortunately, she hadn't brought her irons with her.

She smiled at her error. Here everything was supplied, it was only in their own mess that they had to provide cutlery and mugs. She looked longingly at the counter and then with a sigh, hurried out and returned to the garage. A tall officer, a captain she thought from his epaulettes, was waiting for her and he wasn't happy, but looked livid.

'Where the hell have you been all morning, Corporal?'

She saluted but he ignored this and continued to glare down at her. He was quite old, probably almost thirty, had dark hair, regular features and the most terrifying slate-grey eyes that were boring into her.

'I apologise if I've kept you waiting, sir—'

He didn't allow her to finish.

'Waiting? I've been stuck here for the best part of an hour. I didn't want this job; I have better things to do than drive around the countryside with a female.'

If he'd been a horse, steam would have been puffing out of his nostrils. She was about to attempt to explain where she'd been, but again, he didn't give her the chance.

'It might have escaped your notice, Felgate, but there's a war on.' He pointed not to an Austin but to what was obviously his own vehicle, a dark-blue, open-topped sports car. 'Get in, and if you so much as scratch my car, I'll be very unhappy.'

Clara should have meekly trotted across to the expensive, highly unsuitable car and shown him just how good a driver she was. But instead, she looked up at him.

'Then I've nothing to worry about, sir, as that will be an improvement on your present state of mind.'

She didn't wait for his reply but ran across to the car, jumped over the driver's door and dropped into the seat. She had the engine purring sweetly by the time he arrived in similar fashion in the adjacent seat.

She didn't dare look at him, but released the clutch and moved off smoothly but rather faster than was wise. There was a sharp intake of breath from beside her and Clara laughed. She was already in so much trouble that whatever happened on the drive wouldn't matter.

Her cap flew off as the powerful car roared down the narrow lane that ran along the rear of the camp. She was in her element. Her uncle had owned exactly the same Alfa Romeo and she'd driven it many times.

She wasn't reckless, so slowed the car and turned onto the larger road at a sensible speed. After ten minutes, she indicated and pulled onto a clearing at the side of the road. She braced herself, waiting for the bad-tempered officer to let rip. He remained ominously silent. After a few seconds, she risked a sideways glance at him. Her mouth rounded. He was smiling.

'You've driven one of these before.' It was a statement, not a question.

She nodded and only then remembered she was without her cap. Nervously, she touched her head as if it might somehow miraculously reappear.

'Turn round here, Corporal, and take us back. I know exactly where your missing hat is located.' He laughed. 'You've passed your test.'

She smiled, delighted that she hadn't upset this fierce officer by what he might have considered her reckless driving.

The car had excellent lock and she completed the manoeuvre expertly, then, bubbling with excitement, she took them back to the camp. She'd expected to be failed, deserved to be put on a charge for insubordination, but for some reason, the captain had found her antics amusing.

As she was slowing down to turn into the driving school, he suddenly shouted, 'Stop.'

Thinking this was a test of her emergency stopping ability, she slammed on the brakes. If he hadn't reacted instantly and braced his arms on the dashboard, he would have been thrown forward.

'What the f... What the dickens are you playing at? I almost pitched over the windscreen.' Now he was certainly not amused and was back to being the terrifying officer she'd met earlier.

Her knuckles were white on the steering wheel and for a second, her tongue seemed to be stuck to the roof of the mouth and she couldn't answer. 'I thought you wanted me to do an emergency stop, sir. I'm sorry...'

'Fair enough, my fault. I was just telling you your missing headgear is in the hedge just there.'

She was about to jump out and get it but he forestalled her. 'No, stay where you are, I'll get it. Take the car in and park it where you found it.'

Surprised but pleased, Clara did as he ordered. Her heart was still thumping and her hands were clammy. It was a good thing he'd already said she'd passed the driving test as after that performance, he would probably have failed her. She could have seriously injured him.

She barely had time to scramble out of the car before he strode in and solemnly handed her the missing cap. 'Thank you, sir. I really enjoyed driving your car.'

'Did you indeed? Can you drive anything else?'

'Well, I did drive the lorry back, but I doubt I could reverse it safely. I can drive a tractor and a motorbike and, as I've just demonstrated, a car.'

'If you learn how to reverse a lorry then you could become an instructor. They don't have enough of them here and drivers are desperately needed, particularly for convoy work.'

'I'd also like to become proficient at driving an ambulance, although I expect it's a lot easier than a lorry and not much harder than a car.' He frowned and hastily, she continued. 'Of course, I'd be honoured to become a junior instructor if that's going to be helpful.'

Whilst she was talking, she'd been reattaching her cap and not looking directly at him, which was almost certainly another black mark.

'No time like the present, Corporal; there's a lorry parked over there. I've missed my meeting so I've got another hour to waste here.'

Clara looked at the lorry and back at him, not sure if he was serious or not. His eyes flashed dangerously and belatedly she realised he'd meant that she should actually get in the lorry.

She took off like a startled rabbit and was halfway into the cab before he reacted. She hastily slammed the door, adjusted the seat, and tried to look confident and as if she was eager to begin. It was all very well demonstrating her skills as a car driver, but she just knew she was going to make a complete fool of herself behind the wheel of a lorry if he was sitting next to her glaring at her in that unnerving way.

She didn't dare look at him as he settled beside her. They sat like a pair of stuffed dummies, neither of them speaking. She could hear him breathing but didn't dare look across.

'Felgate, I said I had an hour, not a week to spare. For God's sake, get a move on. You do know where the reverse gear is, I take it?'

Clara assumed this was a rhetorical question so didn't answer. Then she did. 'I don't need to reverse here, sir; I need to go forwards.'

He laughed and she relaxed. 'Then, Felgate, please do so. I'm eager to see your prowess behind the wheel of this vehicle.'

By some miracle, she managed to move without stalling or crashing the gears. 'Which direction, sir?'

'Turn right, then drive for about a mile and turn left into the field.'

* * *

Captain Peregrine Harrow stretched out his legs and swivelled slightly so he could watch this extraordinary young woman handle the lorry. He'd volunteered to test her driving skills after hearing about her stepping in and bringing her squad safely to the camp yesterday.

He was temporarily at Camberley in order to select half a dozen suitable ATS drivers who were needed to transport secret documents between senior officers, the Americans and the PM as well as driving VIPs about the country. He'd thought this girl was exactly the sort of driver he was looking for but now he wasn't so sure. She was far too ready to offer unwanted comments, and this wouldn't go down well with the important men she'd be driving.

The lorry was heavy to drive but she was handing it easily. She was stronger than she looked. There were no electric indicators on this old vehicle so she did the correct hand signal and turned into the field.

He pointed to the white-painted stones set out to mark a route that all learners followed.

'Right, I want you to reverse into that turning. You'll have to use your mirrors.'

She nodded but didn't answer and he heard what sounded suspiciously like a snort. He ignored it.

It took her two attempts to complete the manoeuvre without hitting any stones but he'd expected her to make more errors than she had.

'Good. Have you done any night driving? Driven in a convoy?'

This time, she turned to look at him. 'Of course I haven't, sir. What civilian would drive in a convoy?'

She, fortunately for her, didn't add 'for heaven's sake' but it was implied. Time to establish exactly who was in charge and how a lowly NCO should speak to an officer.

'Felgate, do you know to whom you're speaking?' As soon as he said this, he realised it was a mistake.

She shook her head and smiled sweetly. 'Actually, I don't, sir, as you haven't introduced yourself. I know you're a captain, but not who you are.'

He took a deep breath. He'd asked for that and it wouldn't be fair to snarl at her. 'I am Peregrine Harrow. *Captain* Peregrine Harrow.' He emphasised the word captain and her smile vanished.

'I apologise if I've offended you, Captain; it wasn't intentional.'

His anger evaporated. She wasn't an insolent squaddie but a sweet little ATS corporal. 'Good, I'm glad we understand each other. I was tempted to turf you out of the lorry and make you walk back.'

She opened her mouth as if about to speak but then hastily closed it again. He laughed. 'Go on, Felgate, you have my permission to speak freely. What were you going to say?'

'I was going to say, sir, that I'd much rather walk than drive this horrible lorry.'

'No, you weren't. You were going to say that you doubted I was capable of driving it.'

Her cheeks coloured and she nodded. 'I was. How one earth did you know that?'

He raised an eyebrow and she quickly added the word *sir*.

'Drive around the field, following the arrows, and then take me back. You said that you can ride a motorbike. I would like to see you do that before we finish.'

* * *

Felgate was as proficient on a motorbike as she had been in the car and the lorry. They'd missed lunch but the NAAFI was always open so she could find something to eat and drink there. He could get something in the officers' mess.

'You are now passed to instruct in daytime driving but need to get some experience driving at night. I'll arrange for that. Thank you, I've enjoyed this morning.'

She saluted and he walked off, wondering why he'd thanked her. She was there to follow orders and he was there to give them. Thanks weren't needed.

By the time he entered the mess, he'd forgotten about the girl and sent an orderly to find him some sandwiches and a pot of coffee. This was now available to officers as the Yanks were supplying it.

'I'll be in my office; bring it there.'

The office wasn't his but belonged to a captain on leave. Perry got out his notebook and began to scribble down the things that had transpired that morning. Despite his personal reservations about the suitability of this ATS girl, she was, on paper, a perfect candidate.

His food duly arrived, and he was munching through it when a slightly inebriated lieutenant burst in. 'I say, Perry old bean, when's Adrian going to be back? He owes me a guinea and I need it.'

The only acceptable thing about this buffoon's interruption was that Selbourne had remembered not to call him Peregrine. He hated his name and wasn't fond of Perry either, but it was better than the alternative.

'James, I'm only here for two weeks so presumably Adrian, whoever he might be, will be back then.'

'I don't suppose you can lend me a fiver, old bean?'

'No, I bloody can't. Go away, I'm busy. If you address me as "old bean" again, I'll put you on a charge.'

James didn't take offence but waved and tottered off, leaving Perry to continue to write. He wanted Felgate to be an instructor as then she could select the girls she thought would be suitable for this special group of drivers. The girls had to be reliable, discreet and happy to move about the country as needed.

That wasn't an issue really as all members of the armed forces were obliged to serve where sent. They had no choice in the matter. He wanted to get her driving in a convoy and also at night as these skills were essential for the role she would have to play.

The other troop of trainee drivers had finished the preliminary training and were about to start this section. He'd add Felgate to their number. Several of this group would have been weeded out by now so there would be a space for her.

All he had to do now was convince the officer in

charge to include a girl he hadn't trained himself. He snapped his book shut and shoved it back in his pocket and went in search of the antiquated relic who was in charge of the driving side of this camp. Major Bentley was old school, had fought in the last war, and didn't agree with females doing what he considered to be a man's job.

Perry's mouth curved. It was going to be interesting persuading the old soldier to break the rules and add Felgate to his list. He had no doubt that he'd get his way – he always did.

4

Clara wasn't hungry despite having missed lunch. Whatever the captain said, she didn't think she could make an instructor if she couldn't repair the engines of the vehicles that she drove.

Obviously, she had a head start as she was able to drive and some of the others had never even travelled in a private car, let alone driven one. But they were all starting on equal footing as far as the innards of the internal combustion engine and she was determined to spend whatever spare time she had learning how things worked.

On her way to the workshop, she was waylaid by a grey-haired sergeant. 'Felgate, I've just been told I'm to add you to my list of drivers.'

'I'm sorry, Sergeant, I don't quite follow you. What list is that?'

This was clearly the wrong response as he glared at her as though she was being deliberately obtuse. 'Convoy driving, Corporal, convoy driving. Get a bleeding move on – we're waiting to go out.'

What she should have done was nod and trot along behind him but even a lowly NCO like herself was entitled to half an hour's break between assignments. Goodness knows how long she'd be out driving around the country in a convoy and she needed at the very least a visit to the loo.

'I've just got back from a whole morning doing three driving tests. Captain Harrow mentioned that he would try and get me into convoy training but that was only fifteen minutes ago. Thank you very much for coming to find me so promptly, Sergeant, but if you don't mind, I'll—'

'You'll do as you're bloody well told. Are you refusing a direct order?'

Clara swallowed the lump in her throat. She'd read all the pamphlets and knew she was in the right. If they were in the middle of an air raid, an emergency of some sort, then obviously the rules were ignored, but she really couldn't risk spending several hours in a cab without dashing to the WC.

She could hardly tell him why she couldn't come with him immediately – mentioning something so personal just wasn't done.

'I'll only be five minutes, Sergeant.'

She didn't wait for him to roar at her again but raced behind the huts and into the latrines. She was out in less than two minutes and raced back, expecting to find two red caps waiting to arrest her.

The sergeant was still there and though not exactly friendly, he didn't glare at her. 'Right, understood. Are you ready now?'

'Yes, sorry to have kept you waiting.' He'd actually spent longer shouting at her than it had taken her to spend a penny.

He nodded and marched off and this time, she did march behind him. Clara followed him through a maze of passageways and into a large, concreted central square in which there were two dozen lorries waiting to leave.

Accompanying them were half a dozen motorbike riders and these she looked at with more interest. This was what she wanted to do and if she had to jump through all the hoops before she was given the opportunity then so be it.

The drivers, mostly men, were lounging about smoking, leaning on the side of the cab. There was one lorry with no one next to it and without being told, she doubled across the space and stood next to it.

The sergeant blew a whistle and immediately, everybody clambered into the cabs. Her lorry was exactly the same as the one she'd been driving earlier, which was a relief. The fact that it was sunny and wouldn't be dark for several hours was also going to make this a lot easier.

As she sat in the shuddering cab, waiting for the vehicle in front to move away, she wondered if the other drivers had been told where they were going or had some inkling of the kind of terrain they would be covering.

There was nothing she could do about it so there was no point in worrying. It was unlikely to be off road and as long as she was following another vehicle on tarmac, she'd be fine.

The snake of lorries wound up and down narrow country lanes, turned right and left and so far, Clara had found it remarkably simple. All she had to do was avoid stalling the engine and keep a few yards from the vehicle in front. They didn't travel fast, which made it all so much simpler.

The dispatch riders' role was to stop traffic at crossroads and convey messages from the front to the back of the moving column. Those she saw were all men, but what they were doing wasn't difficult and she was confident she could do it just as well as they did. Their job seemed a lot more interesting than just driving behind another vehicle for hours.

She was a little concerned when after a while, the column turned onto a busier road. Clara thought it was a good thing there were so few private vehicles on the road as anybody stuck behind them would be held up.

They were driving through a small town, Clara had no idea which one, when disaster struck. The vehicle in front of her suddenly slammed on it brakes, veered onto the pavement and drove into the front of a greengrocer's shop, sending vegetables and fruit in all directions.

Clara reacted instinctively. She spun the wheel whilst braking hard and prayed she'd be able to avoid a collision with the rear of the crashed lorry. It was too late to avoid hitting the lorry but at least the impact wasn't too hard, but the driver behind must have been daydreaming as he drove straight into the two stationary vehicles. Fortunately, they'd been travelling at less than twenty miles an hour, so the impact wasn't too violent.

She had been bracing herself so wasn't thrown

into the windscreen. However, her knees cracked painfully on something hard and she thanked God she was wearing battledress trousers which offered a lot more protection than lisle stockings.

It took her a few seconds to recover her breath, then she stopped the engine and checked the hand-brake was pulled on. It took her two attempts to open the heavy driver's door and she narrowly missed knocking the sergeant over as she'd forgotten to check it was safe to do so.

'Are you all right? Any injuries?'

'No, bit bruised and shaken. What can I do to help?'

'Stay with your vehicle, Felgate. The lorries be-hind you are going to reverse and give you room to straighten up. Do you think you've got any mechan-ical problems?'

'The engine was running smoothly after the acci-dent so no, Sarge, I don't think there's anything wrong with it.'

He nodded. 'Well done, Corporal, you reacted well and avoided an even worse catastrophe.'

From somewhere at the head of the convoy, a medical orderly had appeared and was dealing with the driver of the lorry that had crashed into the shop. Clara ignored the instructions to stay with her vehicle as if she only went a few yards away, she could still return when she had to.

The driver of the lorry that had been behind her was receiving an earful of abuse from the sergeant and it served him right. If the man had been paying attention, she was sure he could have stopped without hitting her and making things worse.

Clara was curious as to why the lorry in front had initially crashed and when she saw a local constable propping his bike against the wall of the butchers on the other side of the road, she called over to him.

'Excuse me, constable, has anybody been hurt? Do you know why the lorry in front of me crashed?'

The policeman looked up and down and then smiled. 'He didn't have a chance, Corp; three kiddies ran out from the newsagents straight in front of him. None of them were hit, thank the good Lord. You can rebuild a shopfront; nobody's going to blame him for the damage. I could be dealing with three fatalities if the dozy bugger in the lorry behind you had been the one at the wheel.'

'Golly, I'm so glad the children were unharmed. What about the driver?'

'He's tickety-boo, Corp; your medic's just checking him over before he lets him out. I shouldn't think any of these lorries will drive. The high street will be blocked for blooming ages.'

Clara thanked him and returned to her cab as the lorry behind had just begun to reverse slowly.

One of the rear lights was broken, there was a dent in the rear bumper but apart from that, she thought her vehicle was unscathed. With luck, the idiot who'd run into her would also be able to extricate his lorry.

With extreme caution, she reversed until the tailgate was almost touching the front of the haberdashers, which was next to the butcher. She'd felt the rear wheels bounce over the edge of the pavement a few seconds earlier.

She was pleased with her performance. She heaved on the wheel and managed to be facing in the correct direction without having to reverse. The only problem with this was that she was now the only lorry not reversing.

The high street was just wide enough for two large vehicles to pass safely and she decided it would make more sense for her to drive past the reversing column and return to camp. She doubted very much that the convoy would continue to wherever it had been going after the accident.

After driving carefully past the slowly reversing

column of lorries, Clara drove off but had travelled only a short distance when she realised she'd no idea where she was or how to get back to the camp. It seemed to be one disaster after another since she'd arrived. Was the man upstairs trying to tell her something?

There were two options but neither of them appealed to her. She could find somewhere to pull in and wait and then tuck in at the end of the line or keep going and hope to see a local she could ask directions from. The removal of all signposts made it all but impossible for strangers to find their way about the narrow Surrey lanes. There seemed no point in wasting petrol so she drove a little further until there was a gap in the hedge just large enough for her to get off the road.

Her stomach rumbled and she regretted not having gone into the NAAFI for something to eat because now she wouldn't be hungry. Also, it was quite likely the sergeant wouldn't have found her so she wouldn't even be here in the first place.

* * *

Perry had bumped into Sergeant Pullman on his way to the mess and given him the order to include Felgate in his next convoy. He was just finishing his sandwiches and coffee when the telephone on his desk jangled noisily.

'Captain Harrow.'

'Captain, the convoy's caused chaos in Farnham. Nobody hurt, thank God, but I need you to go over there immediately and smooth any ruffled feathers. Assess the damage and get back to me. Sergeant Pullman used the public telephone to inform me of this disaster and he's waiting for you.' The speaker was his CO, Brigadier Russell, and one didn't argue with him.

In his Alfa Romeo, Perry could be there in twenty minutes. He vaulted into the driver's seat and roared out of the gate without stopping to show his papers and then put his foot down.

He'd been to Farnham a couple of times – a small market town surrounded by manor houses and woods. He'd studied the maps of the area and was confident he'd not get lost. He had an excellent visual memory and knew what buildings and landmarks to look out for.

He didn't drive dangerously but accelerated when the road was clear and there were no blind bends to negotiate. There was always the danger of a herd of cows or a flock of sheep blocking the road in these rural areas.

He was nearing Farnham when ahead of him, he saw a lorry parked on the side of the road. This had to be from the convoy but what exactly it was doing marooned here he'd no idea and didn't intend to stop and investigate as he'd been ordered to go directly to Farnham.

But when he was close enough to recognise the driver, he stamped on the brakes. The car skidded but he maintained control and pulled up. Felgate smiled when she saw him.

'Thank goodness, sir, I've no idea how to get back to base.'

'To say that I'm surprised to see you is an understatement. Briefly explain what you're doing here.'

'The lorry in front of me crashed because some children ran in front of him. The driver behind me then ran into my vehicle. I didn't run into anyone.'

He grinned. 'I see – but that doesn't explain what you're doing here, does it?'

'No, I suppose it doesn't, sir. I was ordered to turn my lorry round as I was blocking the road. I ended up facing this way, the column is reversing out of the town, so I decided it would be sensible to continue in this direction and not try and slot into the column going in the opposite direction.'

'Right. Wait here, the other lorries will be along eventually. As you know, they'll be led by a motorbike – join the head of the column. How bad is the damage to the other lorries involved and more importantly to the buildings?'

'The one that went straight into the greengrocer's will have to be towed back. The idiot who drove into us then veered across the road into the butcher's opposite. I don't know how badly damaged that one is.'

Perry was about to drive away but there was something else he needed to say. 'I'm sorry about all this, Felgate; I spoke to the sergeant but really didn't expect him to insist you joined his convoy immediately.' He reached into the glove compartment and pulled out half a packet of custard creams. 'Here, eat these, you must be starving.'

Her eyes widened and she smiled. 'How spiffing! I don't suppose you've got a flask of tea in there as well as I'm absolutely parched.'

He tossed the biscuits up to her and she caught them neatly. 'Sorry, can't help you with that. Sit tight, Felgate, and well done.'

* * *

As expected, the lorries had reversed until there was somewhere they could turn, and he passed the rear of the column driving behind the motorbike. The other half of the convoy would have to continue and return to camp on the route that had been planned before the accident.

He tooted the horn and raised a hand as he sped past. He parked next to the accident and Sergeant Pullman was delighted to see him.

'Thank God, sir, someone needs to calm down the local populace. You'd think they'd be congratulating the driver for not killing the children instead of creating a fuss about the damage.'

'Are the drivers still here?'

'No, sir, I thought it better to send them back. Those in front have already gone.'

'Excellent, I'm hoping you've retained a dispatch rider. I need to send him to the nearest farm for a tractor. This road needs to be made passable as soon as possible.'

The sergeant nodded. 'Already done that, sir; hopefully, he'll be successful and return soon. Things are getting a bit ugly on the other side of the blockage. There's the bus waiting to get past, the local doctor and the milk lorry.'

'Thank you, Sergeant, I'll take it from here. By the

way, I passed Felgate waiting on the side of the road and told her to join the head of the column when it reaches her. I didn't expect you to put her into this convoy – although I appreciate you doing so.'

'She wasn't best pleased. I don't hold with girls doing a man's job but, in her case, I might make an exception.'

Perry nodded. 'She's exceptional, I agree. When can she go out on a night manoeuvre?'

'The day after tomorrow, sir; I'll make sure that she's on my list.'

* * *

It took Perry an hour of being charming, polite and humiliatingly apologetic to the various dignitaries who'd gathered to make their complaints about the disgraceful behaviour of the army. He'd pointed out several times that the accident wouldn't have happened if the three children hadn't dashed out from the shop without looking, but this fell on deaf ears. As far as they were concerned, only the army were to blame.

A farmer arrived with his ancient tractor and pulled the lorry out of the front of the shop as if it was something he did all the time. He then did the same with the second lorry, which wasn't as badly damaged.

'Thank you, Mr Robinson, your help's most appreciated. If you could be kind enough to tow the undriveable lorry out of Farnham and leave it in the first clearing you can find, that would be splendid.'

'What if I take it back to my farm, Captain? It'll not be in the way there and you can collect it whenever you like.'

'Even better. I think Farnham has seen more than enough of our lorries for this week.'

The farmer touched his cap as if he was a peasant greeting his noble lord and this made Perry smile. He was a product of Eton and Oxford, from a wealthy upper-class family, and sounded like it.

'Make sure you send your bill to Camberley. I can assure you that you will be well recompensed for your assistance,' Perry said, glad that everything was now organised. He'd sent the sergeant to telephone the brigadier so his commanding officer was aware that the incident was now closed.

He hated having to be so conciliatory to so many people when, if the driver of the lorry hadn't been so alert, three children would now be lying in the morgue. The army needed to keep the support of the civilian population as it prepared for the invasion of

Europe next year or the year after. Defeating Hitler was all that mattered, and he would grovel and smile as much as necessary if that would help even in the smallest way to achieve this.

Pullman had wisely kept out of the way but now everything was smoothed over, he appeared. 'I'll drive the other lorry back, sir. I found a couple of local blokes who are going to sort out the damage to the buildings. The shopkeepers weren't the ones making the fuss; it was a load of busybodies, folk not involved with any of it.'

'Not to worry, Sergeant, you've done well. Do you want me to drive behind you just in case your lorry packs up?'

'No, sir, ta. I've got the dispatch rider – if anything goes wrong, he can fetch help. The damage is superficial; we'll have it tickety-boo in no time.'

Perry reclaimed his car, did an expert three-point turn and was halfway back to Camberley barracks when he recalled something he'd said to the sergeant. Why the hell had he called Felgate exceptional? The sergeant had said that he'd consider her an exception – not that the corporal was exceptional. He frowned and wished the words unsaid. He hoped he'd not given an erroneous impression: that his unguarded remark indicated he had a personal interest in this girl. He shook his head. Officers and other ranks didn't fraternise, so even if he was interested, Felgate was out of bounds.

Usually when driving at speed with the top down, the wind whistling through his hair, the engine purring under the bonnet, he forgot for the duration of the drive that he was a disappointment to his father who, if he knew, would think his only child should be back on the front line fighting in Libya and not pussyfooting about in England like a coward. Not that he had any respect for his parent; in fact, since he'd gone to Sandhurst, he'd not seen or spoken to his father. He wasn't going to earn any gongs working for the War Office, but did that really matter? He'd been seconded there to recuperate after a burst appendix from which he'd nearly died. He'd been fighting fit for the past two months and as soon as this assignment was completed, he'd try to wangle an overseas posting, although it was unlikely he'd ever be able to rejoin his regiment.

5

Clara slotted into the pole position as instructed by the captain and followed the motorbike to the camp. If she was fully trained, she would take her lorry to the garage and repair it herself, but as she couldn't, she parked it where indicated and dashed off to her billet.

Battledress was hot and she decided to have quick shower and put on her other uniform. A skirt, even with the horrid lisle stockings, was cooler than what she was wearing now. She then headed for the NAAFI as she was too late for tea.

She was anxious to catch up with her squad as it was her responsibility to see they were settled and didn't have any queries. It was all very well being rushed through a variety of tests, but it wasn't fair on the girls she was there to look after.

The NAAFI was enormous, noisy and full of blue smoke and steam from the hot water urns. The doors at either end were open but the interior was still hot. There was a separate hatch for the ATS and a dozen tables set aside for their sole use. She didn't expect to see many of them there as they'd only just finished their tea.

She was pleased to see Emma and Gladys were at one of the tables and they waved to her. Clara rushed over.

'Sorry I've been absent all day. How have you got on? Emma, is there anything you couldn't deal with? Anything I should know?'

'All tickety-boo,' Emma replied.

'You look knackered, lovie; you sit down and I'll get you something to eat,' Gladys said and immediately stood up.

'That's kind of you but I'll get it. I'm not sure what I want.'

Gladys was determined. 'There's corn beef hash and ham salad; I'd go for the hash. It's what we had.'

Clara sank on the nearest chair. 'In which case, please do fetch it for me. Tea as well, please.' She already had more than enough change in her hand and gave it to Gladys. 'That should be enough. Get something for yourself and Emma too.'

Emma grinned. 'Tea and any cake. Anything that's going, please.' She turned to Clara. 'We missed tea as we were in the workshop. We didn't want to leave until we'd finished.'

'Good for you. What was the actual driving like?'

'We went out in an Austin, one driving, two of us in the back. The instructor was harsh but fair. I reckon we did okay.'

Clara thought things had gone as well as they could have, even with their corporal absent. Gladys returned with the tray and, as always, food first and then conversation.

She drained her mug, dropped her cutlery and sighed. 'That was scrumptious. All I've had today was half a packet of biscuits.'

The two listened avidly to her adventures but for some reason, both were more interested in the captain and his involvement in the proceedings.

'We've not seen this officer. Is he young? Handsome?' Emma asked, her eyes alight with curiosity.

'Was he a bit of all right? Did you fancy him?'

'Gladys, what a thing to ask. He's an officer and even if I did find him attractive, he's absolutely out of bounds. Officers and other ranks can't fraternise.'

They both laughed and continued their interrogation.

'Describe him to us. All we've seen so far are old men with bad breath,' Emma said.

Clara thought for a moment. 'Do you know, I really can't tell you much about his appearance. He's tall, that much I noticed. He's obviously rich; his uniform has been tailored to fit him and he drives a very expensive car. He's intelligent, funny and very authoritative.'

Emma snorted. 'He'd better be; his job is to boss us around.' She exchanged a look with Gladys. 'I don't think he can be much to look at; he obviously didn't make much of an impression on you.'

Clara smiled and shook her head. 'Actually, you're wrong. He made a real impression on me. But not as a man: as an officer. He's the sort of person I'd like to serve under.'

Gladys sniggered. 'Lie under, more like.'

Clara's cheeks coloured at this crudeness. 'I'm sorry, I really ought to go and speak to the others.' She was on her feet and across the room before either of them could protest.

Gladys was a good sort, but Clara was uncomfortable with those sorts of references. She'd left boarding school with her higher school certificate and immediately signed up to the ATS. This hadn't given her any opportunity to mix with young men of any sort apart from the occasional grand event that she'd been forced to attend.

Strangely, though, she wasn't nervous about being surrounded by thousands of men as they were all wearing the same uniform as her. There'd been an unpleasant incident when she was training and two local girls had been attacked by soldiers doing their basic training – however, she thought this was a rare occurrence and hadn't taken it to heart.

She was hoping that her squad would be in the hut even though it was early as they would have been given a lot of information to study. Although they couldn't make up the beds during the day, they could do so now as it was after five o'clock. There was also a table and several chairs at the end of the hut where they could sit and talk, play board games and cards and which would be ideal for studying.

When she approached, she saw that the door was propped open and the chairs had been brought out-side. She could hear the girls laughing and talking and they had pamphlets and sheets of paper with them so were mostly discussing their work.

'Corp, we wondered where you were,' one of them said.

'I've been taking various driving proficiency tests but for the next two days, I'll be in the workshop alongside you all. Do any of you have any problems you need to discuss with me?'

Nobody did, which was a relief as Clara wasn't exactly sure where they could have gone to talk privately. She went inside, hoping to talk to the remaining six but there was nobody there. They must be in the rec room – they certainly hadn't been in the NAAFI and there were no passes to leave the base until next week.

There were plenty of girls in the recreation room, but they belonged to the group that were finishing their training and would be taking their written and driving tests over the following days. Considering they were about to discover if they would be returned to base or posted as a driver, they seemed remarkably cheerful and relaxed.

Clara spoke to one or two and then left, now seriously concerned about the whereabouts of the others. Maybe there was some clue as to where they'd gone in their billet and she was on her way back there when she heard the sound of laughter and voices from the ablutions.

This evening was their slot for using the showers and baths. Her heart slowed and her stomach stopped churning. She really wasn't very good at this being in charge business. If she was going to panic before she'd investigated a problem, then she wasn't going to keep her stripes for long.

* * *

Clara spent the next day learning the mechanics of a car. Each group had a car on blocks without wheels into which they rummaged with enthusiasm. Some of the long-suffering instructors were tearing their hair out by the time they were dismissed. Not all the girls were as enthusiastic about getting greasy and oily under a bonnet, but they'd have to get used to it if they wanted to become a qualified driver.

Ellen, the friendly sergeant she was sharing a billet with, was waiting to speak to Clara.

'Captain Harrow wants to talk to you. He was most insistent that you came as soon as you left the workshop. I'm afraid you're going to miss your tea again.'

'Not to worry – I can get something in the NAAFI like I did yesterday. Do you know what he wants?'

'Good heavens, officers don't tell us why they want something done. Did you know that he's not permanently based here but is on an assignment for a few weeks?'

'I'm not sure that's relevant but thank you for telling me.' As Clara was checking she looked as smart as she could in battle dress with oil stains down the front, she asked a question. 'Do you think the captain's a good-looking man?'

Ellen laughed. 'If you like tall, dark and handsome, then yes. But he's out of reach even for someone as pretty as you.'

Clara flushed. He wished her cheeks didn't turn pink so easily. 'Goodness, that's not why I asked. One of my squad said he was attractive but to be honest, I couldn't even tell you what colour his hair is. His eyes I did notice as they're an icy grey.'

'You didn't take to him, then. I think you must be one of the few unattached girls who aren't swooning every time he strides past.'

Clara laughed, rubbed a smudge she'd missed earlier from her nose and was ready to discover why she'd been summoned. She was a bit cross that for the second time, his interference in her life was going to cause her to miss another meal. He might be an efficient officer, but he wasn't a very caring one.

'Golly, I nearly left without asking exactly where I'll find him.'

Armed with the directions, she marched off, curious to know what Captain Harrow wanted with her.

* * *

Perry was in a foul mood. There was not a single girl in the intake that was passing out today that would fit the stringent requirements he'd been given by his CO. Four of them had failed their tests and several others had barely scraped through. If he couldn't find the six he'd been sent to find from the group that had just arrived, he'd have failed his mission.

He hoped this wasn't going to happen. If he went back empty-handed then his chances of getting reassigned to his regiment were negligible. He'd no option but to take Felgate into his confidence and hope that she could help him make a decision. If there weren't five other girls in her squad that she considered suitable then he'd abandon his quest. Even to fulfil his assignment, he wasn't going to appoint substandard candidates.

He'd spent the day completing the investigation into the accident yesterday and hadn't had time to speak to Felgate until now. He glanced at his watch. She should be with him imminently as the trainees finished at five so they had the evening to study for the next day.

Perry stood at the window checking his watch impatiently every few seconds. The third time he did it, he swore. His door was open, and he thought it quite likely his appalling language would have been heard by the female clerks working in the next office.

He was furious with himself. This was the second time he'd caused Felgate to miss a meal. Unforgivable. Maybe there was something he could do to put it right.

He walked to the door of his office and smiled apologetically at the three girls typing away industriously and avoiding looking at him.

'I need a favour and I apologise for my disgraceful language a few moments ago. My intervention caused Corporal Felgate to miss all her meals yesterday and I've just sent for her so now she's going to miss another one.'

They were looking at him and listening carefully.

'I was hoping one of you would go to the NAAFI and get some sandwiches and buns if possible. I can make a pot of tea myself in the kitchen.'

A plump, smiley girl stood up. 'It would be my pleasure, sir. I don't think there are any other officers here would even consider doing the same.' She nodded and then continued. 'Is that why you used that bad language, sir?'

He grinned and shrugged. 'Mea culpa. Why don't two of you go and then you can get yourselves something as well?' Perry handed over a ten-shilling note which was far more than would be needed even to feed five of them.

The girl beamed. 'Thank you, sir, that would be a treat.'

He noted that she was a lance corporal so was presumably in charge of the other two who had no stripes.

'Mary will make your tea, sir; there's no need for you to bother yourself.'

'Thank you, that's very kind.'

* * *

He'd only been in his office a few minutes when there was a knock on the door that opened onto the corridor. Instead of calling for Felgate to come in, he opened the door himself.

'Excellent, Felgate, thank you for coming.' They both knew she'd no choice but it didn't hurt to show his appreciation. He expected her to smile, to appreciate his uncharacteristic behaviour, but instead she snapped to attention and saluted.

He'd no option but to return the gesture. He wasn't irritated – she couldn't tell him what she thought about his inconsideration but forcing him to salute was making her feelings clear without risking being put on a charge for insubordination.

He gestured towards the chair he'd put at the end of his desk – not opposite – and this should have shown her his intentions were friendly.

Felgate marched across and remained stationary next to her chair until he'd resumed his own seat. He hoped the peace offering arrived soon or this was going to be a rather prickly interview.

The girl sat ramrod straight on the chair, staring straight in front of her. As she was positioned at his side, she didn't have to look at him. All he could see was her profile and there was a smudge of oil on her cheek.

'God, I'm so sorry. I didn't even give you time to change or wash...'

This got her attention and she swivelled and stared at him. He wasn't sure if she was offended or amused.

She raised an elegant eyebrow. 'Are you suggesting that my appearance is unacceptable, sir?'

He dropped his head in his hands for a second. Then looked at her, trying not to laugh. 'Well, Felgate, you not only have oil on your face but also down the front of your battledress blouse. However, in the circumstances, I believe the fault, if there was one, is mine.'

She giggled – not something he'd expected her to do – and suddenly, he realised just how painfully young she was.

'If you really want me to, Captain, I'll go back to my billet and sort myself out. Maybe you would allow me fifteen minutes so I can grab a cup of tea and a sandwich on the way.'

He heard the distinct rattle of crockery on a tray and leaned back on his chair and smiled at her. 'That won't be necessary – I've arranged for your tea to be brought to you. I can hear it approaching now.'

He expected her to exclaim in delight or even in astonishment but for the first time since he'd made her acquaintance yesterday, she was silent. He looked at her more closely and her eyes glittered with un-shed tears. His small gesture had moved her, and he was pleased he'd done it. She started to stand up, but he shook his head.

'No, stay put.' He noticed there wasn't a lot of

room on his desk for a tray. 'Make a space; I'll collect the food.' He'd issued orders rather than requests.

She nodded solemnly. 'That's better. I find you even more unnerving when you're being pleasant.'

He was still laughing at her highly inappropriate remark when he collected the tray. He thanked the girls and kicked the door shut behind him.

'This looks appetising. Unlike other ranks, officers have dinner in the mess at a sensible time. However, this will be more than enough this evening.'

He put the tray down in the cleared space and sat down. She remained immobile, as did he. Why wasn't she dishing out the food?

'Are you waiting for me to be mother?'

Her gurgle of laughter was infectious and he smiled. 'Good gracious, perish the thought. I don't expect you to serve me. Not only am I a lowly NCS, I'm also a woman and it's my place to wait on a man.'

His smile told her he appreciated her humour.

'Exactly so, Felgate. Don't just sit there letting the tea get cold.' He folded his arms and looked down his nose at her. She sniggered and stood up.

'I didn't know that the NAAFI served tea in a teapot – I thought it always came in the big mugs. This is a real spread. We only get beans on toast and a slice of indifferent cake. I'm glad now that I missed tea in the mess.'

Perry had been thinking that the NAAFI had produced something out of the ordinary and had a nasty suspicion why that was. He leaned forward to look for the expected change. There wasn't any. For a moment, he was annoyed then decided to accept the fact that the lance corporal had blown the entire ten shillings. His fault – he should have specified how much she had to spend.

* * *

'Thank you so much, Captain Harrow, I enjoyed every morsel. I can't remember the last time I had actual cheese and pickle in my sandwiches and they were made with real butter and not margarine. What a treat!'

Perry watched her efficiently stack the empty plates, brush any stray crumbs from his desk and then take the tray into the clerks' office. He was about to push himself onto his feet and open the door for her but she balanced the tray on one arm and did it herself. She returned immediately and resumed her place and then looked expectantly at him. Time for business.

He quickly explained the reason he was at Camberley and what he wanted her to do for him. Again, she surprised him by her reaction. He'd expected her to be honoured, delighted that he'd singled her out for this prestigious role, but the reverse was true.

'Thank you for thinking of me, sir, but as you've told me that this posting is voluntary, I'm sorry, but I must politely decline. However, I'll be very happy to look at the other girls and see if there are six who would fit your stringent requirements.' She shook her head. 'I think I'd better warn you that I doubt that there are more than four in my squad.'

He pushed down his disappointment and annoyance at her refusal. 'Why don't you want to do this? Members of the team will get rapid promotion, be paid above the specified rate and be doing an important job for the Prime Minister himself.'

'I appreciate that, sir, but I want to be attached to a unit that's going to be part of the invasion plans. I'd prefer to be a dispatch rider but think if I want to go abroad, I'll have to be an ambulance driver instead.'

'I see. Is there anything I can do to change your mind?'

'Sorry, no. My goal from the start was to serve abroad, be where the action is. Can I speak freely, sir?'

He nodded. The girl really did nothing else.

'If the four girls that I'm thinking of do as well as I expect then why not take these? I'm sure you'll find the other two somewhere. Have you looked at drivers that are already fully trained?'

'My brief was to select newly qualified girls, not take experienced drivers away from a job they're already doing.'

She nodded. 'Are you quite sure there weren't any at all in the cohort that finishes today?'

He frowned. He wasn't accustomed to having his judgement questioned and especially not by a female corporal. This particular ATS member got under his skin. He'd no idea why and it irritated him.

'Thank you, Felgate, I'll take your suggestions under advisement.' He stood up, making it clear she was dismissed.

She was on her feet and the dratted girl snapped to attention and saluted as she'd done before. This time, he ignored the gesture, which was bad form. She about turned and marched out. For some reason, the room seemed emptier when she'd gone.

6

Clara marched briskly through the camp and into the area at the rear of the base where the ATS were billeted. What was it about this man that made her so angry? Officers were often unpleasant, as were sergeants and warrant officers, but this captain was in a class of his own.

If he behaved consistently, remained aloof and issued orders as others did, things would be simpler. He treated her like someone of equal rank at one moment and then reverted to being a fearsome officer the next.

Why wasn't he leading from the front in Africa? He was certainly fighting fit and messing about looking for special drivers didn't seem a sensible way to use his abilities. He must have offended someone further up the chain of command to have been given such a mediocre task.

It wasn't her place to judge an officer and certainly not to be offended by anything he did. She stopped and her stomach clenched. He hadn't returned her salute, which was a requirement, and there could only be one reason why he hadn't. He'd known why she'd put him in that position and refused to be provoked, even if it meant breaking the rules.

Other ranks initiated the salute and the officer responded. However, in the sort of situation she'd been in, there was no need to salute. She'd been technically correct but deliberately provocative. Clara was ashamed of herself. She knew how things worked, had obediently followed the orders of the prefects when she was a junior at her boarding school and given them effectively when she was one herself.

What had possessed her to intentionally annoy this formidable officer? It was out of character, and she didn't understand why she'd behaved as she had. Her intention had been to mingle with her squad, start making an assessment of the character and abilities of the four she thought would be suitable, but she wasn't ready to talk to anybody right now. The course had barely started, had many weeks to go before the girls knew enough to be passed as competent drivers and mechanics.

Instead of joining the girls, she skirted their billet and walked around to the workshop. She still had the booklet she'd been given this morning by the instructor and decided to spend an hour looking into the engine of the car she'd been allocated to.

'Corporal, there's no overtime when you're training. Push off and enjoy your evening – no need to be here now.' The speaker was the same rank as her but a fully qualified instructor.

'I'm not going to touch anything, but I missed yesterday's session and I want to be familiar with everything before tomorrow.'

'Fair enough. What do you want to know?'

After an hour working with Dan – they were on first-name terms now – Clara was confident she knew as much as the others in her group, hopefully more.

'Thank you, I appreciate you giving up your time, Dan. Sarge said he wants me to be an instructor as soon as I'm better acquainted with the infernal combustion engine.'

He smiled at her deliberate error, as she'd hoped he would. He was the same height as her, a few years older, not exactly handsome but was pleasant looking. He had ginger hair and green eyes – a pleasing combination.

Dan wiped his hands on his battledress trousers and shook his head. 'No need to thank me, Clara; it was a real treat spending time even if we were head-first in an engine.' He smiled shyly. 'There's a dance tomorrow night for NCOs – don't suppose you'd consider being my date?'

She was about to refuse as she'd decided she would go to the social in the village but changed her mind. 'Yes, but only as a friend. I hope you understand I'm really not interested in having any sort of relationship.'

He didn't seem bothered by her rebuff and grinned. 'That's fine by me; it'll just be a rare treat having the best-looking girl on the base on my arm even for one evening. Girls of any sort are in short supply round here, I can tell you.'

'Thank you for the compliment and for inviting me. Before we go our separate ways, could I ask you if you think there were any exceptional drivers in the group that just finished? Not just good drivers but reliable, responsible sort of girls.'

She'd expected him to query her reason for asking but he just frowned, closed his eyes for a few seconds and then nodded. 'Actually, there are two, but they didn't perform brilliantly in their tests today. I've trained lots of girls over the past year and know that some of them don't do well in tests.'

'Twelve weeks is barely long enough to learn everything and I'm surprised more don't fail. Could you give me their names? I need to pass these on before they leave tomorrow morning.'

She wrote them down in her notebook and rushed back to the main building, hoping that Captain Harrow would still be there. He wasn't in his office, and neither were the three friendly girls at their desks.

She dithered for a few minutes and then decided to steal a sheet of paper and write him a note. She'd checked and knew that the transport for the girls who were leaving wasn't coming until mid-morning so he'd have ample time to see the note on his desk when he came in and could take the recommendations or ignore them.

Dear Captain Harrow,

I spoke to Corporal Higgins who was the chief instructor for this cohort and he gave me two names of girls who would be ideal for your purposes. They are excellent in every way but just don't perform well on tests.

Private Jean Smith and Lance Corporal Mary Simpson.

I'd also like to apologise for my insubordination.

Clara couldn't think of any way to end the letter – yours sincerely, yours truly or any of the other accepted closing words just didn't seem appropriate. In the end, she just signed her name and left the paper in the centre of his desk.

It hadn't taken her long to write it but all the time she'd been doing so, she'd been watching the door anxiously, knowing she'd be in trouble if anyone found her in here. Relieved she done what she came to do, she bolted for the door and collided with what felt like a solid brick wall. She bounced backwards, hit the back of her head on something, lost her balance and ended up on her backside.

Mortified, thinking in her haste that she'd run into the doorway, she remained seated, trying catch her breath and her dignity. Then she was lifted to her feet and her eyes flew open.

'I'm so sorry, sir, I didn't see you,' she managed to whisper, even though her head was spinning and her vision a little blurred.

'That much was obvious, Felgate, but I'm curious to know what you were doing in my office.'

His calm voice steadied her and she began to feel more stable. Belatedly, she realised he was still holding her elbows.

He smiled. 'Good, I thought you were about to pass out. No, don't move; I'll carry you to a chair.'

The idea of being lifted by him cleared her head instantly.

'No, no, I'm fine.' Her voice was a terrified squeak, and she pulled her arms free but had to grip the door frame to remain upright.

'God damn it,' the captain muttered. 'Heaven preserve me from foolish females.'

Then she was picked up and carried into his office and put firmly on the nearest chair. She winced and didn't quite disguise it as her bruised behind landed on the hard, wooden seat.

She was hideously embarrassed, expected to be put on a charge, so did what she'd always done as a small child in trouble. She closed her eyes and pretended she was somewhere else. She couldn't prevent the slow trickle of tears.

Then strong fingers cupped her chin and a soft handkerchief was used to wipe her wet cheeks.

'You can open your eyes; I'm not angry.'

With considerable reluctance, she did, and flinched away, pressing herself against the chair back. The back of her head touched the chair and this time, she yelped. Her reaction had been caused by the fact that he was crouched beside her. Too close.

His friendly smile vanished. He reached out and gently touched her head with his hanky and it came away red.

'You're injured. God, I'm sorry; I didn't know you'd cracked your skull. I'm calling a medic.'

Clara's head hurt horribly but her eyes were a bit clearer and the dizziness wasn't as bad. 'There's no need, sir, I'm fine. Head wounds bleed a lot but I'm sure the one on mine isn't bleeding all that much.'

He ignored her and she heard him ordering the doctor to come at once with an ambulance. This was getting worse by the minute. Clara was tempted to sneak out whilst his back was turned but wasn't entirely sure her legs would carry her.

'I'm going to hold this folded handkerchief on the wound. It will stop the blood loss. You might think you're fine but I can assure you that you're not. You're deathly pale and your speech is slightly slurred.'

She did feel a bit woozy and suddenly really tired. Maybe she'd doze for a few minutes until the doctor arrived. She closed her eyes but opened them again when he squeezed her shoulder hard.

'No sleeping. You're concussed, I think, and need to remain awake.' He kept his hand on her shoulder and she rather liked the pressure; it was reassuring somehow. 'I've read your note; thank you for doing that. I had left but saw someone in the office through the window so returned to investigate. That's why I was running.'

He was talking a lot, but she liked the sound of his voice so didn't object. What had he said? He was running. Where to? What for? Had she missed something?

He said something very rude and it shocked her awake.

'Don't swear. I don't like it.'

He didn't apologise but squeezed her shoulder a bit harder. Not painful, but firm.

'It worked, though, didn't it?'

Then the clang of the arriving ambulance had the same effect, stopped her dozing off. From a distance, she heard heavy footsteps and then everything blurred again.

* * *

Perry was cursing inwardly that he'd inadvertently caused this accident. The poor girl had come back to help him and had been sent flying for her trouble. She'd left angry with him and yet had still gone out of her way to find him these two girls.

'Don't nod off, Corporal Felgate; you need to stay awake. The doctor is here and wants to talk to you.'

He squeezed her shoulder and she regained consciousness – thank God. The young medic, Lieutenant Sawyer, fresh from medical school, rushed in accompanied by two medical orderlies with a stretcher and carrying his smart, new, leather medical bag.

'How did this happen?' Sawyer barked. 'You didn't bother to give any details.'

The medic didn't address him as sir, which under different circumstances would have aggravated Perry. He explained what had happened and Sawyer nodded.

'I'll take it from here, Captain Harrow.' The young man directed the orderly to place a folded, sterilised gauze pad on the head wound. 'Do it as soon as the captain removes his hand.'

Perry was impressed – this chap might be young, but he appeared to know what he was doing. He changed places with the orderly and shifted swiftly out of the way. He'd no intention of leaving. He wanted to be sure the girl wasn't as seriously injured as he feared. He'd never forgive himself if that was the case.

From his vantage point in the doorway, he watched the medic use his small torch to check the reaction of his patient's pupils, before carefully examining the head wound.

'This cut is deep, Corporal, and will need stitching. You have concussion – I'm going to transfer you immediately to the camp hospital so we can keep an eye on you.'

The girl muttered a reply but Perry couldn't hear what she said.

Sawyer quickly put a gauze bandage around her head so that it held the pad of material securely. This was already stained red so the sooner the stitches were put in, the better, Perry thought. Once this was completed, the two men put the stretcher on the floor and were about to put the girl on it.

'No, it'll be much quicker and more comfortable for the patient if I carry her to the ambulance.'

Perry didn't wait for any disagreement from the doctor but stepped in and scooped her from the chair. To his surprise, she looked up at him, her eyes clear. He'd thought her semiconscious.

'Thank you, sir. I'm sorry to be such a nuisance.'

He didn't answer, just smiled and nodded whilst he cautiously negotiated his office door, the central vestibule and then out through the front door and around to the rear of the ambulance.

He'd expected the interior of the vehicle to be better equipped than the ones that were used on the front line, but it was exactly the same. For some reason, he was reluctant to put his burden down and was tempted to sit on the seat used for the walking wounded and hold her himself rather than put her on the lower padded bench on the other side of the ambulance.

Perry did the sensible thing and gently put her down in the cocoon of waiting snowy white sheets and khaki blankets. He backed out of the vehicle and the doctor jumped in. One of the orderlies slammed the doors and then ran round and jumped into the passenger seat.

The ambulance sped away and thoughtfully, he watched it go. He knew this girl's first name – thinking of her as Felgate didn't seem right any more. He returned to the office and straightened the chairs but there was nothing he could do about the blood on the door frame and the back of the chair. That would have to be dealt with by an orderly tomorrow.

Clara had got under his skin somehow and despite the disparity in their ages – he was twenty-seven and she only nineteen – despite the fact that officers and other ranks were forbidden to fraternise, he was beginning to think of her as an attractive, intelligent, desirable young woman, which would be disastrous for both of them if he acted on his feelings.

He collected the note she'd left for him and headed for the ATS admin office, hoping there might still be someone there who could convey a message to these two girls. They would be given no option about this posting, and letting Clara believe her appointment was entirely voluntary was incorrect. He should have made it clear that he'd misled her, had thought she would jump at the chance to have such a prestigious posting and that like every other ATS, she was obliged to go where she was sent.

Yet he knew he wouldn't do this. This was uncharacteristic – he wasn't known as a sentimental or particularly sympathetic officer – but something about her had made him feel protective, not wish to order her to join this elite team of drivers if she didn't want to do so.

As he strode through the camp, he frowned. This slip of a girl had been seriously injured trying to help him and even if he changed his mind about allowing her to refuse his offer, he wasn't going to do anything about it. But if the brigadier discovered how Perry had breached regulations, there'd be hell to pay.

The office was occupied by a junior subaltern, the ATS equivalent of lieutenant, and he explained his mission.

'Yes, sir, the girls haven't been given their postings as yet – that happens first thing tomorrow. It's an honour that I'm sure they'll appreciate.'

He nodded. 'Good. Make sure they understand that they'll be here until I've completed my quota. Use them as instructors.' Something else occurred to him. 'You'll have to find them an alternative billet. That won't be a problem, will it?'

'No, sir, it won't.'

From her expression, it would, but that wasn't his concern. These girls would have to remain here for another ten weeks whilst the other four completed their training. They were short of instructors so having them here would be of benefit. He hoped the girls wouldn't be dismayed at having to remain here when the rest of their group moved on to permanent posts. Perhaps he'd make an effort to speak to them, tell them a little about the important role they would be playing.

Perry nodded again and strode off. He was going

to make a detour to the hospital and see how Clara was progressing. Concussion was unpleasant but not life-threatening – but what if she had some sort of brain injury? No – he refused to consider that possibility. He didn't want to think that Clara wasn't going to make a full and permanent recovery and rapidly so.

7

Clara drifted in and out of consciousness and when she was awake, she was horribly sick and her head hurt abominably. She wasn't sure how long this misery lasted but she eventually woke up feeling almost normal.

'Good, you're finally fully awake, Corporal Felgate,' a cheerful nursing orderly greeted her. 'I'll give you a bedpan...'

'No, I'm going to the WC.' Clara sat up and something pulled at her arm.

'Just a minute, I'll take out your drip,' the nurse said and deftly did so. 'I'll come with you. You've been rather poorly for three days and you'll be unsteady for a bit.'

The nurse was right. Clara was relieved to return to her bed and lie back on the pillows to recover. She remained like this until she was roused by the appetising smell of hot toast. She pushed herself up and waited eagerly for something to eat and drink.

She ate the single slice and drained the mug of tea but was still hungry and thirsty. 'Is there any more toast or tea, please?'

'No, you've not eaten for three days so small amounts to begin with. If you keep this down then you can have more later.'

After another slightly faster trip to the bathroom for a wash, Clara was exhausted. How could just doing something so small have made her so tired? She flopped back into the bed, now with crisp, fresh sheets, and fell asleep.

* * *

It took another three days for her to be well enough to want to ask the medic if she could be discharged.

'I understand that I'm not fully fit for duty, but I really don't want to remain in hospital.'

'I'm not signing you off for another week. However, Corporal, you can be discharged from here. You had a nasty concussion, that can have lingering side effects and although you might feel better, you're really not.'

'Goodness, what sort of things can I expect?'

'Headaches, dizziness, loss of memory, extreme fatigue are the most common. If you overdo it too soon then you'll end up back here.'

'Can I do desk duties?' Clara was dreading being told she had to go home to recuperate. A military base wasn't the place for semi-invalids, but she was persona non grata at her family home. She'd been told by her parents that she wasn't welcome there. Joining the ATS against their wishes had caused a permanent rift.

The doctor thought for a moment then nodded. 'Yes, light duties only and half a day, not a full one. I need to check on your progress every day and your sutures have to come out in two days. Agreed?'

'Yes, sir. Thank you. Can I get dressed and leave now?'

'I'll sort out the paperwork whilst you do so. Call in at my office on the way out.' He paused and smiled. 'You have my permission not to wear your cap.'

Clara didn't rush but got ready slowly. The medic was correct; she was still not fully fit. Her battledress had been laundered and no longer had the oil and grease stains on the front, her boots were polished and everything else was ironed and fresh.

As she was heading for the office to collect her discharge slip, she saw the captain striding towards her.

'Thank God, I was beginning to think you'd taken root in that bed, Felgate,' he greeted her. His smile was friendly, not at all officer-like.

'I'm on light duties for another few days. I don't remember much of what happened but I think I have to thank you for helping me.' They were standing a few feet apart and causing an obstruction in the busy passageway.

'I want to talk to you. Will you come to my office when you've got your slips? I'll order some refreshments.'

'Yes, I'll be there as soon as I can.'

He nodded, about turned and strode off. Why did he want to speak to her? It couldn't be anything bad as he'd been too friendly. She shrugged and regretted it as it pulled her stitches. She had six which meant the gash had been significant.

* * *

By the time she'd walked across the camp to the admin building, she was a bit dizzy and ready to rest. Knowing the captain was waiting, but more importantly that he'd ordered refreshments, kept her marching forwards.

She stopped outside and put out a hand to steady herself. She'd only banged her head, for heaven's sake, so how was she so exhausted just walking a couple of hundred yards? Once recovered, she straightened her shoulders and marched, head up, into the building. His office door was open and he was standing in the doorway. From his expression, she wasn't sure if he was cross that she'd taken so long or worried that she had.

He stepped aside to let her walk in and then closed the door behind them. The heavy clunk made her anxious. She wasn't comfortable being shut in with him but she'd no idea why this was.

Then her nervousness evaporated as she saw the spread set out on his desk. Her stomach gurgled loudly and he chuckled.

'Excellent, I'm glad you're hungry. You've lost a lot of weight. Hospital food isn't palatable. I lost a stone when I was recovering from my burst appendix.'

She spoke without thinking. 'Oh, that explains why someone so obviously fit is wasting his time here.' Her hands flew to her mouth as if she could push them back. She waited for the well-deserved reprimand, but it didn't come. He ignored her words.

'Sit down and I'll serve this time.' He pulled out her chair as if he was a waiter and she an important guest. Her pulse skittered and she almost collapsed on the seat.

To add to her bewilderment, he gently squeezed her shoulders as he walked around to his side of the desk. She really didn't know what was going on and wasn't sure if she was excited or nervous.

* * *

Perry had had almost a week to think about Clara. Seeing her so ill, knowing that he'd caused her injury, added to his dilemma. An officer wasn't supposed to have a relationship with a girl in the ranks. This wasn't the problem – as she wasn't in his chain of command, the rule didn't apply – what was giving him sleepless nights was the disparity in their ages and life experience.

She was far too young to be involved with him. She needed a few years to gain more knowledge of the world before embarking on a relationship with him or with anyone. If he completed this mission successfully then he'd be back overseas anyway and not in a position to start any sort of relationship. This was what he'd been wrestling with for the past few days and went to visit her, not as a potential lover, but in his capacity as the man who'd knocked her over, and see how he felt then.

However, things hadn't gone to plan. Perry hadn't expected her to be up and dressed and walking towards him, bright eyed, but pale and so much thinner, and this had made the decision for him. An unexpected rush of emotion overwhelmed his good intentions and so here they were.

'I hope you're not back on duty,' he hesitated, then continued using her first name, 'Clara, as you're not fit enough.'

Her eyes widened and colour flooded her cheeks. Had he made a colossal error? Then she smiled.

'If we're to be informal then shouldn't I know your given name?'

The tightness around his chest slackened. 'Peregrine, but I'm called Perry.'

Her laughter filled the room. 'I should think you are. I love Perry; it suits you.' She smiled shyly. but didn't look away. 'Why have things changed between us?'

He considered himself a confident man but for an

inexplicable reason, his throat closed and he was unable to answer. He busied himself pouring tea to cover the awkward moment. By the time both cups were full, he still didn't know what to say.

'I think I've guessed, Perry.' She seemed to savour the word, stressing each syllable as if trying it out, seeing if she liked using it. 'You're thinking of me a bit differently.'

He handed her the cup and saucer and looked directly at her, trying not to show how happy her words had made him. He wasn't going to rush things; that would be unforgivable.

'I am. I know I'm too old for you, that you're out of bounds to me, but I want to get to know you better.'

Her eyes flashed and she looked at him in a very sophisticated way. 'Good heavens, if men younger than me are fighting and perishing for their country, then I'm quite old enough to be friends with you.'

He smiled in what he hoped was a nonthreatening manner. 'I was hoping that we'd become rather more than friends, Clara.'

She looked puzzled for a second and then stood up abruptly. 'Oh, I'm so sorry but I couldn't possibly consider you as more than an ordinary friend. I don't understand how you can suggest that we might become romantically involved when you know it's absolutely forbidden for officers and other ranks to fraternise.'

Before he could reply, she'd gone, closing the door firmly behind her. What had possessed him to suggest something she wasn't ready for? No wonder she'd fled – he didn't blame her – up until that moment, she'd seen him as just an officer. Expecting her to adjust her view so suddenly had been asinine.

Sadly, he picked up his cup and drained it. He glared at the laden table as if it was to blame for the monumental mess he'd made of everything. He wasn't hungry but he could hardly send this food back. Waste not, want not – the posters were everywhere and it was even a criminal offence to feed breadcrumbs to the birds. Everything had to be eaten or added to the pig swill.

Someone tapped on his door and he was about to roar at them to go away when it slowly opened. Clara came in, closing it behind her. She appeared composed. He held his breath, waiting to see what she said.

'I'm sorry I rushed off like that. It was such a shock – I know most of the girls on here consider you the catch of the season. I'm sorry but I'm not one of them.'

This wasn't going well, wasn't what he'd hoped to

hear. He didn't respond but waited for her to finish. She'd obviously returned to explain how she felt and he must allow her to do so.

'I can see that you're an attractive man; I'm not blind. But we both know that to be more than friends is impossible even if I wanted things to change even more than they have already.'

He nodded. 'I understand. God knows why I sprung that on you. Please, won't you at least stay and share this feast with me? I couldn't possibly eat all of it myself.'

She looked at him and then down at the food and also nodded. 'I'm absolutely ravenous and it does look very tempting. If you promise not to say anything you shouldn't then I'd be delighted to stay.'

Small steps – he was going to be extremely careful what he said or did as he didn't want her to bolt again. He wasn't giving up hope that eventually, once she knew him better, she might come to see him differently but for now, he'd settle for just spending time with her. Even this was risky for a man in his position but also for her. If either of their COs got wind of this, they'd both be in trouble.

* * *

They talked about the progress of the war, the weather, the two girls she'd suggested to him and a variety of other innocuous topics. The more time he spent in her company, the better he liked her. They chatted as they ate and everything was going swimmingly until she told him that she'd accepted an invitation to go to the NCO dance.

Now her reaction made sense. It hadn't occurred to him that she'd made a connection with another chap already. He swallowed his disappointment. She was unaware that her casual remark had been so significant. She chatted on as she munched.

'I'll have to find the corporal who invited me and apologise as he must think I'm very impolite not to have turned up.'

'He'll have made enquiries and be aware of your accident. I have to tell you that you knocking yourself out here has raised a few eyebrows.'

'Then inviting me to tea will just have fanned the flames. I really shouldn't have come, and you shouldn't have asked me. A man of your age should know better.'

He choked on his cake, and it took him some time to stop spluttering and coughing. 'Good God, how old do you think I am? I'm not Methuselah.'

She tilted her head and pursed her lips. If she

knew what that was doing to his pulse, she'd run off again.

'Let me see, thirty something?'

'I'm twenty-seven.'

'Really? You look so much older.'

He was about to reply when she laughed.

'Good grief, I was worried for a moment.'

'You know very well that you don't look your age. You're too easy to tease.'

'I admit I'm not famous for my sense of humour.' He surveyed the wreckage of their meal. Nothing left for the birds even if they were allowed to feed them. It was time to end this meeting and somehow return to just being an officer. Belatedly, he grasped the fact that Clara hadn't used his name since her return.

As she stacked the dirty plates on the tray, he moved away to give her room. He didn't want to inadvertently bump into her.

'I've only been here a few days and first the driver of our transport was delivered to the hospital with concussion and then two days later, I joined him. I'm afraid I'll be known as a Jonah from now on.'

He wasn't sure if she was serious or teasing him again. 'Does it matter? You'll be gone from here in a few weeks and the stories won't go with you.'

'I'd better go. I'm supposed to report to my CO for desk duties.'

'Not today, surely? You've only just been discharged.'

She didn't deny it. 'I've got to go. Thank you for the super spread.' She turned at the door and smiled.

'It's the least I could do as it was my fault you were injured,' Perry said.

Her eyes widened at his words as if they surprised her. Then she nodded and marched off.

Clara had stirred something in him and it wouldn't be easy to continue as if nothing had changed between them. It certainly had for him. She was the responsible one, she'd done the right thing, but he really wished she hadn't.

* * *

Clara walked quickly to her billet where she was certain she could be alone. Her heart was racing, her eyes damp, and she needed privacy to recover. Until he'd suggested he wanted to be more than friends, she'd not even considered the possibility, not thought of him as a potential boyfriend. Her lips curved. Boyfriend was hardly a suitable term to apply to the captain. He was a man, a very large, formidable one and, she was forced to admit, a very handsome one.

She flung herself on her bed and closed her eyes. Her head was spinning and not just from the after effects of her concussion. She couldn't understand why someone like him was interested in her. She was unsophisticated, pretty but not beautiful, and tended to talk too much and frequently didn't consider her words before she spoke.

Talking to him had been fun, he made her laugh but that couldn't be what had made him say what he had. Golly! Her eyes flew open as she understood his real motivation. He actually believed that he had caused her accident, hadn't just said it to be polite, and thought that he might have killed her. This had made him guilty and overreact by suggesting they go out together.

He'd done nothing really, just been in her way. She shouldn't have been running and should have been looking where she was going. If anyone was culpable, it was she.

She sat up slowly, knowing that to do it fast would make her dizzy, and then collected her stationery wallet. She certainly wasn't going to speak to him; that would be too embarrassing. Writing a letter would be easier for both of them.

Dear Captain Harrow,

Thank you for the delicious tea; it was absolutely wonderful. I'm sorry I rushed away but I was overwhelmed by what you said. I am flattered that you suggested I go out with you and have now realised why you did so.

There's no need to feel guilty about the accident; it was no one's fault. You are not to blame. I do appreciate your kindness, that you wanted to make it up to me, but that's really not necessary.

She chewed the end of her fountain pen as she tried to think of a way to finish the letter. Should she reassure him that she did find him attractive, that if he wasn't an officer and so much older then she'd be thrilled to go out with him?

She'd already given him the names of the four girls she thought would fit the bill so ended the letter, hoping her explanation would help.

If the circumstances were different, if you were younger and not an officer then I would have given you a different answer.

Yours sincerely,

Clara blotted the page, folded the paper and stuffed it in the matching envelope. This was the last of her expensive stationery; from now on, it would have to be Basildon Bond like everyone else. She was glad she'd had this last sheet and envelope left as she knew he'd appreciate the quality. Would he understand her motives for writing, or would he be offended and revert to his terrifying other self?

8

Perry read the letter from Clara and smiled ruefully. Her two reasons for not wanting to change things were insurmountable. It was small consolation that she apparently liked him too. He must expedite this assignment and return to the War Office; he had a nasty suspicion that his feelings for this girl were more than desire, that he was halfway to falling in love with her. As soon as he was confident the four girls Clara had recommended were suitable, he'd leave. There was no need for him to hang about until they qualified in a couple of months.

Romance had passed him by. He'd had girl-friends in the past but nothing serious. There wasn't the time, and he was concentrating on his career, not on personal things. He'd been at Sandhurst, then the war had started and since then, he'd been fighting on the front line. At least he had been until his appendix had burst and he'd been shipped home, not expected to recover. He'd defied the quacks and was hoping that he'd return to active duty as soon as this mission was completed. Apart from seeing the ragged scar across his belly every day, his near miss with the grim reaper was forgotten.

If he was going to kick the bucket, then it would be fighting the Nazis. He was a soldier to the core but knew his chances of survival were not good once he was back in Africa. Far more sensible to remain unattached until this conflict was done. He had envied the chaps who'd received regular correspondence from wives, girlfriends, fiancées, and mothers. His own mother was dead and he had no contact with his father.

He read the letter from Clara again and smiled. Even if they couldn't be involved, maybe she would agree to be his penfriend. He'd suggest it if he got the opportunity.

The telephone on his desk jangled and he picked it up. His focus was immediate, all other matters forgotten.

* * *

A few days later, he'd disregarded his whimsical idea to ask Clara to write to him. If he'd seen her, it might have reminded him but she was presumably still on desk duties. He had been following the group of trainees and had decided she'd been correct in her assessment of these four's capabilities. He'd got his six and all he needed to do was hand his request to the ATS officer and his job was done and he could return to London later today.

He went back to his desk and wrote the names, ranks and numbers of those he wanted and then headed for the ATS admin building. He strode in and saw Clara sitting at the reception desk.

He shook his head as she was about to jump to her feet and salute. 'As you were, Corporal. Are you almost recovered?'

'Yes, sir, I'm back to full duties in two days' time.' She looked at the paper in his hand and he nodded.

'I've selected the girls you recommended. Will you ensure this list is logged and those on it are posted, with the other two, at the end of their course?'

'Yes, sir, I'll enter their names in the system myself.'

She was alone but he didn't want to discuss personal matters where there was the remotest possibility they could be overheard.

'I need to talk to you before I leave. When are you free today?'

'I'll be relieved here in half an hour, sir. Perhaps we could meet on the golf course? It will be deserted today as it's too wet underfoot to play.'

'Good. Half an hour.'

This gave him time to send someone to tell his orderly to pack his gear immediately and to inform his CO he was leaving. The brigadier wasn't in camp today so Perry scribbled a note explain that as his task was completed he was returning to the War Office immediately. He thanked him for his hospitality and put in a note of praise for Clara for finding him his team.

He headed for the green, wondering how he would find her as they'd not agreed on a specific location. He followed the treelined track made by the unfortunate girls trekking back and forth every day from their billet off camp. When he emerged through the bushes, he saw Clara. Her smile was bright; she appeared as happy to be alone with him as he was to be with her.

'Thank you for coming and thank you for your letter,' he said as he walked up to her.

'I'm actually glad you suggested this meeting. I would have been sad if you'd left without speaking to me.'

Being close to her, knowing no one from the camp could see or hear them, gave him the confidence to reach out and take her hands. She didn't snatch them back.

'There's something I want to tell you, Clara. You might not be aware the no fraternising rule only applies to officers and other ranks in the same chain of command. I'm leaving immediately after I say goodbye to you and, if you want to, we could remain friends. I was hoping you'd consider writing to me when I'm back in Africa.'

She squeezed his hands. 'That's one of the problems solved but there's nothing we can do about your age.' She said this seriously, but her eyes were dancing.

'Well, next year we'll both be in our twenties. The year after that, you'll be legally an adult and who gives a damn about ages after that?'

Her delightful laughter echoed across the empty, waterlogged area. 'Goodness, do you really expect us to still be involved in two years' time?'

He couldn't help himself. He gently tugged on her

hands and she tumbled into his arms. She tilted her head and he kissed her.

A highly satisfactory few minutes later, they were both breathless.

His heart was pounding. She was pressed tight against his chest. Common sense prevailed and he raised his head and increased the distance between them. Not far, but enough to stop him doing something they would both regret.

'Should I apologise?'

She shook her head. 'No, that was divine. Maybe having an older escort has its advantages.' Her smile was radiant. 'That was my very first kiss and I'm so glad it was from you.'

The idea of her never having had a boyfriend pleased him. He'd rather hoped he'd be her first. 'We can't hang about here, Clara; we might be seen. I'm leaving right away. Will you write to me?' Even to him, this didn't sound right. He should have responded in kind, not barked at her about letters.

She giggled. He loved to hear her do so. 'Now that's a tone I recognise. If I was hoping for a romantic boyfriend then I'd definitely be looking in the wrong place.'

He couldn't resist and swept her back into his arms and kissed her again passionately. He heard the sound of voices approaching and just managed to step away from her and turn his back before the speakers appeared on the track behind them.

They saluted and he reciprocated. There was no sign of Clara. Where the hell was she? Slowly, he scanned the bushes, the stretch of greensward for a glimpse of her but she appeared to have vanished.

'You're looking in the wrong direction, Perry,' she said from somewhere above him.

'Good God! How did you get up there?' She was peering down at him through the lower branches of an oak tree. He moved to help her but she shook her head and her shoes appeared – no battledress and boots when working in an office – then her delectable ankles, calves and she was swinging from her hands and dropped neatly to the ground in front of him.

'I was a champion tree climber as a child. That was such fun, don't you think?'

Grudgingly, he smiled. 'I'm impressed at your prowess, my dear, but—'

She pulled face. 'No, don't call me that. It makes me feel about five years old and you sound like my uncle.'

Now he laughed out loud. 'A bloody good job I'm not, don't you think?'

For a moment, she looked puzzled then her mouth rounded. 'Good heavens, I didn't think of the connotations.' She ignored the distinct possibility that if two girls had just used this path then others might also be about to do so and was back in his arms.

She felt his hesitation and he couldn't prevent his nervous glance down the track.

'I don't care, Perry. I've decided that if we're going to truly be a courting couple then we've got to make the most of the time we've got.'

He rested his head on the top of hers and sighed. 'So a court martial for me and disgrace for you. So be it. Shall we make love behind that tree over there?'

Her sharp intake of breath made him smile. She was out of his arms and almost running down the path before he could call her back. 'My love, I was joking. Hang on, we've got to say goodbye properly and make arrangements for when we can see each other again.'

She stopped and scowled. 'I don't appreciate your sense of humour. I nearly had kittens...'

With a straight face, he replied, 'It wouldn't have been kittens you had, my love.'

In one smooth motion, she scooped up a large piece of wood and threw it at him. He didn't have time to duck and it hit him in the chest, painfully. He lost his balance and went backwards into a prickly bush.

He heard her laughing as she ran off. He was still smiling when, somewhat dishevelled, he arrived back on the camp.

If he was going to leave immediately then he had to think of a way to be able to talk to her. A telephone call would work admirably. He returned to the office he'd been using for the past few weeks and asked the operator to connect him to the ATS admin desk.

'I fell into a bush; I'm not at all happy.' He didn't announce himself. She recognised him.

'I see, how unfortunate. I'm on duty and shouldn't be taking personal calls.'

He was about to tell her he knew that when she sniggered. She was teasing him again.

'You're impossible but adorable. I'll be in London faffing about until I can get this team of girls working. Then I'll be back with my regiment. I'll get embarkation leave, two weeks; will you marry me then?'

Until he'd proposed, he'd not known he was going to ask her. The idea was preposterous, insane, but as soon as he'd spoken, he'd know that he wanted to marry her, be sure she was waiting for him if he was fortunate enough to return in one piece at the end of the war. He shouldn't have blurted it out; she was now in an impossible position. He was the older one; he should have had more sense.

There was an ominous silence. Why didn't she answer? Then she laughed. 'Good try, Perry, I was almost fooled. It would have served you right if I'd thought you serious and said yes.'

He somehow managed to laugh too. 'So you would have said yes. I'll bear that in mind for when we know each other better.'

'I didn't say that. I don't know you well enough to commit to a lifetime as your wife. I might be young but I'm not foolish. When I marry, it will be for love and it will be forever.'

'Right, I'm about to write to you and give you my London address. It's a small hotel, caters solely for those working at the War Office. You could be posted anywhere when you finish here. Will you come and see me in Town? We'll have afternoon tea at the Ritz, catch a show and go to nightclub. How does that sound?'

'That sounds spiffing. I know you said that for us to be involved, once you're elsewhere, is allowed but I'm not comfortable with anyone knowing about it whilst I'm here. Would you mind if we kept it between us until I've left here?' She paused. 'They'd know we met here and draw the correct conclusion.'

* * *

Clara's hand was trembling as she held the receiver, waiting for Perry's answer. She wasn't sure if this was because she was talking to him or because she was afraid someone would walk in and hear her. She really liked him but the idea of being romantically involved with someone like him was overwhelming.

She was out of her depth. He was a head taller than her, nearly eight years older, extremely handsome and charming as well as being an officer. Was she silly to think she could hold the interest of a man like him?

'Clara, are you still there?'

'Yes, sorry, I thought I heard someone coming and was distracted. I missed your reply.'

'I agree. We'll keep it between ourselves for now. I'll let you get back to work. Goodbye.'

The line went dead. Clara stared at the receiver in shock. She couldn't recall what she'd asked him, didn't know what he'd agreed to. The conversation had ended so abruptly, there'd been no chance to ask him. She replaced it in the cradle thoughtfully. He was so difficult to understand and she didn't think that was just because of the differences between them.

She smiled. Maybe this behaviour was normal. She'd no experience with men of any age and sincerely wished that she'd not chosen such a formidable one to be her first boyfriend. She'd have been better off with the young corporal she'd intended to go to the dance with. He certainly wouldn't make her nervous and, if she was being honest, so excited, when he spoke to her.

* * *

At the end of this final shift in the admin office, Junior Commander Fergerson thanked Clara for her help. 'I'm sorry to lose you, Felgate, but understand you need to complete the mechanical side of your training now you're fit for active duty. I gather you'll be a junior instructor as well.'

'Yes, ma'am, that's correct. As I've passed the driving side, I've got time to help out. There seems to be a shortage of instructors.'

The officer ignored this and changed the subject. Was this what all officers did?

'Your group are doing well enough, but they need

their NCO back in charge. Several of them have been put on fatigues for various misdemeanours. Make sure this doesn't happen again, Felgate.' She pursed her lips. 'I've not had an officer free to inspect them; do that now.'

'Yes, ma'am.' Clara saluted and marched out of the office. She'd been ignoring her duty, allowing her personal life to interfere with her responsibilities and that would stop right now.

She had spent time in the mess with them but that wasn't the same as being in charge. Emma had only just been promoted, had no real experience, so would have found it hard to keep them in line. She smiled wryly. Her promotion was almost as recent so there was no reason Emma couldn't do an excellent job.

Tonight was 'night in' night when the girls had to do their mending, darn their stockings, polish their boots and so on, which meant they'd all be in their billet. Not that any of them would be wearing stockings as they drove and worked in battledress or overalls. Clara had reverted to normal uniform since coming out of hospital as she'd been working in the office.

The weather had been warm, far too warm for the heavy woollen skirt and jacket she'd been obliged to wear. Battledress and overalls were far more comfortable in such hot weather. As expected, the girls were outside, the door propped open, and some were in their flimsy PT kit. This should only be worn when attending the gym classes; they knew this, and so should Emma. The area was untidy, the girls loud. There was no sign of Emma. This would not do.

She stalked across and glared at the offenders. 'You four, back into your uniform. The rest of you return these chairs to the billet. Collect the mess and go inside. I can see standards have slipped in my absence.'

She looked at each one in turn before continuing. 'There will be a full kit inspection in ten minutes.'

She braced herself for a barrage of complaints, rudeness even, but without a murmur, they gathered everything up and within minutes, the area was clear and not a girl in sight. The four improperly dressed had been the first to vanish.

She returned to her own billet to check she was looking as she should. She waited for the ten minutes to drag by and then marched briskly to do her first kit inspection. Why hadn't there been an officer available to do the inspection? More importantly, where was Emma?

She marched into the hut and was surprised and

delighted to find the girls standing, perfectly dressed, some in battledress, others in overalls, but all as they should be. Only then did she realise that Gladys was also missing. Two beds stood unattended, no kit displayed.

She walked slowly down the centre of the room examining all the kit laid out neatly. She discovered nothing out of place, no items missing. At least that was one thing she could make a positive report on.

'Excellent, well done, girls. You can put your kit away.' She paused. 'Before you do so, someone needs to tell me where the missing two are.'

Clara had expected blank faces, avoidance of direct eye contact but without exception, all the girls looked at the empty beds as if surprised Emma and Gladys were missing.

'Never knew they wasn't here,' one of them said.

'Were they at tea?' Clara asked.

Again, puzzled looks. Another girl shook her head. 'I ain't sure, Corp; we just grabbed our scoff and fetched it over here. Too blooming hot to stop inside if we don't have to.'

'Right, I'll investigate. Are you sure nobody knows anything about their absence?' She looked directly at Gladys's friend, who didn't look shifty but shook her head. 'Right. You will remain here doing your repairs and any homework you might have. Nobody will be outside, is that quite clear?'

This wasn't greeted with enthusiasm but that was only to be expected.

'The door can be wedged open, but you do your mending indoors.'

Clara wasn't unduly worried, but it was odd that an NCO, who was ostensibly in charge of the hut, would be breaking the rules herself. After initially working well with Emma, there'd been little opportunity for further contact between them. Then Clara had been injured and Emma hadn't visited; in fact, no one from this group had done so.

Now she came to consider this omission, Clara began to think that something more serious was going on with her squad. But surely she was being ridiculous, wasn't she?

9

Clara decided that the first thing to do was check who'd been put on fatigues. In fact, this was probably where the missing girls were. Her only reservation being that the others would have known and mentioned it; also Emma was an NCO and was unlikely to have broken the rules. Gladys was a fierce East Ender, spoke her mind and could well have annoyed her instructors.

The charge sheet proved her wrong. The four girls who'd had to spend two evenings peeling potatoes and cleaning latrines were the same four she'd ticked off for being improperly dressed.

She replaced the clipboard on its hook and frowned. She marched to the workshops and found they were deserted; not even the friendly corporal she'd worked with last time was there. As she was leaving the garage, something occurred to her. All the vehicles used for training were logged in a book and whenever they left the camp, this was recorded, as was their return.

She quickly scanned the half a dozen sheets and on the third sheet, she saw an Austin was out. It had left the base two hours ago, destination not recorded, but the driver was Emma, and presumably Gladys was with her.

Her hands clenched and her stomach lurched. To steal, as that was what it amounted to, an army vehicle was a court martial offence. The two of them were AWOL and she wasn't sure which was the worst offence.

Then common sense returned. If their journey was illegal, then they wouldn't have signed the car out. She swallowed the lump in her throat and went in search of the sarge who was in charge. Eventually, she found him in his tiny office drinking tea and smoking a Woodbine. His boots were on the desk and his shirt was covered in what looked like sausage roll crumbs.

She'd expected him to slam his feet down, tidy his shirt and snarl at her for interrupting him. He did none of these. He grinned, remained as he was, and waved her in.

'There you are, Corp; I was expecting you. Would have been disappointed if you hadn't come here looking for your two girls.'

'Where are they, Sarge?'

'I sent them into Guildford. I needed a few things collected for me missus and it's part of their training.' He gestured over his shoulder to the noisy kitchen clock on the shelf. 'Timed drive with an unexpected breakdown to contend with on the way.' He grinned. 'All the squad get to do this test. These two were the first.'

Now Clara was interested. 'Golly, what did you do to their car?'

'Loosened a plug and put a slow puncture in the offside rear wheel. It shouldn't have gone flat until the return journey. I expect them to be able to identify the mechanical problem and rectify it and change the tyre. They carry tools with them.'

'Did you remind them to take their bags?'

'No. If I had, they'd have known something was going to happen.'

'When did they leave? The shops would have closed ages ago. Shouldn't they be back by now?'

Sarge's happy grin faded, and he jumped to his

feet. 'Bugger me, you're right, Corp. They should've been here an hour ago.'

'If they were unable to get moving, wouldn't one of them have stayed with the car and the other hitched a lift or found a telephone box? Shall I go and look for them? I can find my way to Guildford easily enough.'

He nodded. 'Good point, one of them ought to have contacted me.' He shrugged. 'Still, the blooming car might have waited until they were in the middle of nowhere before stopping. There's a short cut down a lane that's rarely used; if they took that, well, they'd be there all day without seeing a soul. Show us your map and I'll point it out. Look down there first. I've got to stop here; someone has to be on duty at all times and it's my turn, or I'd go myself.'

Clara nodded. 'I'll change into battledress. I won't be long.'

She didn't ask for permission, ran to her billet and was out again in minutes and racing back to the garage. Sarge was standing beside a sturdy van.

'Take this – you might have to tow them back. The tools and spare wheel are in the back in case the one they've got is duff for some reason.' He scowled. 'I don't suppose they thought to check there even was one before they left.'

* * *

Clara had her map open just in case she got lost, but she was sure she'd not miss the small turning into the lane. It wouldn't be dark for several hours so finding them should be simple.

There was little civilian traffic on the roads but plenty of army vehicles. If Emma and Gladys had broken down or had an accident on any of the roads around Camberley barracks, they would have had no trouble flagging down assistance. An army vehicle would stop automatically if they spotted one of their own in a mess. Therefore, the car must be somewhere in the small lane she was about to turn into.

The hedges were high, the lane twisted and turned with several blind corners and her pulse was racing every time she slowed down, hooted and turned, expecting to meet a tractor or horse and cart. Reversing would be difficult and places to turn were few.

Then the lane widened slightly and straightened and to her delight, she saw the Austin parked at the side of the road in a convenient farm entrance. At first, she thought it abandoned then two red, oil-smeared faces appeared and the missing pair were waving and grinning.

'Thank God, we thought we'd be stuck here all night,' Emma greeted her. 'The bloody car's got a flat tyre and we've got no spare.'

Gladys chimed in. 'First the bugger packed up on the way to Guildford, had to tighten the spark plugs, then on the way back, this bloody happened.'

'I've got a spare wheel with fully inflated tyre in the back. It won't take long to change it. Sarge is beside himself. I'm afraid it looks as if you've failed this part of your training.'

The girls gawped at her and then Gladys's language made Clara's ears burn. When she finally stopped swearing, she glared at Clara.

'This ain't fair. We should have been told it were a test.'

'Then it wouldn't have been one. The idea was for you to deal with the incidents and return in good time. If you'd checked the car before leaving as stated in the manual, then you'd have known there was no spare and also that a spark plug was loose,' Clara said. 'The engine wouldn't have idled properly, and you should have noticed the performance was poor.' She was sorry they'd been marooned for so long, but it was their own fault. 'Emma, I expected better from you.'

'To be honest, I don't think this driving lark is for

me. I'm sick of being covered in grease and oil. I'm going to ask to be sent somewhere else. I'd rather work in the stores than drive. Gladys is a dab hand at the mechanics; she spotted the plug problem almost immediately and soon sorted that out.' She shrugged. 'I was supposed to check the car, but I thought as Sarge was sending us out, it would be fine.'

Whilst Clara had been talking to Emma, Gladys had recovered her temper and collected the spare wheel. The Austin was already on the jack and the flat removed. It didn't take Gladys long to put the new one on and expertly tighten the wheel nuts.

'There, all tickety-boo, Corp. Sorry for the language. Was a bit upset.' She stowed the jack and the tools in the boot and wiped her hands on a bit of rag. 'I love learning about engines and that and really want to be a driver. Will this get me chucked out?'

'No, absolutely not. Emma's failed this test, but you've passed,' Clara told them. 'Emma, you can opt to retake this, but I'm assuming that you'd rather be failed and be reposted.'

'I would. Do you think I'll lose my stripe?'

'It's possible, but unlikely. I'll let you go first, then I'll reverse into the farm track and follow. Gladys, you drive.'

* * *

It was dark by the time Clara had written her report and returned to her own billet. Ellen was on leave, so she had the hut to herself. The first thing she saw was a letter on the chest of drawers addressed to her.

She snatched it up, knowing it must be from Perry. She examined the envelope; the bold, black writing suited him. Not many people favoured black ink – most used blue or blue-back to fill their fountain pens – and she liked that he didn't.

After carefully opening it, she removed the two sheets of paper, surprised it was so long, and smoothed them out before starting to read. It began:

Dear Clara,

The first page was just information: his address, his service number, the telephone number of the hotel he lived in – exactly what he'd said he would send her. It ended with:

Best wishes

She was rather deflated as secretly, she'd hoped for something more romantic. After all, he'd kissed her several times and this letter could have been for his maiden aunt, not his girlfriend.

Then she turned to the second sheet and her heart skipped a beat.

My love,

    I cannot quite believe that I now have the right to call you my love. I'm not an emotional man, not given to flowery sentiments or romantic nonsense, but for some inexplicable reason, I'm now overcome with a desire to do both.

    However, I draw the line at writing a sonnet to your eyebrows, which was the expected thing in Jane Austen's time. Not that they aren't very elegant eyebrows, of course.

    I miss you already and can't wait to show you the delights of London. I'll be the envy of every man we meet with you on my arm.

    Tell me that you miss me or I'll be forlorn. I'll fade away without a letter from you.

He signed his name with a scrawl, no best wishes, yours sincerely or your obedient servant, just *Perry*. She read it again and was smiling when she slipped it back in the envelope with the other boring page.

Somehow, he'd combined humour with romance and at the same time revealed quite a lot about himself. All this on one short page. She held the envelope to her nose as if a faint whiff of his masculine aroma might remain but sadly it didn't.

He'd asked, no, demanded, that she reply at once, but she didn't know how to write as he had, to be amusing, heartfelt and loving in the same letter. She feared whatever she wrote would seem childish and demonstrate her lack of worldly knowledge and everything else and widen the gulf between them.

* * *

Perry returned to his office in London, shared with another captain also waiting to be redeployed after injury, and was immediately buried in paperwork. Several days went by before he had time to give Clara more than a fond passing thought. He was free at weekends and only now did he notice her lack of reply to his letter.

Had he written something that upset her? Frightened her off by almost declaring his feelings? Feelings? He didn't know exactly what they were himself. When he'd been at Camberley, had seen her in person, spoken to her on the telephone, then things had been clearer. Since his return three weeks ago, her image had faded a little, his interest slightly waned, and military life had taken over. He was almost convinced that boredom had prompted his out-of-character behaviour and her lack of response was probably for the best.

He should never have kissed her, asked her to become involved with him. Thank God she'd not taken his proposal seriously, although in that moment, he'd meant it. If he was able to become so immersed in his work that he scarcely thought of her then his feelings couldn't be genuine.

Surely if he was in love with Clara then he'd be thinking about her all the time? Checking his pigeonhole at the hotel every evening, and this just hadn't been the case. Her lack of reply was a good thing as it indicated that she too was having second thoughts. Clara was young, but a sensible girl and would have realised being involved with him wouldn't be good for either of them.

He'd invited her to visit him here, offered to escort her to the best places; what would he do if she held him to that promise? He was ashamed. He wasn't going to write again but if she eventually responded then he'd put his reservations aside and do the gentlemanly thing. He sincerely hoped he would be posted abroad soon and then they would become merely penfriends. She was a lovely, intelligent young woman and wouldn't be without an escort for long.

For some reason, the idea of her dancing with another man didn't please him but he pushed this thought aside and took his book, a new Agatha Christie, down to the lounge. Gallivanting around Town didn't appeal this evening but a quiet night in listening to the wireless and reading did.

He was sipping a rather good claret in the bar when a waiter approached him.

'Excuse me, Captain, there's a young lady on the telephone for you.'

'Thank you, it will be my secretary.' Perry followed the black-garbed, tailcoated man to the foyer and picked up the waiting receiver. 'Captain Harrow speaking.'

'Perry, it's me. I'm so sorry I've not replied to your lovely letter. I decided to ring instead.'

His fingers tightened. He'd forgotten that he'd given Clara his contact number. He wasn't often lost for words but this time, he was.

'Perry, are we still connected?'

He gathered his wits and answered. 'Sorry, I was

rather surprised to hear your voice. How are you? I wasn't expecting you to call.'

This time, there was a pause at the other end. A sharp intake of breath. 'I'm sorry, I shouldn't have called. I'm sorry to have disturbed you. Don't worry, I won't bother you again.' There was a clunk and the line went dead.

He didn't understand what had happened. What had he said to upset her? He reviewed the brief conversation and swore, causing a couple of female guests to tut at him as they walked by.

How ham-fisted of him. He couldn't ring her back and apologise, attempt to put things right, as he didn't know where she was ringing from. Wasn't this a good thing? Hadn't he decided he didn't want to be involved with her?

'Is everything all right, sir? Was it bad news?' The waiter was beside him, looking anxious.

Perry forced a smile. 'No, thank you, all tickety-boo.'

He resumed his seat and swallowed his wine in one gulp. It didn't help. He knew, far too late, that Clara meant a lot to him, and now he'd ruined things. His only excuse, and it was a flimsy one, was that he'd never been in love before, hadn't recognised this feeling for what it was, and had pushed her away.

The barman refilled his glass and Perry looked up and nodded his thanks. At this rate, his bar bill was going to be massive. He'd intended to treat this glass with more respect but downed it in two gulps. The only thing he could do now was write to her and try to apologise and put things right.

Clara must be so confused, humiliated, upset by what he'd said. He'd left her what was tantamount to a love letter and then spoken to her as if she was a stranger. He prided himself on his good manners, on being unfailingly polite even when provoked and had just behaved like an imbecile and a very ill-mannered one.

He took the stairs two at a time and dropped into the chair in front of the antique roll-top desk in his bedroom. Headed notepaper, ink, and envelopes were supplied by the hotel. He always carried his Burnham 65 fountain pen in his inside pocket. It had been a gift from his father on Perry's majority. The only gift he'd ever received from him.

He didn't know what to write but thinking about it would make it harder. He had to speak from the heart, pray he could persuade this wonderful girl to reconsider. He made several botched attempts before settling on a version that he believed would work, not daring to read it through as what he'd written revealed too much and he might well tear it up if he did so. He'd never even spoken such sentiments, and this bothered him. What if she showed the letter to a friend? He'd be ridiculed and...

He shook his head at his selfishness. This wasn't about him. His feelings weren't important; Clara's were. He closed his eyes briefly and her image filled his mind. He had asked her to marry him, for God's sake; how could he not have understood that he'd fallen in love with her?

He sealed the envelope and strolled down to the foyer and handed it to the concierge. The man stored it somewhere behind the desk and informed him that it would be transferred to the nearest pillar box that evening. It couldn't come soon enough.

10

Clara had walked into the nearby village after the mass exodus of girls who were on their way to the village hall for some sort of event. This hadn't appealed to her. The sun had been setting, but it wouldn't be full dark for another hour. Plenty of time to get to the village and back.

She hadn't wanted to use the public telephone at the barracks and risk being overheard when talking to Perry. Someone might have known this was the first name of a recently departed officer. She was being over cautious as there was little chance of there being an eavesdropper on a Saturday night. The men off duty had a film show of some sort for their entertainment and the ATS trainee drivers had the evening off and had decided to join the villagers at their family-orientated social.

Clara was pleased to find the telephone box empty; hanging around, being seen and possibly asked difficult questions was not a good thing. Her hands were clammy, her heart pounding. The thought of making a call to Perry made her unsteady. Surely she shouldn't be so nervous waiting to speak to him?

She asked to speak to Captain Harrow and waited for the concierge to fetch him. He was so off hand, so cool that she'd cut short the call and put the receiver down. She pushed open the heavy door and stumbled out of the kiosk.

There was a housewife with a small, ginger dog on string waiting outside. Clara had forgotten to press button B and reclaim her unused coins.

She was walking away, blinking furiously, when someone called out.

'Here, love, you've not got your money.' It was the woman who'd been waiting for her turn to use the phone.

'Never mind, you keep it. Thanks,' Clara called without turning. She didn't want anyone to see her tears.

'Ta, that's kind of you,' the woman yelled back.

It wasn't dark enough to need a torch and if she walked fast, Clara was confident she'd be on base before that was necessary. As she'd shown her ID card on the way out of the main gate, she was waved in by the armed guard and didn't have to stop.

On the twenty-minute walk, she'd had time to review what had actually been said by both of them. She'd begun to think that Perry hadn't really said anything so bad that she'd needed to hang up on him. He'd sounded surprised, had not been expecting her to ring, had possibly thought he was about to speak to someone else.

It was too late to go back and ring a second time; curfew was in half an hour. If only she'd written the promised letter, then she wouldn't have ruined things. One thing she was certain of was that he would be furious at her hanging up on him.

She would write, apologising, but not post it for a few days to allow him to calm down.

Gladys saw her approaching and rushed up to speak to her.

'I was looking for you, Corp. Did you recommend me for these?' She pointed to her newly sewn on lance corporal's stripe.

'I did; you deserve it. I wasn't sure when we first met, but you've proved me wrong.'

'I reckon my crowbar put you right off. Me dad gave it me, said I could see off any buggers what tried it on. But I ain't no burglar.'

'I admit I did consider that for a moment but thank goodness you had it. We couldn't have been able to stop the lorry otherwise.'

'It's tucked away in me locker. I was hoping to buy you a char and a wad to say ta for recommending me. The NAAFI's still open.'

'A mug of tea and a bun would be perfect. Are we the only two who didn't go out tonight?'

'Reckon so, I'd have liked to see the Charlie Chaplin and Keystone Cops films but the others wanted to go to the social. Didn't want to go on me own.'

'I'll go with you to the next film show, Gladys. I'll explain what your new responsibilities are whilst we eat.'

'I've got a bleeding great pamphlet to work through; never knew there was so much to learn.' She grinned, her uneven teeth white in the almost darkness. 'The extra money will be handy; I'd not have accepted the stripe if it weren't for that.'

* * *

Clara was headfirst in an engine when Sarge called her over. 'Your squad will be doing their first convoy tomorrow. You've passed this section so don't need to participate. However, we need an extra dispatch rider. That's going to be you. Get over to the stores and collect the necessary uniform.'

'Will it be taking the same route as the first time I went?'

'Crikey, we're banned from that village after the fiasco last time. Don't worry, I'll not have you leading the convoy; you'll just have to drive up and down making sure there're no problems.'

'That seems simple enough. To whom do I report if a lorry breaks down or something like that?'

'There'll be a couple of warrant officers accompanying the convoy. Find one of those. Use your initiative. You've still got to do two night trips. You'll be doing the first the day after tomorrow.'

'Yes, Sarge, thank you.'

'You did know that you could have trained to be a dispatch rider and not done the basic training?'

'I did, Sarge, but I wanted to be able to drive everything. I'm not applying to join dispatch until I've got experience with all vehicles. My aim's to serve overseas.'

'Good for you, Felgate. When you've completed

the night driving test, I'll get you attached to the local ambulance service. Do you have any first-aid experience?'

'I did the preliminary St John's certificate at school, but I'd be happy to take a more advanced one. I know an ambulance driver isn't a medical orderly or nurse but I'm sure having basic first-aid knowledge would be useful.'

'Certainly would. Off you go. Be here at twelve-thirty sharp to take out your three. They're moving onto lorries tomorrow but have to pass the basic driving test first.'

* * *

The three girls Clara had been sharing the innards of the engine with had overheard the conversation and waved as she dashed off to the stores. Half an hour later, she returned to her billet with yet another uniform. This one she had to return when she left.

She quickly dressed in the smart jodhpurs, jacket and cap and pulled on the bright-yellow gauntlets all drivers wore. They were this colour to make it easier for other motorists to see their hand signals.

Once back in her battledress, she headed for the canteen. Normally, she'd wait for the others, but she only had twenty minutes before having to report to the workshop and collect the three trainees. Two of them were already reasonably competent but the third constantly stalled the engine and Clara had already decided that if the girl didn't dramatically improve today she'd be leaving Camberley to be reassigned to something less taxing for her.

The three girls she was instructing were already at their table, which meant the lesson would start on time.

The heavens opened as Clara arrived outside the garage. It was her responsibility to check the car was roadworthy before they left the barracks.

Everything was as it should be, apart from the fact she was unpleasantly damp as she hadn't had the forethought to bring her wet weather cape. The storm clouds had cleared by the time the girls arrived.

'Good, Smith, you're with me in the front,' Clara said. This was one of the two girls who were already good drivers after only six hours' training.

'Yes, Corp, I'm glad it stopped peeing down; those wipers aren't much cop.'

'There are a lot of puddles; some of them could conceal deep potholes so take care,' she replied.

Clara was able to relax and just issue directions as

this driver was more than ready to move on to driving a lorry, as was the second competent girl. With some trepidation, she invited the third girl to take her place behind the steering wheel.

The other two passengers were equally tense as they were well aware of how bad this girl was. 'Right, Private, you know the routine. I don't need to tell you how to pull away safely, do I?'

The girl's fingers were gripped around the wheel as if by clinging on, she might somehow master the tricky gearbox and overcome the car's tendency to veer from one side of the road to the other. She hadn't yet grasped the fact that the vagaries of the vehicle were her fault.

The poor little Austin jolted forward but this time, Reynolds didn't stall the engine and there was a collective sigh of relief as they increased speed and were travelling in a relatively straight line down the narrow lane.

All four windows were wound down and there was a pleasant breeze blowing through the car. The air smelt fresh after the rain shower.

'Slow down, change down and indicate left,' Clara said firmly as they approached the turning.

Reynolds managed both successfully but then disaster struck. A friendly cow poked her head over the fence and mooed loudly. The car veered violently and went straight through the hedge.

* * *

The two girls in the back ended up jammed behind the front seats, Clara had managed to brace herself just before the accident and Reynolds was also unscathed. It was the unfortunate Austin that was damaged. Someone was always put on a charge when something like this happened, and it was almost certainly going to be her. She sighed. As she was in charge, it was her fault so she couldn't complain.

'Right, girls, extricate yourselves if you can.' She'd already glanced over her shoulder and seen that those in the back were shaken but unharmed.

'Bloody hell fire,' one of them said. 'This is a turn-up for the books.'

The driver said nothing at all and made no attempt to get out.

'Move yourself, Reynolds; we need to get this car out of the field.'

The girl shook her head. 'I don't like cows, Corp; I'm not getting out. I can't get out. I won't get out.'

'This field is full of potatoes. Not a cow in sight. I gave you a direct order, Private: get out of the car.'

The girl remained glued to her seat. There was an ominous smell of petrol and it wasn't safe to remain inside. The petrol tank was at the rear, the impact at the front so Clara was mystified as to how this had happened. 'You two, get her out. It doesn't matter how much she fusses; she can't stay in there.'

* * *

Clara surveyed the car from a safe distance. It looked all right from the outside; the radiator and the front bumper were festooned with greenery but apart from that, there didn't seem to be a lot of external damage.

'Blimey, Corp, the back half of the car's sticking out in the road. Should we push it right through, get it out of the way?'

'No, I'm going to have a closer look. It has to be the pipe that feeds the petrol into the engine, but it's still dangerous.'

As long as the car didn't burst into flames, it was repairable – she prayed for the dark clouds approaching to hurry and douse the engine and the leaking tank with water and thus avoid a fire.

'The three of you march back to Camberley. It's no more than a couple of miles. I have to stay here and warn other road users.'

Reynolds was sullen and refused to look at her. Clara decided she might as well get the unpleasantness over with.

'Private Reynolds, you will be returned to basic training immediately. You might well be facing a disciplinary hearing for your actions before you leave.'

'I don't care, Corporal Felgate, as long as I never have to sit behind a wheel again. I should never have volunteered for this trade.'

'I agree, it was a serious error of judgement on your part. You will remain in your billet until I return. Is that clear?'

The girl nodded. The other two chivvied Reynolds back to the road, which involved walking along the high hedge and then clambering over a farm gate.

'Smith, tell Sarge what happened and that I need a tow truck.'

'Okay, Corp, I'll let him know what's what.'

Clara watched them until they vanished around the bend. If a lorry wanted to pass, it would be unlucky – there just wasn't room – but she thought a car could probably manage it.

Then she reconsidered. Maybe it wouldn't be safe for anyone to pass apart from a bicycle just in case the car caught fire. With any luck, Sarge would send out a tow truck and mechanics as soon as he received the information. It shouldn't take the girls more than half an hour to march back and no more than a further ten minutes for the truck to appear.

Was this accident her fault? From what she'd heard, the driver was always held responsible but the fact that Reynolds was a trainee and Clara had been sitting next to her as instructor might mean she was equally culpable.

She positioned herself a safe distance from the protruding rear of the vehicle, facing the way they'd come. Twenty minutes dragged by and no other road users had appeared when she heard the distinct sound of a large lorry but it was approaching from the other direction.

Hastily, she ran back and waved her arms frantically. It wasn't a British lorry but an American one – it was still the same khaki colour but bigger and newer than the ones she was familiar with.

There were three Yanks sitting in the cab and from the racket coming from the canvas-covered rear, it was full of GIs. This was her first encounter with the friendly invasion of US allies.

The lorry rocked to a halt, both front doors opened and two young men dropped to the ground. One of them was an officer, which was a relief. There were already several heads peering from the back making ribald comments and patronising remarks about women drivers.

The officer strode up with a friendly grin on his face. 'Corporal, would you like me to get my men to pull your vehicle out of the hedge?'

'No, sir, thank you. There's a strong smell of petrol and I don't think it's safe to move it. There should be a team of mechanics and a tow truck arriving from Camberley very shortly.'

'Would you mind if I had a look? I don't doubt your word, Corporal, but I really do need to press on if possible. These men are engineers and urgently needed to construct a runway the other side of Guildford.'

He was going to look whether she wanted him to or not. 'Yes, but if you don't mind, I'll remain where I am.'

He nodded, walked up to the car and then dropped onto his back and shimmied underneath. She held her breath – it was really dangerous, not to say foolhardy, to do what he was doing.

The young, fair-haired lieutenant wriggled out and regained his feet. He nodded and then rejoined her.

'Too much gas, you're right to stand clear,' he said

as he leaned against the hedge on the opposite side of the road.

She was about to answer him when the same cow that had caused the accident poked her head over and mooed loudly right behind him. She hid her smile as the officer literally left the ground, causing those watching to screech with laughter.

He recovered and spun round to face the cow. He reached up and scratched her between her ears. 'Jees, you sure startled me.'

'I'd forgotten about her, sir; she was the cause of her mishap. The girl driving lost control – not that she had very much in the first place.'

He grinned. 'Then we've no option but to wait.'

He was half a head taller than her, had a better view of the road, and his expression changed suddenly. 'Rescue's arriving. Though it's going to be a hell of a job extracting that dinky car from the hedge in so small a space.'

* * *

It took Sarge and his men ten minutes to drain the petrol tank and make it safe and then he commandeered the GIs and they lifted the car out of the hedge and between them manhandled it onto the rear of the lorry.

'Right, in the back with your car, Corporal, and you can guide us as we reverse.'

There was a farm entrance after a hundred yards which allowed the Americans to squeeze past and then the lorry to turn safely.

As soon as they reached the workshop, Clara scrambled down and waited to be told to report to whichever junior commander was on duty that day.

'Well done, Corp, couldn't have handled it better myself. This old girl just needs the petrol feed replacing and she'll be good to go. As Reynolds has already left, I've decided not to pass this up the chain of command.'

'Golly, that's a relief. I need to wash the petrol from my hands. Do I have another trio to take out this afternoon?'

'No, no car available. You're free for the rest of the day.'

Clara thanked him and returned to her billet to collect her wash bag. The first thing she saw was a letter on the chest of drawers. She recognised the black scrawl. Perry had written to her.

11

Clara was overjoyed to see this letter from London and relieved she hadn't posted one to Perry herself. She forgot about washing her hands, snatched up the envelope and opened it.

> Clara, my love,
>
> I wish you hadn't hung up on me. I wish I'd known the number you were ringing from so I could ring back. I am so sorry you felt you had to disconnect so abruptly.
>
> I'd been eagerly awaiting your first letter, not expecting you to telephone the hotel as I'd forgotten that I'd given you the number. When I

picked up the receiver, I expected to hear my secretary.

That's the only reason I sounded offhand. By the time I'd recovered from the surprise, you'd gone. I wrote this letter immediately afterwards and hope you haven't torn it up without reading it.

Of course, if you have then I might as well have sent you an empty sheet of paper which would somewhat defeat the purpose of my trying to apologise and put things right.

I keep forgetting that you're so much younger than me, so inexperienced; as far as I'm concerned, we're equals on every level. Well – not quite on every level as I'm definitely a lot taller than you.

Clara stopped reading and laughed. He was such an entertaining correspondent and was apologising in such a wonderful way when he didn't need to at all. It was she who should be writing a letter like this to him as she'd misunderstood and not done the sensible thing and waited to hear his explanation.

She started at the beginning again before continuing the letter. Her eyes glistened at his use of the endearment and understood that his feelings were engaged, that he was in love with her, if she responded to his letter, it would be committing herself and she wasn't quite sure she wanted to.

He made her pulse race, she wanted to see him again, but she was still firmly focused on her goal to be either an ambulance driver or a dispatch rider overseas. If their relationship became official then it was quite possible he wouldn't want her to follow her dream.

> *I want to speak to you in person – please telephone the hotel tonight if you can and promise not to hang up. As soon as you finish your training in September, come and see me, please; there's so much I want to say to you and writing it is just not adequate.*
>
> *If I don't hear from you in the next few days then I won't pursue this.*
>
> *I apologise again for upsetting you,*

As with the first letter she'd received from him, he didn't end with anything but his scrawled name. For a man like him to apologise twice was a testament to his good character and his strong feelings for her.

She couldn't leave the camp today so if she was going to ring him, it would have to be from the telephone in the admin office where she could be over-heard. As Perry was no longer in her chain of command, she supposed this didn't really matter; however, she still wasn't sure she was going to ring him at all.

Perry had given her an easy way to end the relationship. All she had to do was ignore his letter, not telephone him, and they'd both get on with their lives. She'd got two or three days to make up her mind, but he would already know her feelings weren't the same as his if she didn't respond immediately.

Therefore, she had to decide before eight o'clock tonight what she was going to do.

* * *

Perry had known that his letter to Clara would take a couple of days to reach her; it might get there in twenty-four hours but that didn't always happen. This meant he could expect a call anytime from tonight.

Although he'd said he would give her a few days to decide, if she didn't telephone the hotel tonight then she wasn't going to contact him again. If she was unsure of her feelings towards him then his wretched letter would just have made things more difficult.

He didn't regret writing so passionately but with hindsight understood that by so doing, he'd pushed her into making a decision. She might do something – or rather not do something – today that she might have done differently in a week or two if she hadn't been pressed.

He remained in the bar after dinner and heard the telephone jangle twice but neither call was for him. Sadly, he retired to bed at eleven knowing that it was highly unlikely he was now going to see the girl he'd fallen in love with ever again.

He joined in a game of bridge the following evening with no expectation of being called to the telephone. The evening was enjoyable, he was able to concentrate on the cards, and from that point on didn't check his pigeonhole in the hope of a letter or remain in the hotel in the evenings.

Being in love was supposed to be euphoric but for him, it was the reverse. It was a damnable business and he wished he'd never met Clara as he rather thought that he'd never meet another woman he could feel the same way about. Anyone else would be second best so maybe he wouldn't get married at all, just concentrate on his career.

* * *

Four days after writing the letter, he put in a request to return to his regiment, now serving in Egypt somewhere. He was summoned to the office of his commanding officer the next day.

'Look here, Captain Harrow, you can't shove off until I'm satisfied that these special dispatch riders are satisfactory.'

Perry bit back a sharp retort. He thought the agreement was that he'd find the girls, not that he had to hang about until they were in situ.

'They finish their training in ten days. They'll not be at their new post until after they've completed their leave – I'm not sure how long that will be.'

'Then you'll have to remain here until after that date. I know you're not happy to be kicking your heels in Blighty when you could be in the frontline. I give you my word that you'll rejoin a regiment in the New Year. I need you here until then. I have another project for you.'

Perry couldn't restrain his exclamation of dismay. 'That's another bloody six months, sir. I'll have been away from my men for almost a year by then. It's unlikely there'll be a place for me after so long away.'

The general nodded sympathetically. 'I understand your frustration. What do you say about the fact that you have to be a major to do this?'

'Thank you, that's good of you. We both know I have to follow orders whether I want to or not.' Perry shrugged and pulled out the chair that General Pickering had set out for him that so far he'd ignored.

'Good man. I knew I could count on you.' He pushed a manila file across the desk. 'Read this and whilst you do, I'll rustle up some coffee and so on. I think despite your disappointment about not going overseas right now, you'll enjoy taking point on this.'

Perry flipped through the pages and was reluctantly forced to agree with the general that what he was being given to do was almost as good as returning to his regiment.

The general wanted someone currently unattached to travel around the country making a personal inspection of the readiness of the troops who'd been idling their time in barracks all over the shop. Those in charge were supposed to keep the men fit and active, ready for embarkation at any point. It was quite possible that some barracks would be doing this better than others and it made sense for this to be addressed if this was the case.

Perry frowned. In his opinion, no colonel would allow his regiment to drop standards or let morale collapse. Also, he wasn't prepared to spy, even for his CO.

Neither could he see why it would take him several months as there weren't that many barracks and camps; he did a rough count in his head and thought no more than a few dozen. It shouldn't take an observant and efficient officer more than a couple of days to make an assessment. If you added travelling time then these inspections would take a minimum of three months, probably four, to complete. He was going to politely refuse to be the man who spied on his comrades.

As he couldn't start this next project for another four weeks, that would mean it would be New Year by the time he was finished. At least he wouldn't be moping around in London thinking about Clara, wishing that he'd handled things better.

The general had left the office door open and returned followed by a waitress from the canteen downstairs carrying a large, wooden tray. The smell of fresh coffee wafted towards him. Even a tempting array of refreshments wasn't going to make this next conversation easy.

He did, fortunately, think that he had an acceptable alternative that he would suggest after they'd eaten.

'Put it down on the desk; we'll serve ourselves. Come back for the tray in an hour,' the general said.

The girl smiled nervously, curtsied and dashed off.

'Don't snigger, my boy; I can't help it if the girls treat me like royalty,' the general said as he returned to his chair on the other side of the desk.

'I was smiling at the thought that you'd gone down in person to arrange this – not something I expected. Aren't there orderlies and privates knocking about just waiting to run errands for you?'

'I wanted to give you time to peruse the documents. You certainly look less peeved, Captain; am I to understand that you're happy to undertake this new project?'

Perry didn't answer as he leaned across and poured them both a drink. He took his coffee black without sugar but he wasn't sure about his CO.

'White, two lumps, please.'

There was a tempting array of sandwiches, sausage rolls with actual sausage in them, and two generous slices of fruit cake. There was a national shortage of dried fruit but obviously this didn't extend to the War Office.

Whilst they ate, there was no talking – food first, conversation second was the rule in every mess, be it

Army, RAF or Navy. They drained the coffee jug but didn't quite clear the tray of food. Perry brushed the crumbs from his uniform, stacked the plates and put the tray on the table outside the office. He closed the door behind him and resumed his place.

'I can see a major flaw in this plan, sir: I'm not prepared to spy on my fellow soldiers. It's, I consider, dishonourable.'

'Ah, you might consider me a geriatric, young man, but I'm not senile. Naturally, that's been taken into consideration. It's also why it's going to take you months rather than weeks to accomplish this.' The general beamed, waiting to be asked how they could keep the inspections secret.

'Well? Are you going to keep me in suspense or shall I guess?'

'Yes, tell me how you'd do it.'

Perry had been considering this for the past twenty minutes and was ready with his answer. 'I'll go in disguise and use a false name at every camp.' He managed to keep a straight face and for a second, the general believed him.

'You're a buffoon, Harrow, very droll, I must say.'

'Right, couldn't resist. I think lack of essential equipment is more important than whether the men are doing enough drill, firing practice and so on. Our infantry marches; Hitler's don't. Do you know if there are enough socks and boots in the stores for the invasion?'

The general looked thoughtful. 'Actually, I don't. Go on, Captain.'

'I suggest that I visit every barracks and explain to the colonel in charge of the regiment that the War Office wants to know if there are any shortfalls in equipment. I'm prepared to cast a casual eye over the place at the same time.'

'That is an exceptional plan, young man. You're quite right to point out the flaws in mine. Quarter-masters indent for items but as we all know often these things don't arrive.'

'There's still ample time to rectify matters if I find a national shortage of socks or anything else on my travels.'

'Then I'll get the paperwork in hand for your promotion.'

Perry was dismissed. He stood up, saluted, and marched out, pleased with the interview although still disappointed not to be back on active service for another few months. It was possible he wouldn't be able to rejoin his own regiment, his position could have been filled, but also if he did, the boys could be back home and another one out there to replace them.

* * *

By six o'clock, when he left his office, he'd compiled a route for his journey and discovered that his men were still in Libya and not scheduled to return until next summer. He was more cheerful about being able to rejoin them as they appeared to be a couple of senior officers short.

All he had to do now was contact the first half a dozen camps and let them know he was coming and why.

Tonight, he was joining fellow officers for dinner at the Ritz so walked there directly, knowing he could sit in comfort in the bar until the others turned up.

An orderly had already attached his new insignia and removed the old from his epaulettes. He had permission to do the same with his dress uniform and spare, so Perry could consider himself officially a major. The paperwork would take longer, but if he had the pip and crown on his shoulder, that was good enough. He was a career soldier and intended to concentrate on that and put personal things aside.

* * *

Clara tried to forget about her decision to end the romance – if that's what it was – with Perry and threw herself into her work, spending extra hours in the workshop mending engines, joining the girls in the rec room to play pontoon or even silly games like snakes and ladders.

The foray into the life of being a dispatch rider went reasonably well, although there was a heavy summer shower and she did most of it damp to her underwear. Another girl was sent back to basic training to be reposted but the remaining girls passed this particular part of their training with no difficulty.

Two days after receiving the letter from Perry, she was on a night convoy as a lorry driver. It was going to be hair-raising being alone in the cab, in the dark, having absolutely no idea where she was going or when they might be turning right, left, or stopping altogether.

Unfortunately, just before she was allocated her position in the long row of lorries, she'd been obliged to have words with two privates for making improper remarks and being insolent. She saw their delight when they discovered she was to be in the lorry sandwiched between them. From being excited at the prospect of learning another skill, she was now apprehensive as she was quite certain the two unpleasant individuals were going to try to make things as difficult for her as possible.

Things went smoothly for the first few miles and she began to relax and enjoy the experience, then the lorry behind accelerated and bumped into the rear of her vehicle. At the same time, the lorry in front, driven by the other unpleasant individual, slowed down so she was trapped.

She tried braking hard but the driver behind put his foot down, shoving her more forcefully into the lorry in front. Damage to her vehicle would be considered her responsibility – she doubted anyone would believe that these two drivers could behave in such a reprehensible way.

The driver of the lorry in front was obviously concentrating on making her life as difficult as possible and not on what was going on in front of him. Clara had wound down her window and was leaning out and saw what he hadn't: they were about to take a sharp right turn at the approaching crossroads.

This was her opportunity to escape the harassment. The gap between the vehicle in front of her and the rest of the convoy widened. She put her foot down and crashed into the lorry, sending it forward and giving herself enough room to swerve around it and then tuck neatly in behind the rapidly vanishing convoy, leaving the two idiots behind.

The fact that there were probably about a dozen lorries behind them which were now being held up should get them into sufficient trouble to make their life a misery. She was going to make a full report when she returned and was determined to have them charged for their reckless behaviour.

Lorries didn't have rear lights and only a tiny beam of headlight was allowed, therefore if you didn't drive close enough to the one in front to be able to see its outline in your feeble beams then you wouldn't be able to follow successfully.

Clara now found herself the rear of the shortened convoy and smiled happily. Not only was she free from being shoved about by those idiots, she knew that they would now be lost. Hopefully, the dispatch rider that would be travelling at the back would realise there was something amiss but unless they had been given the route beforehand, they wouldn't know whether to turn right or left at the crossroads.

The remainder of the drive was uneventful and she followed the fifteen lorries in front of her onto the concrete square where they were parked and switched off her engine.

After jumping to the ground, she went in search of an officer, but none were present. The man in charge was a sergeant and she marched up to him to explain what had happened.

'Bleeding hell,' the grizzled man swore. 'God knows where the other lot are, but they'll find their way back in the end. Those two little sods will be sent back to basic training pronto. Have you checked the damage to your vehicle?'

'I was going to do that after I explained to you why half your convoy's missing, Sarge. I'll do it right now.'

'Drive it into the workshop over there. I can close the doors and put the lights on and then we can see how bad it is.'

Clara scrambled back into the cab and he hopped onto the running board, held onto the lowered window and travelled to the workshop with her.

He examined the lorry front and back and was muttering and cursing under his breath. She was horrified at how much damage had been done, particularly to the rear of her lorry.

'Bugger me, you're lucky you weren't injured. An inexperienced driver might well have gone off the road. Those two will spend time in the glasshouse, that's for sure.'

'Will I be put on a charge for not taking care of my vehicle properly?'

'No, you certainly won't. In fact, I'll wangle you a couple of days' leave to recover from the shock.'

She was about to tell him that she didn't need special treatment then reconsidered. If she had a forty-eight-hour pass, she could go to London and speak to Perry in person. Despite her earlier decision to follow her dream, to end the friendship, she'd been regretting it ever since.

12

Perry wasn't a heavy drinker and a couple of glasses of wine over dinner was enough for him. His companions were less abstemious and drank heavily. As the evening progressed, their loud voices drew the disapproving attention of the older, more sedate diners at this prestigious establishment. He was becoming uncomfortable sitting with these idiots and decided he really should leave them to it.

The Ritz management had been remarkably tolerant; a group of rowdy young officers was probably a common occurrence there. However, after several complaints, the head waiter came over. He chose Perry to address his concerns to as he was obviously the only one sober.

'Major, I'm afraid there have been several complaints about the behaviour of your friends. If you cannot persuade them to moderation, then I shall have to ask you all to leave.'

'I apologise. I'll deal with it. I should have done so earlier. I'll settle the bill myself.'

The man nodded and smiled sympathetically. 'I'll have it ready for you at the desk, sir.'

Up to this point, Perry hadn't intervened; they were enjoying themselves, were loud but not offensively so but when they began to toss bread rolls across the table, he stepped in.

'Gentlemen, enough. That's an order,' he snapped. He outranked them and at his command, they froze and one by one sheepishly dropped their missiles and were silent.

'Your behaviour is unbecoming of an officer. You will leave now and apologise to the management. Do I make myself clear?'

Perry was standing, glaring down at them. One by one, they nodded and staggered to their feet. He stood aside as the five of them shambled out. He was aware that the room had fallen silent. As the last man fumbled his way through the doors, there was an unexpected round of applause from those remaining.

He turned, half bowed, saluted and marched out,

smiling. He settled the astronomical bill and added a substantial gratuity. The others would repay him when they sobered up.

He stood on the pavement outside the hotel. He could hear the drunken laughter of those he'd ejected fading into the distance. If he hadn't been promoted then he'd not have been in a position to issue orders. Two of them were captains, the other three lieutenants. God knows why they were languishing at the War Office and not with a regiment.

He glanced at his watch; the luminous dial was just viable in the darkness. Ten o'clock – he would go home and read a book. There were nightclubs and other smart drinking places still open, but he had no desire to go in search of one. He walked briskly though the blackout, the thin beam from his torch adequate to keep him on the pavement and travelling in the right direction.

All guests signed in and out of his hotel. This was a hangover from the Blitz when knowing who was in or out might be crucial if a bomb dropped on the place.

The night manager accosted Perry as he entered the foyer.

'Thank goodness you're back, sir; I'm really worried about the young lady who came to see you around seven.'

Perry stiffened. 'An ATS corporal?'

'Yes, sir. She turned up and asked for you, but you weren't here. I suggested she waited in the lounge until you returned.'

'And? Get on with it, man.'

'Captain Ford overheard our conversation and told her you'd gone to the Ritz with friends. She thanked him and rushed off before I could stop her, and she's not returned.' He peered around Perry's shoulders as if expecting Clara to be with him. 'You didn't meet her then?'

'No, I bloody didn't. I need to use the telephone.' Not waiting for permission, he snatched it up. The operator connected him to the Ritz.

'I'm Major Harrow, I dined with you earlier. Has there been anyone asking for me this evening?'

'No, Major, no one. I'm sorry I can't be of more help.'

Where the hell was she? London in the blackout wasn't a safe place for a girl to be out alone. Had something happened to her on the way to the Ritz? If she'd encountered a group of drunken men like the ones he'd ejected from the Ritz, she might...

'Do you wish me to contact the constabulary, sir?'

The anxious voice of the manager dragged him back from his nightmare. 'No, not yet. I'll have a look myself first. Is there a spare room for her when I do find her?'

'Yes, I'll make the arrangements whilst you're gone.'

He was a few yards from the hotel when he was called back. He returned at the double. 'Telephone for you, sir. It's the young lady.'

Perry pushed past him and, his hand shaking, spoke into the receiver. 'Clara, where are you? Are you all right?'

'Perry, I'm so sorry. I got lost and tripped over and sprained my ankle. I'm fine, but I can't walk the rest of the way back to your hotel. I'm not sure what to do now as I can't stay here much longer.'

'Where is here, my love? You've not told me where to come.'

'I'm in an ARP's box on Birdcage Walk. He's allowed me to use his official telephone but I have to hang up now.'

He was pretty sure he knew where this was as he'd stopped to chat to the warden a couple of times. If Clara was in his little box then why hadn't he seen her when he walked home ten minutes ago? Had she had her accident on the way to the Ritz or on the way back?

He thanked the manager. 'I'm going to collect her now. Hopefully I'll be back in half an hour or so.'

The thought of her having walked across St James's Park in the dark wasn't a happy one. He shoved his torch into his pocket and ran down the centre of the road. There was little traffic and he'd see it approaching or hear it coming and would be able to dodge out of the way if necessary.

He pounded past a merry group of GIs and they cheered him on. He was fit, could have run for another mile without difficulty but had no need. The ARP position was just ahead.

A tin-hatted old chap saw him and waved vigorously. Thank God this was the right place.

The man hurried towards him. 'The young lady insists she's not broken her ankle but I'm not so sure. She went a purler just outside my post. I had to half-carry her in.'

'Right. Thank you. How long has she been here?'

'Not long, she rang you just after she fell.'

Perry peered into the hut and Clara waved to him.

'Golly, that was quick. I think I can hop if you can support me.'

He grinned. 'No chance. I'll carry you. Piggyback okay?'

Her eyes widened and she shook her head. 'No, absolutely not.'

'Then that's settled.' He reached down and picked her up. She didn't protest; his plan had worked. If the alternative to being in his arms was a piggyback then he knew she'd let him carry her.

The Westminster Hospital was closest and although severely bomb damaged last year, it still had an emergency room. He wasn't going to tell Clara he was going there first as then she might really protest.

'Dare I enquire what the hell you were doing in the middle of the night in Birdcage Walk? You came to the hotel hours ago. Where the hell have you been since then?'

'Oh, please don't ask me to tell you. I'm too embarrassed.'

He stopped in the centre of the road and smiled down at her. 'I'm not moving until you do.'

'Oh, if you insist. I rushed out of the hotel and immediately got horribly lost. I really should have asked for directions. I've been for tea at the Ritz and thought I knew exactly how to get there.'

He started walking again as he continued her story.

'I knew I had to cross St James's Park but ended up wandering about in Green Park for hours. I never found the Ritz. I can't tell you how happy I was to eventually end up back on this street which I recognised. Then in my enthusiasm, I tripped over the kerb.'

'At least you timed it well. I'd just got back to my hotel.'

He was enjoying having her so close; the heavy warmth of her against his chest was a delight. Now he knew nothing unpleasant had occurred, apart from her ankle, he relaxed.

'Are you very cross with me?'

'Cross? I'm the reverse. I'm so happy to have you here as I honestly thought I'd never see you again.'

'I'm sorry I didn't ring. I thought I wanted to pursue my dream of serving overseas, but then changed my mind.' She tugged at his lapel. 'Aren't you tired? Shouldn't we be there by now?'

'I'm tickety-boo. And we are there, but not at the hotel: at Westminster Hospital. I want a medic to take a look at your ankle.'

* * *

Clara didn't bother to protest. Perry had made the decision, and she couldn't complain after he'd carried her for miles.

'I'm not in a position to argue after you've played Sir Galahad. I'm no lightweight and I'm impressed by your endurance. You don't seem at all puffed.'

His chest vibrated as he laughed. It was strangely personal being able to feel this.

'I'm surprised you haven't noticed before, my love, I'm a positive Hercules. One might say that I could be compared favourably to a Greek god.'

She giggled. There was no need for her to answer as he was bounding up the steps that led to the front of the hospital and every bounce jarred her ankle horribly. She was relieved to be dropped gently into a wheelchair which was conveniently waiting by the doors.

'Right, we need to find someone to examine your injury. I told the chap at the Regent hotel that I would only be half an hour. I think it might be considerably longer than that.'

The place smelt of damp brick, fresh paint, cabbage and carbolic – a strange combination. He pushed her through the corridors and came to double doors that to her relief opened onto the emergency room.

'Where is everyone? Surely there must be someone on duty just in case there's an accident or a bomb drops unexpectedly?' Clara said as she looked round in dismay.

There were screens around a couple of beds and a disembodied voice answered from behind one of them. 'Just a tick, catching forty winks. Doing a double shift tonight,' a cheerful, male voice replied.

The screen was rattled aside, and a bespectacled young doctor appeared, fortunately looking wide awake and reasonably smart.

'I twisted my ankle, Doctor, but I don't think I've broken it. We thought it best to check.'

'Okay, I'll have a look. We don't have an X-ray here – I think the one at St Thomas is working even though most of the hospital has moved to Surrey after the bombing.'

Perry pushed her to the now vacant examination bed and lifted her onto it. He was extra careful not to knock her injury as he did so. The white sheet beneath her was still warm from the doctor's body and Clara wished they'd gone to the other one.

The young doctor had vanished but reappeared a few moments later with a nurse. 'Nurse Jenkins will remove your shoe and stocking, Corporal, then I'll see what's what.'

He stepped out and Perry with him. She'd been a bit on edge about having rather too much of her leg on show.

'I'll be as gentle as I can, Corporal, but I expect this is going to hurt. I can see just how swollen it is. How did you do it?'

Having to answer a series of mundane questions from the young doctor kept Clara's mind away from the acute discomfort that followed. Her eyes were watering and there were beads of perspiration on her forehead by the time the job was done.

'There, you can open your eyes now, Corporal. Just sprained. If you don't walk on it for a couple of days, it should be fine,' the medic said as he stepped away.

'Are you sure?' Perry asked.

'Absolutely, sir, it doesn't need an X-ray. Couple of aspirins and a couple of days' rest and she'll be tick-ety-boo.'

'Do I get crutches or am I supposed to hop for the next two days?' Clara asked, trying to smile and look as if she was amused by the situation.

'You're supposed to remain in one place, Corporal – no need for crutches.' The doctor smiled and vanished, leaving her alone behind the curtain with Perry.

'If you think that you're going to carry me around like a parcel, forget all about.'

'Actually, I was thinking that if we borrow this wheelchair, the problem will be solved. We can return it when you're better.'

'Were you – were you also thinking about exactly how I'm going to get back to Camberley tomorrow morning?' She knew she sounded snippy but she couldn't help it.

'Don't worry about that, my love; as a newly minted major, I shall pull some strings and get your leave turned into medical absence.'

She grabbed his arm, horrified she hadn't noticed the pip on his shoulder. 'Golly, congratulations. I'm delighted for you, but I have to tell you that going out with a captain was bad enough, but to be involved with a major is something I'm not sure about.'

He chuckled, lifted her off the bed and dropped her back into the wheelchair. 'Your carriage awaits, my lady – allow me to transport you to your abode.'

'You're quite ridiculous, and you haven't even asked me why I'm here. If I hadn't come, none of this would have happened.'

They were trundling back down the long corridor heading for the exit. 'Very true, but I'm glad that you did. I assume that you've changed your mind about me.'

She swivelled in the chair, almost tipping herself out, and he laughed as he grabbed her shoulder, keeping her on the slippery seat.

'I did – in fact, I regretted hanging up on you immediately. Can we pretend that it didn't happen?'

'Already forgotten, my love, and we can now move forward, get to know each other better. Is it too soon to talk about a possible future together?'

Clara was glad she was facing forward and he couldn't see her smile. A future together? That was an exciting thought and one she might have rejected a week ago but was now eager to find out if he was right. Seeing him again had confirmed her belief that Perry was going to be someone important in her life. Maybe, possibly, the man she might one day marry?

* * *

Despite the lateness of the hour, the hotel was expecting them. 'Good evening, Major, the room for Corporal Felgate is ready. Our kitchens have been closed for some time but I have had a flask of coffee and a few titbits put in each of your bedrooms.'

Clara was more concerned about how she was

going to get to any bedroom as there was no lift in the foyer.

'There is no guest lift, Corporal, but we have a service lift which you can use.' The night manager – if that's what he was – beamed. 'If we can get a trolley into it then I'm sure your wheelchair will fit just fine.'

He conducted them through a staff door and she was pleasantly surprised at the cleanliness of this part of the hotel where guests normally didn't visit. Her room was on the second floor and the lift moved smoothly up. It was a tight squeeze but not unpleasantly so.

'Here we are, Clara. We'd better be quiet as I know that two irascible old generals live up here,' Perry whispered.

'I wasn't intending to sing the national anthem, were you?' Clara whispered back.

'Don't make me laugh; we need to be quiet, I just told you that.' His breath was warm against her face and sent tingles swirling around her body.

The room was at the far end of the passageway. The door was standing open and he wheeled her in. 'This is a lot bigger and nicer than I expected as it's on the top floor,' she said, looking round at the spacious, well-appointed room.

'I'm not sure where the ablutions are – you won't be able to get there on your own.'

'I'm sure I'll manage. You've done more than enough for me tonight. I know we've got lots to talk about, but I've now got two extra days in which we can do so.' She'd spotted a commode behind a screen but had no intention of mentioning it. She really didn't know him well enough to talk about such intimate things.

He was about to argue but then grinned. 'I see that you've been catered for in every department. If you're quite sure you don't need my capable assistance then I'll bid you goodnight.'

He gave a casual wave and was almost at the door, leaving her feeling abandoned – she'd expected at least a goodnight kiss after all the excitement. Then he turned. His eyes blazed. In two strides, he was standing in front of her and he lifted her from the wheelchair and held her close.

'I can't be in here. Your reputation's important. That's why I've left the door open.'

Gently, he put her on the edge of the bed and then cupped her chin in one hand and pressed his lips against hers in the sweetest of kisses.

'I'll come and see you before I leave. God knows what you're going to do all day.'

'I shall read like a lady of leisure and keep my foot elevated as instructed. I'm sure I'll survive on my own until you return in the evening.'

'I'm sure that you will, my love; you're the most capable young woman I've ever had the pleasure to meet.'

He closed the door quietly behind him, leaving her fizzing with excitement. Was she in love with this wonderful, charismatic man or was it just a physical attraction? She didn't know much about that sort of thing but if a man made a woman glow all over, it had to be a good sign, didn't it?

13

Perry was a happy man. He knew he shouldn't be celebrating Clara's accident but without it, she wouldn't be here; he wouldn't have these two days to convince her that they had a future together.

He drank the coffee and devoured the sandwiches, even though they were somewhat curled and dry. As always, he was asleep immediately after getting into bed, he never remembered his dreams, and awoke at six feeling positive and relieved that he wasn't on route to rejoin his regiment.

The bathroom was empty and he was in and out rapidly. Freshly shaved, his uniform immaculate, he headed down to the reception desk to organise things for Clara. She was going to need room service and a wireless for the next couple of days.

'Good morning, Major Harrow, how can I be of assistance to you?' The night manager, Brown, was still on duty and looking remarkably cheerful for a man who'd been up all night.

He handed over the list he'd made which explained what he wanted done for Clara while she was staying there. It also made it plain that he would be paying the bill.

'I see, very comprehensive and clear instructions, sir; everything will be done as you requested.'

'Excellent. I'm going out for an hour but will be back to take up Corporal Felgate's breakfast on my return.'

The man nodded and scribbled something in his notebook.

Perry marched fast to his place of work, the War Office, knowing there would be somebody on the other end of the phone at Camberley when he rang. Despite the earliness of the hour, the place was busy – officially, most people finished around six o'clock in the evening and weren't expected to report until eight the following morning. However, when there was a flap on, you worked whatever hours were necessary to solve the problem.

Unsurprisingly, he was connected to Camberley barracks immediately but then getting transferred to the ATS administrative building was more complicated. Eventually, a woman answered.

'Junior Subaltern Matthews speaking. How can I be of help, Major Harrow?'

'Sorry to call so early,' Perry said and then explained the reason for his call.

'Corporal Felgate is an exemplary trainee and I've no hesitation in extending her absence for however long is deemed necessary. Missing a week will be no problem at all for her.'

She paused and Perry sensed there was a caveat coming.

'This is the second accident Corporal Felgate has had since she joined us here. Both incidents have involved yourself, Major.'

'And?' His tone was arctic. How dare she question him on his personal life?

The subaltern cleared her throat and decided to continue. 'Felgate is not twenty until next month. Are you quite sure you are being entirely fair to her? She can hardly say no to a senior officer, can she?'

Perry managed to contain his fury. This woman was more or less suggesting he was taking advantage of a vulnerable young woman. He was about to set her straight but didn't trust his self-control. If he said what he wanted to say, he'd be cashiered. There was a click and the line went dead. She'd wisely hung up before he dropped on her like a ton of bricks.

After he'd calmed down, he considered what he'd heard and was forced to admit there was some truth in what she'd said. The first, far more serious accident, when she'd cannoned into him and was concussed had definitely been his fault. And if Clara hadn't come to London to find him then she wouldn't have twisted her ankle so that was down to him as well.

He hadn't pursued her after she'd not contacted him, so the second accusation was entirely untrue. That said, he was forced to admit that he did tend to take over – he'd always been authoritative, which was what made him such a good officer. How much had this influenced her?

There was a sour taste in his mouth and a nasty suspicion that if he was going to do the decent thing then he'd step back, give her a breathing space, before trying to move things on to a more official footing.

* * *

He returned to the hotel less buoyant than when he'd left. He'd decided what he was going to say; however hard it was going to be for him, he knew it was the right thing to do. Eight years wasn't such a big age gap, but if you added life experience into the equation, the difference between the ages and their circumstances was almost insurmountable. In three years' time, she'd be in her twenties and so would he and then things would have evened out a bit.

He was going to be travelling around the country for the next few months, she had to finish her course, so there would be a natural break in the relationship anyway. He would suggest that they wrote to each other occasionally and when he'd finished doing his inspections, they could meet in London if that's what she still wanted.

A waiter appeared with a breakfast tray immediately after he walked in. He thanked the boy – he was probably only about thirteen or fourteen – and carried it carefully upstairs. He saw at once that her door was open, which made things easier.

'Good morning, Corporal Felgate, I bring your breakfast and good tidings,' he said as he stepped in.

The bed was empty, neatly made. He froze for a horrified moment, thinking she might be behind the screen, which would be hideously embarrassing for both of them. Then he heard her voice outside in the passageway.

She entered using two walking sticks to support her and keep her injured ankle from the floor.

'Hello, sorry, I was using the ablutions. The charming old gentleman who resides next door to me has loaned me these sticks. Isn't that kind of him?'

He shook his head. 'You were told to stay off that foot; if the doctor had wanted you to use crutches, he would have given them to you.'

'No, he wouldn't – they can't afford to hand them out willy-nilly. There's a shortage of everything and I'm quite sure that crutches and walking sticks are included in that list.' She smiled and nodded at the tray he was still holding. 'That looks and smells scrumptious. Have you eaten? There's more than enough for two on here.'

Perry hadn't really looked at the tray contents but now he glanced down and saw that it had been set for two. 'There certainly is. I'll put it on the table by the window.'

Once they were seated, she poured the tea and then helped herself to a boiled egg and freshly made toast – real bread and not the disgusting British loaf.

'You didn't tell me what your good news was? Tidings is very old-fashioned – I thought for a moment you were pretending to be the angel Gabriel.'

He grinned, swallowed a mouthful of toast, and then told her about her extended leave but obviously didn't mention what else her officer had said to him.

'Actually, Perry, I've been thinking that I'll go back today now I've got these sticks. I've only got my haversack so don't have a kit bag to carry. I can work in the office and do administrative duties until I'm able to return to my training.'

'I know that nothing I say will dissuade you once you've made up your mind.'

She nodded and smiled. 'Good, you are finally beginning to see how I tick. Was there something else you wanted to tell me?'

'Yes, there is. I'm sorry but I'm going to be away for several months. There's no point in you writing every week as I'll be travelling from place to place and the letters will just be chasing me around the country.' He drained his tea and poured himself another cup whilst he thought about the best way to break the bad news. 'I'm sorry but we won't be able to meet until November or December.'

'I see. That's probably for the best as I've got to concentrate on finishing my course. I have to be able to repair and service all the vehicles that I drive, and I've missed a lot of the mechanics' course already.'

Perry was confused by her calm acceptance of what he'd thought would be upsetting news. 'You'll probably be posted to your permanent base before I finish what I've got to do. If you send a letter here then it'll be waiting for me when I get back.'

Clara continued to munch her breakfast, drink her tea and he thought her unmoved by what he'd told her. Then he glanced down and saw that she was gripping her butter knife so hard, her knuckles were white. She looked up, her eyes glittering with unshed tears, and smiled bravely.

'But you can still write to me when you have time, can't you?'

A rush of relief enveloped him. He knew his feelings wouldn't change during the intervening months but for a moment, he'd not been sure of hers.

'I'll write every week – let you know how I am. I know I said there's no point in you replying but actually, I would really like to hear from you even if all the letters arrive at once.'

Her smile was brilliant. 'It'll be fun having our letters cross. I love the way you write; it makes me laugh.'

'I aim to please. Now, are you going to eat that other egg or can I have it?'

'No, you don't, Major Harrow; that's my egg. I can't remember the last time I was offered two whole eggs for breakfast. I also want two slices of that toast but you can have the last two. I don't suppose they'd have any real coffee going?'

'I'll shoot down and get some.'

When he returned, it wasn't only with the jug of coffee but also a selection of freshly baked scones accompanied by actual butter and some sort of red jam.

'I come bearing gifts,' he said, trying not to laugh.

'How extremely biblical of you,' she said, smiling. 'How did you know I was still hungry? I'm not sure which smells better: the coffee or the scones.'

He casually glanced at his watch and was shocked to see he was going to be late if he didn't leave immediately.

'I wonder if they've got any cream to go with these scones. I won't be a minute.' He didn't remain in the room long enough for her to tell him she didn't need it.

The manager allowed him to use the telephone and Perry was fortunate to be connected at once to the general. He quickly explained the circumstances and as he'd hoped, his CO gave him the morning off.

'Get your young lady to the station and then come in, Harrow.'

'Thank you, sir. I appreciate your understanding.'

He dropped a handful of loose change into the little wooden box that was put by the telephone for guests to pay for their calls and ascended the stairs even quicker than he'd come down a few moments earlier.

* * *

They spent a delightful hour eating every crumb and drinking every last drop of coffee before they both reluctantly agreed it was time that she left.

'If you can find a taxi then I can do the rest myself, Perry. I don't want you to be in bad odour because you're not at your desk.' She smiled. 'You haven't noticed the absence of the wheelchair. A very young waiter offered to take it back for me and I gave him sixpence.'

'I was going to do that later. I told you: I've got the morning free.' He stood up and gave her his fiercest stare. 'Either I carry you down all three flights of stairs or just to the service lift which no doubt we'll have to share with chambermaids and their equipment.'

'Good gracious, even a Hercules like you would do yourself no good at all carrying me down so many stairs. It's the service lift. Remember, I've got to get on and off the train and then catch a bus the remainder of the way.'

'I'm well aware of that.' She was busy stacking the tray and brushing the crumbs from her lap. He backed up and quietly closed the door shut with his heel. There was something he needed to do before they left.

She must have heard the faint click of the catch as she looked up, her eyes wide. She pushed herself upright and held out her hands. In two strides, he was beside her and crushed her close.

He wasn't a praying sort of chap but he sent up a quick message to the Almighty that this wouldn't be the last time he held the woman he was hopelessly in love with in his arms.

His intention had been to kiss her tenderly, not frighten her with his passion, but she responded to the touch of his lips on hers. In that second, things changed. A frightened girl not sure of her feelings wouldn't react the way she was doing.

He wanted to make love to her, show her what

real passion was, but pushed these thoughts aside and with considerable unwillingness, gently set her back on her feet.

Her smile told him all he wanted to know. She was in love with him. He was going to stick to his decision and give her space to be sure that she wanted to be his life partner.

'I'm going to miss you so much, Perry, but we're both going to be busy and the months will soon fly by.' She reached up and touched his cheek. 'Having this time apart will settle any doubts either of us have about taking this further.'

He handed over her haversack whilst she pinned on her cap and then they were ready to leave. Neither of them had said anything about love or marriage, but sometimes the idea didn't have to be spoken out loud to be understood.

* * *

Clara travelled first class at Perry's insistence and the porter and the guard couldn't have been more helpful when she disembarked from the train. They even managed to find her one of the very few remaining taxis.

The officer in charge today was surprised but delighted to see her. 'Good show, Corporal, that's the spirit. I am a clerk short today so it's fortuitous that you decided to forego your extra leave.'

'Actually, ma'am, I'm supposed to be on medical leave for another two days. However, I really don't want to sit about twiddling my thumbs in my billet. Do I have to get clearance in order to work?'

'If you managed to get back from London then I'm quite sure you can sit at a desk and answer the telephone and type a few letters. I will let the medic in charge today know that you're here.'

Clara smiled wryly – she'd spent an inordinate amount of time on medical leave since she'd been here, almost as much as she had actually working. It was strange that until she'd met Perry, she'd never had an accident of any sort. Even when she'd tumbled from her pony, she'd got up and scrambled back into the saddle completely unhurt.

Was it a sign of some sort that being involved with him wasn't good for her? Surely God was far too busy to involve himself in the life of somebody like her? She was still smiling at her thoughts when the telephone jangled.

There was no time to think about anything but the matter in hand until finally at six o'clock, her shift was done.

* * *

They had agreed to write but she wanted to have a letter from him first. Despite his assurances, she wasn't really expecting to hear from him for a few weeks. Therefore, she was surprised and delighted when a letter appeared in her pigeonhole the day she was back on full duty. He must have written it almost immediately for it to have arrived so soon. She tucked it into the inside pocket of her battledress jacket as there was no time to read it now.

Today, she was back to instructing three girls from the new cohort in the little Austin which was now fully recovered from its experience with the cow.

'Ta ever so, Corp,' one of the girls said as she scrambled out of the car after a very successful lesson. 'It's much easier having an ATS instructor. We ain't so nervous with you.'

'That's good to know, Private, and all three of you are going to be ready to move on to driving lorries. It won't be me with you in the cab, I'm afraid.'

Tonight was to be her second experience of a night convoy. She was really looking forward to it and it would be another thing to tick off on her list of accomplishments. This time, everything went smoothly and she was told when she turned up at the workshop the following morning that she'd passed.

'You're going to be driving ambulances for the next couple of weeks,' Sarge informed her. 'Then you can concentrate on learning all the other things you need to know about servicing and repairing various engines.'

'Thanks, Sarge, I'm looking forward to it. I wonder if any ATS drivers will ever be in charge of a tank. I'd really like to drive one of those.'

'I've heard on the grapevine that some of the best girls are going to be trained up to service a tank – I don't know about driving one, though.'

It wasn't until she was getting ready for bed that night that she remembered the letter she'd received that morning. Her battledress jacket was hanging on one of the six pegs at the end of the bed and she hurried over to eagerly rummage through the pockets. But the letter wasn't where she'd put it that morning.

Ellen was on a course so the room was Clara's for a few weeks, which was fortunate as otherwise, she couldn't have looked for the letter. She turned each pocket inside out but failed to find the missing envelope. When did it fall out? And more importantly – where? She sat on the end of the bed and went through every place she'd been to that day and concluded it had to have fallen out when she was in the cab of the lorry. It was too late to go to look for it now as it was pitch dark.

Tomorrow, she'd get up early and find the one she'd driven and hope it was still in there. If the lorry was out on manoeuvres first thing then whoever was driving it was bound to have found it. She just had to pray they wouldn't even consider opening it is the thought of anybody knowing about her and Perry wasn't a comfortable one.

She usually fell asleep easily but tonight, despite it being so late and being so tired, she tossed and turned. When she eventually fell asleep, she dreamed of Perry but he wasn't smiling at her but angry. She woke the next morning with a frightful headache but tumbled out of bed and was dressed and out without a second thought. She prayed the lorry was still where she'd left it last night.

Clara searched the lorry she'd driven but there was no sign of the letter and when she enquired in the workshop, it hadn't been handed in. It was a mystery what had happened to it but she wasn't going to dwell on it any longer. She was resigned to the inevitable fact that she and Perry were unlikely to meet in person for a while.

14

Perry was enjoying his perambulation around the country and was pleased that he'd uncovered several discrepancies in the quartermaster stores that probably wouldn't have been noticed otherwise.

The days were shorter as winter approached but it had been unseasonably warm at the end of September – not quite an Indian summer, but definitely hotter than usual. Two letters from Clara had eventually caught up with him in the middle of October.

In the first, after explaining that she'd lost his first letter, she entertained him with amusing anecdotes of her trials and tribulations as a newly qualified ATS driver. She'd been posted to Colchester and was driving a large lorry from one barracks to another in the region, collecting and transporting whatever was needed.

It was the second one that made him smile. This had been written just last week.

Dearest Perry,

Since I last wrote to you, I've been posted to Lincolnshire. Initially, I was still driving a lorry but I'm about to become a dispatch rider.

You won't believe what happened the other day so I'll tell you. I picked up a very handsome sergeant and an ATS bombardier. She turned out to be a friend of my friend Grace, the one that I told you about – the one whose wedding blessing I attended in Chelmsford recently.

Then Sam, the handsome sergeant, was hit by a car and hurt his ankle and Ruth, Grace's friend, asked me to give her a lift to his base just outside Lincoln on the back of my bike. What a small world it is. We've agreed that we're going to meet up in London if we can in December.

I think you told me that you will be in Lincoln at the end of the month. I've been saving my leave and have seven days owing and

could take it when you arrive. Would you be
able to get a few days off too?

I know we said we wouldn't meet until you
have finished doing whatever you're doing but
this seems like too good an opportunity to
miss.

Clara had added the address of her billet as well
as the telephone number where he could leave a
message. He'd not taken any free time since he'd
started this jaunt and was probably owed two or
three weeks' back leave. As he didn't have to report to
anybody, was a free agent more or less, he would definitely book into a hotel in Lincoln as soon as he got
there.

He was naturally thrilled that he'd be meeting his
beloved Clara a few weeks earlier than he'd thought
but what was even more pleasing was the fact for the
first time in their correspondence, she'd addressed
him as *dearest*. He occasionally sprinkled his letters
with endearments but never overdid it.

He didn't confirm his arrival at whatever barracks
he was visiting until he was actually on his way as he
never knew how long it would take to complete his
inspection. He couldn't speak to the rank and file –
they wouldn't tell him anything derogatory about

their regiment anyway – but he was able to see for himself that every place he'd been to so far was up to scratch as far as discipline and the performance of the men was concerned.

There were major discrepancies in several areas of crucial equipment – not because of any fault of the quartermaster but because his requests had been ig-nored or the wrong items delivered. At one barracks, the unfortunate sergeant had been sent thirty pairs of boots but for some inexplicable reason, they'd all been for the left foot. This meant that somewhere in Britain, another quartermaster was tearing his hair out because his boots were all right footed. So far, Perry had not discovered the missing right boots but hoped he could put the two men in touch and they could sort it out themselves.

He returned to the letter.

Even though I'm an experienced NCO, I have no girls directly under my command as I'm constantly on the move. I love being on a mo-torbike but it isn't enjoyable when the weath-er's poor. It's going to be horrible over the winter especially if we have sixteen-foot snow drifts as we did last year.

Please contact me as soon as you get this

letter so I can request my time off. I can't tell
you how much I am looking forward to seeing
you again. I really didn't expect to miss you
quite as much as I have.
    Yours affectionately,

Not exactly a loving sign-off but a lot better than
yours truly or *best wishes*.

The barracks that Perry visited always managed
to find him an empty room and a willing orderly to
take care of his laundry and polish his boots. He was
wined and dined in style in the officers' mess but
after having the previous few months living in a hotel
away from the racket and jollity of the mess, he found
it all a bit tiresome.

The majority of the regiments that he'd come in
contact with hadn't been overseas since the evacua-
tion of Dunkirk. The men had recovered their spirits,
were fighting fit, but boredom was a major handicap
to keeping them battle ready.

It was an open secret that the invasion of Normandy would take place either next year or the one
after and it was going to be difficult for the men
who'd seen no action for so long to be pitched head-
first into a collision with the German army. The Luftwaffe might be virtually destroyed but their army was

still better equipped and better organised than they were.

He could be in Lincoln the following week if he expedited this visit. He'd been given an office with a telephone which was connected to the main switchboard. All he needed now was the name of a decent hotel so he could make his reservation. After speaking to the lieutenant in the next office, he had the name of the White Hart hotel. This was a historic building that had been in Lincoln for over 600 years and was a stone's throw from the lovely cathedral. It sounded perfect.

As soon as he'd made the reservations, he rang the number on the letter Clara had sent him and left a message telling her when he would be at the White Hart. This gave her just over a week to apply for her leave so he was confident that she'd be there.

Yesterday, Perry had spent time talking to the various officers that he met, hearing what they thought they needed but hadn't been able to get for their men. Today, he cut out the chatter and marched around the barracks totally focused on the job in hand.

The young captain who'd been designated to accompany him on his inspection, his role to make a note of anything pertinent that was said or requested, was obliged to run in order to keep up. The poor chap was so exhausted, Perry took pity on him and explained why he was in a hurry.

'Keep this to yourself, but I'm going to be able to see my girlfriend for the first time in months if I can get this inspection completed by tomorrow.'

The young man grinned and mopped his brow. 'Jolly good, sir. I won't slow you down. If we carry on at this pace, we'll be done by lunchtime.'

They were heading for the quartermaster stores – the most important stop on the tour.

'Major Harrow, just the man I wanted to see,' the sergeant in charge of the stores said as Perry walked in. 'I was told to check supplies and I've only got a couple of dozen pairs of socks. I've indented for hundreds of pairs over the past few months but so far, they've not come.'

The captain was busy scribbling this information in his book.

'Unfortunately, Sarge, you're the third man to tell me this. There appears to be a national shortage of khaki socks. God knows where the missing items are, but I aim to find out. You have my word that you'll have what you need by the end of the year.'

This might have sounded a long time to wait but

no one in the army expected things to happen quickly.

'Best news I've had all year, sir. There are a few other things I'm going to need before things kick off.'

Perry completed his inspection in record time, collated the information the helpful captain had recorded for him, and was ready to head for Lincoln.

* * *

Clara found a note in her pigeonhole saying that there was a message for her to be collected from the office. It had to be from Perry. She'd had a long and tiring day delivering messages, mail and on one occasion a lieutenant to various Royal Artillery batteries.

Fatigue was forgotten as she marched briskly across the depot, praying that there would still be somebody there who knew what the message was or where it could be found. She was lucky and a cheerful private sitting behind the desk smiled and nodded when she asked.

'Ever such a lovely voice your young man has, Corp. He never said his name. I wrote down his message. He's going to be at the White Hart hotel in Lincoln from next Friday.'

'That's the best news I've had for months. I need

to fill in the required form to book my leave. I don't suppose you've got one of those lurking in a drawer somewhere?'

'I don't, but I'll get you one. I won't be a tick.'

Clara thanked her and ten minutes later handed in her request and was heading for the Victorian rectory where the female dispatch riders were being accommodated. This was the only time that the girls were able to mingle and talk about their day.

That night, she was bubbling with excitement. She didn't have a snapshot of Perry as it hadn't seemed appropriate to ask him to send her one when they hadn't made a firm commitment to each other. When she saw him on Friday, the first thing she would ask for was a photograph and she had five days to try to get one of herself to give him.

The days were still relatively mild for October but at night, there was a nip in the air and she shivered. She was glad that she'd just been issued her winter gear as she was going to need it soon. She wore a tin helmet with a soft leather neck covering, goggles and the bright-yellow gauntlets so her face and hands were warm enough. The knee-length leather boots kept her feet and lower legs warm and dry too. It was the bit in between that got cold and though the jodhpurs were thick twill, they weren't waterproof.

It would be so much easier to get to Lincoln if she could use her motorbike but that was forbidden. She would also have to wear her normal skirted uniform – battledress of any sort was forbidden when you left the base unless you were on duty.

She hadn't seen the man she loved for months and was positively fizzing with anticipation. Was he as excited as she was at their forthcoming reunion?

* * *

Clara wasn't sure if she'd be staying for all four of the days that she'd been given – when she met Perry, they might decide that they didn't suit after all. Her pulse raced. Unless, during the interim, she'd somehow exaggerated her feelings and built Perry into something he wasn't, then she was absolutely certain she wanted to be his real girlfriend.

Although she was supposed to have her respirator with her at all times, nobody bothered when they were going on leave. If Hitler had been going to gas them then he'd have done it at the start of the war and anyway, he was far too busy trying to defeat Russia to send the Luftwaffe to England with gas.

She was fortunate and managed to scrounge a lift with one of the girls who was collecting an officer from Lincoln station. Clara was dropped off several streets before they reached the station and then had to ask for directions to the hotel.

What would she do if Perry wasn't there? It would be embarrassing hanging around in the foyer so if this happened then she'd go in search of a café and return later. She could see the three magnificent towers of the cathedral on the skyline so knew she was getting close to the hotel as it was in the same area.

There was the sound of a car approaching from behind her and she recognised the sound of the engine. Her heart pounding, she turned. It was indeed Perry in his smart, dark-blue sports car. It screeched to a halt beside her. She'd expected him to lean across and open the passenger door, but he didn't.

Leaving the engine running and his door swinging open, he raced around the car and snatched her up in the air. She clutched his lapels and gazed into his face which was on a level with hers.

'You haven't changed one jot; you look even better than I remember. I'm so happy to see you,' she managed to gasp before he stopped her words with his mouth.

She was dizzy, breathless, tingling all over when eventually, he was forced to put her down as a horse-drawn milk float wanted to pass and couldn't because of the open door.

Laughing, Perry waved a hand to apologise. 'Quickly, darling, hop in before the old chap gets violent.'

She scarcely had time to slam the door before he drove off. 'Goodness, slow down – these streets are far too narrow to travel at this speed.'

He glanced across and grinned, his eyes wicked, and she laughed. He did, however, reduce the pace so they arrived at the hotel without terrifying any further road users or pedestrians.

'I can't believe we've turned up at the same time, my love; it has to be a good sign that we're going to have the most amazing few days together,' he said.

'They only allowed me four days of my owed leave – how long have you got?'

'As long as I damn well please. I've not had even an afternoon free since I started. Anyway, I'm not reporting back to anyone so nobody would know if I was gone for a month.'

The car park was behind the hotel and surprisingly, there were already three other civilian vehicles. 'I thought there was no petrol, yet there are now four non-military vehicles parked here.'

'How observant of you, Corporal Felgate; I wouldn't have noticed if you hadn't pointed it out.'

She punched him playfully. His free arm snaked around her and she was soundly kissed for a second time. She wasn't sure if she could handle so much passion without doing something she really shouldn't.

'No, Perry, somebody might be watching. I really don't like such public displays of affection.' She hadn't intended to sound like a prudish old spinster and regretted her words immediately.

Unrepentant, he kissed her again. 'I don't care who sees, darling; your coming here means I've got my dearest wish.' He sat back but remained twisted in his seat so he was facing her. 'Will you marry me, my darling? I love you and have done from the moment I met you.'

Before she had time to consider her answer, he reached into his pocket, removed a little leather box and slipped a lovely antique diamond ring over her finger.

She looked down. It fitted perfectly but she wished that he'd waited for her to answer and not just assumed she'd say yes.

'It's beautiful, and I love it.' He looked so happy, she wasn't going to ruin the moment by saying what she felt about his unorthodox proposal. She should have said that she loved him but he didn't seem to notice the omission. He had taken her by surprise; she hadn't been expecting him to propose so suddenly and certainly not in his car.

'Come on, let's check in. They only had two rooms for three nights so we'll have to find somewhere else for the last one. I'm sure there are plenty of other places we can stay.'

He took her hand and kissed the ring and they walked into the hotel where they were greeted warmly. An ancient bellboy conducted them to their adjacent bedrooms. She felt a flicker of unease when she saw this.

'These rooms have their own facilities, which is why I reserved them. Don't look so apprehensive, darling; you can lock your door at night.'

'Are you saying that unless it's locked, I'm not safe from you?' She was teasing him, her worries gone for the moment.

'Are you saying that you don't lock your door when you're staying in a hotel? Good God, that's an absolute given for a young woman staying on her own.'

'Of course I do, nitwit. Don't look so fierce; it doesn't suit you.'

He chuckled, ruffled her hair and tossed her the key to her room. He'd handed the ancient retainer a shilling and told him they could find the rooms themselves as they were both concerned the poor old chap might collapse as he ascended the stairs.

'Don't be long – we're having lunch in twenty minutes. I'll see you down there.'

'Okay. But Perry, I'm really happy to be here with you, but everything's happening too fast for me.' She hadn't meant to say this but was glad that she had as immediately, his expression changed to one of concern.

He took her hands in his and shook his head. 'I've made a complete ass of myself, haven't I? I didn't even give you a chance to answer before shoving the ring on your finger.' Again, without asking her opinion, he removed it and carefully put it back into the box. 'I ambushed you. I'm absolutely not going to pressure you into doing something you might not be ready for.'

As soon as he said that, things fell into place. 'I thought a marriage proposal was done on one knee.' She raised an eyebrow and nodded at the floor.

He released her hands and immediately dropped to one knee. Only then did she realise they had an interested audience of two old ladies and a Pekinese dog. Too late to stop him now.

'Corporal Felgate, will you do me the inestimable honour of becoming my wife? Will you make me the happiest of men and accept my proposal of marriage?'

His eyes were sparkling with amusement and she understood he was well aware of their audience. The wretch – he'd done this on purpose. It would serve him right if she said no.

'Major Harrow, how kind of you to ask. I would be thrilled to become your wife.'

He made a noise which sounded like a laugh, surged to his feet and spun her around like a child. As he returned her, somewhat dizzy, to her feet, she saw the smiling faces of the old ladies and knew she'd made the right decision.

Perry loved her and she loved him. He wouldn't do anything to upset her intentionally and before they actually tied the knot, she'd know him better, be more comfortable with him, and would explain that she had a mind of her own and he didn't have to make her decisions for her.

15

Perry bowed to the old ladies and was going to lean down and stroke the smelly little dog but it growled so he refrained. Clara had already gone into her room. How could he have almost ruined things again? She might be young, but she wasn't immature and if he wanted this to work, then he had to do better.

In future, he'd do everything he could to suppress his instincts, try not to make assumptions but ask what she wanted to do before he made decisions for her. He looked around the room, which was adequate, but the ceilings were lower than he liked. Anyone taller than him was likely to knock himself out on the beams.

After tossing his suitcase onto the bed, he checked out the ablutions. No bath, but a reasonable-sized shower and WC.

There was no point in going down for a bit so he strolled to the window and peered out over Lincoln. The hotel was on a hill close to the impressive cathedral. They'd go and look around after lunch. He must ask her if she wanted to visit the cathedral, not tell her she was going.

He turned as he heard sounds from next door. Having her so close but not being able to be with her was going to be torture. He anticipated a lot of cold showers over the next few days. There was a knock on the door. He strode across and opened it, expecting to see a minion of some sort, but it was Clara.

'Perry, before we go down, we need to talk. This seems as good a place as any. Leave the door open if it bothers you – it doesn't me. I think there's more leniency for an engaged couple, don't you?'

'Come in, we've got fifteen minutes – is that long enough?'

She nodded and looked around with interest as she stepped in. She chose to sit in the comfortable armchair on the right of the small fire and he took the one opposite.

'Despite the letters we've written to each other, I

know absolutely nothing about your family, how you grew up and you know nothing about mine. I really think we should have talked about this before, don't you?'

'It didn't occur to me, but I agree. I'll go first if you like. I'm an only child from a wealthy upper-middle-class family. My father was something important in the city, and my mother was a leading light at the tennis club. She died many years ago. I've not seen or heard from my father since I went to Sandhurst. I'm assuming that he's still alive, but he might not be and it makes no difference to me either way.'

He'd been blunt, waiting to see if she was shocked, but she nodded and smiled sympathetically. 'I have two younger brothers; they are twelve and thirteen and at Eton. I doubt I'd even recognise them if I met them in the street as they rarely came home even when I was there. I went to boarding school from the age of seven, I did my highers, would have gone to university but war broke out so I joined the ATS instead. Since then, I've been disinherited and disowned.'

They exchanged a smile. 'Then neither of us will be expecting a big turnout for our nuptials and there will be no interfering in-laws or doting grandparents from either side when we eventually have children.'

She nodded, not at all put out by his summary. 'I can't marry until I'm twenty-one unless I ask for permission, and they'd never give it. Therefore, we'll have to wait until next September.'

'To have children?'

'No, you buffoon, to get married. I prefer not to have children until after the end of the war as I want to serve overseas.'

Perry was about to tell her she'd leave England over his dead body but managed to bite back the words. 'That reminds me, I've got something for you.' He reached into his jacket pocket and gave her a similar leather box to the one the ring had been in. He'd bought it at the same time, knowing that she'd have had a birthday whilst they were apart.

She frowned and took it. This wasn't the reaction he'd been hoping for. He watched anxiously as she pushed back the little silver catches, revealing a simple but elegant gold locket.

'It's beautiful. I don't really like jewellery, but this is perfect. If I had a small snapshot of you, I could put it on one side.'

He flicked open the catch on the locket, revealing that a photo of him was already there. 'I'm hoping we can find a photographer to take a picture of us together and also one of you that I can have in my wallet.'

'You don't have to as I've managed to get one done.' She handed him a snapshot and his eyes misted. She was so beautiful, so young, and he knew he was lucky to be engaged to her.

'Thank you. I've got another slightly larger version of the one in the locket. I thought it might be presumptuous to give it to you but...?'

'Please let me have it. Maybe I can buy a frame somewhere and then have it on my locker so that everybody can see the handsome man I'm going to marry.' She giggled and he loved to hear her do so. 'I don't believe there could be any other corporals engaged to a major. I'll be the talk of the depot.'

She stood up gracefully and held out the locket. 'Could you put this on for me, please? I think I can have it under my uniform and nobody will be the wiser. I don't think I can wear an engagement ring and especially not one as valuable as this. Do you think I could have the box so I can put it away when I'm on duty?'

* * *

They made their way down to the dining room, which was full, the only vacant table being the one that Perry had reserved. They were ushered to it like VIPs and after a lot of fuss and flapping of napkins, they were left alone to peruse the menu.

'Are we having dinner here as well, Perry?'

'I was told this is the best place to eat but we can go somewhere less formal if you prefer.'

'No, I like it here. But if we're eating again then I only want a main course and coffee if they've got it.'

He glanced down and saw there were lamb chops, fish pie and a steak and kidney pie. 'I'm going to have the steak and kidney – what about you?'

'Yes, I can smell it from here. I think everybody's having the same.'

He thought the meal was probably excellent but he was scarcely aware of what he ate. He couldn't remember ever being so happy – if he was being honest, he'd never been happy. This was a fresh start for both of them and he intended to make the most of it.

'Would you like to stroll over and look at the cathedral after lunch, darling?'

'I was going to suggest exactly the same. I'm not especially religious but I do like historical buildings.'

The coffee was barely drinkable but at least it wasn't the artificial muck that was sometimes served in the officers' mess – a concoction made from acorns. The meal would be added to his bill and he'd settle it when they left. One thing he hadn't mentioned to Clara was that he didn't have to rely on his pay – he was independently wealthy.

Perry wasn't sure why he hadn't included this information when they were talking earlier. Probably because nobody in his family talked about money as it was considered vulgar. He hadn't even known that he'd be a comparatively rich man on his twenty-first birthday; he'd received a letter from the family solicitor in the final months of his time at Sandhurst.

Neither of them had asked why they'd had such a miserable childhood but he suspected her background was similar. As they were walking hand in hand towards the cathedral, something occurred to him.

'Your brothers, are they your half-brothers by any chance, Clara?'

She wasn't upset by his question and nodded. 'How did you guess?'

'The age gap and how you talked about your home life. I think my parents resented me because my grandmother – I never met her – left the family fortune to me in trust and not to them.'

Now he had her full attention. 'Are you telling me

that you're not just a major but a wealthy major? How exciting – as soon as we're married, I'll be in Harrods every weekend spending your inheritance.'

He ignored her reference to shopping and latched onto her mention of marriage. 'About that – if you're agreeable then I'm pretty sure we could get permission from the CO of your depot. We don't actually have to wait until next September.'

'I don't know. I've not quite got used to being engaged yet. I do love you, but I think we should both concentrate on doing our bit and put our personal wishes to one side at least until next year.'

It had been worth a try and her answer was what he'd expected. 'Your wish is my command, my love: next September it will be.'

Her eyes sparkled and she smiled. 'As I know that you're a man of your word, I have several requests. The first being...'

He sighed theatrically. 'Well? What have I let myself in for?'

'Actually, I can't think of anything I want you to do. I'm content with how things are.'

Ignoring all the rules of etiquette that had been drummed into him since he was a small boy, he gathered her close and kissed her, loving the way she responded, knowing that she was enjoying it as much as he was.

'Disgraceful behaviour, young man,' a woman in a mink coat and extraordinary hat said sharply as she waited for them to move so she could walk past.

He grinned. 'We've just got engaged, ma'am, we've only got three days' leave and then might not see each other for months.'

He'd hoped she might smile and wish them well but she pursed her lips and glared at him as she stalked off.

'Golly, what a nasty old biddy. I don't mind if you kiss me whenever you want, Perry, even if we do get a ticking off for doing it in public.'

A young woman holding a small child smiled at them. 'Don't take any notice of lady muck; she might be rich but she's nothing special. You make a lovely couple; reminds me of when me and my Den were first courting.'

* * *

Clara was captivated by the cathedral and would have been happy to wander about for hours but she sensed that Perry was not as enthralled as she was.

'Shall we explore the city or go back to the hotel and order tea?'

He couldn't hide his look of relief and she giggled, drawing several disapproving looks from other visitors. 'Yes, stunning as this place is, as far as I'm concerned, one cathedral is very like another.'

This was blatantly untrue but she wasn't going to argue the point until they were outside. She stopped and turned to have a last look, determined to return if she got the chance and maybe attend a service if possible.

'The choirs at cathedrals are quite wonderful. It's worth going just to listen to that even if you don't enjoy the service. A sung Eucharist would be perfect,' she said as they strolled back to the hotel.

'We'll be here on Sunday. If you'd like to go then I'm more than happy to accompany you.'

'Matins would probably be best as it's shorter. Let's not decide right now as we might well have something else we want to do instead.'

His arm tightened around her waist and she pressed against him. 'I realise now that I've never been really happy until now,' he announced and for a second, she thought he was joking.

'That's so sad, I hate to think of you as an unhappy little boy. My stepmother wasn't unkind; she just didn't care for me. My father didn't like any of us but that's how things often are in my sort of family.'

'Are you happy now?'

She stopped, making him do the same. 'Look at me, look at my face; I'm sure it's written all over it. I feel as if I've swallowed a bottle of pop and could take off and fly about in the sky at any moment.'

She saw his eyes darken and hastily stepped away. 'No, we've caused enough scandal already today. If you don't behave then I won't hold your hand.'

His smile was electric. Her heart was trying to escape from her chest. Would she unlock the door tonight if he tapped on it? The way she felt at that moment, she knew that she would.

* * *

Clara became more confused as the day progressed. It wasn't because Perry had even hinted that he expected to be sharing her bed that night; he couldn't have been more gentlemanly if he tried. He used endearments, touched her face, kissed her hand a couple of times but for some reason, even when they were alone, he didn't kiss her the way she wanted to be kissed.

Had she done something to offend him by

seeming over eager? She didn't know exactly about what went on between a man and a woman in the privacy of their bedroom; of course she knew the mechanics but not how it was actually achieved. But one thing she was quite certain of was that girls from her sort of background didn't sleep with their boyfriends or even their fiancés. They waited until the knot was tied before doing that.

'Clara, you're daydreaming – I've asked you three times if you want to go and explore the city before dinner.'

'I'm sorry, I'm finding this unexpected engagement terribly confusing. I never expected to fall in love and certainly not with you – it's a mystery to me why we've ended up together as we're so different.'

He raised an eyebrow and she giggled. When he did that, he looked like the sort of man who should have a monocle, a deerstalker hat and a pipe.

'I'd say that we're very similar: we come from the same background, had a bloody rotten childhood, are no longer in contact with our family and are both in the army.'

Clara smiled. 'I thought you were going to say that we're both spectacularly good looking, incredibly intelligent, witty and popular – why didn't you?' It was her turn to raise an eyebrow and he laughed out loud, making the two nice old ladies with the smelly dog look round. Unlike the unpleasant woman outside the cathedral, these two nodded and smiled – it was only the dog who didn't like them.

'That goes without saying, my love. Why don't you spend the rest of the afternoon in your room, write to a couple of your friends and give them the good news? I've got some paperwork with me which I can get on with. Hopefully, when we go down for dinner, you'll feel more settled.'

For some reason, instead of replying to his kind suggestion, she changed the subject. 'I've told you my birthday, but I still don't know when yours is. Also, do you have any middle names? I shudder to think what they might be if your first name is Peregrine.' She pulled a face and he pretended to look cross.

'I'm Peregrine George Harrow. What about you? Do you have any horrors lurking in the middle of your name?'

'I'm afraid I do – I fear if I tell you that you might disown me. My full name is Clara Elizabeth Agatha Brownlee Felgate.'

'That's a mouthful – if we do marry in church, it will take the vicar five minutes to say that lot.'

'Are you in fact a lot older than you've told me? Twenty-seven seems very young to be a major.' She loved teasing him and he enjoyed it as much as she did.

He puffed out his chest and crossed his arms. 'I'm really twenty-seven. I was promoted because I'm the best officer they've ever had and am destined to be a brigadier by the time I'm thirty.' Then he smiled almost shyly and looked a little self-conscious. 'I wasn't going to mention it, but it's my birthday tomorrow. I'll be twenty-eight.'

'Then we must do something to celebrate – I wish I'd known as I would have tried to find you a gift of some sort.'

'Just having you here, hearing you say that you love me as much as I love you, is all I want.'

Her eyes filled. 'Then if we can get permission, I'll marry you when we meet in December. If you're rejoining your regiment in Africa it might be years before you're back.'

She didn't say so but they both knew it was quite possible he might not come back.

'Are you quite sure? I don't want to you to do anything you're not absolutely sure is the right thing for you.'

She nodded. 'I'm absolutely sure. I wasn't until now, but things have somehow fallen into place.'

'I'll speak to my CO – I think he can probably

swing things with your officer which will make things easier for you.'

Clara leaned across and kissed him – not anything passionate – just a touch of her lips on his but this was enough to send spirals of what she now recognised as desire flowing through her veins.

'Will you knock on my door when you've finished your paperwork?' Clara asked him.

'It shouldn't take me more than a couple of hours. I thought maybe we could wander down into the centre and post your letters. There might be somewhere else we can have dinner tomorrow night. What do you think?'

She tilted her head and put her finger on her lips as if seriously considering her answer. His smile made her catch her breath.

'I think this time, I'm going to let you decide. After all, if you're the shining star of Sandhurst; it hardly seems right that a lowly NCO decides anything at all.'

He didn't follow her upstairs as his papers were in the car and it gave her a few moments to gather her thoughts. She knew exactly what she was going to give him for his birthday. He wouldn't dream of knocking on her door but at one minute past midnight tonight, she was going to knock on his.

16

Perry completed his paperwork in a couple of hours. He'd heard Clara moving about next door so thought it likely that she'd finished writing her letters. The contents of his briefcase weren't actually classified as top-secret but if it fell into enemy hands, it would be a disaster.

Hitler knowing that there was a national shortage of socks might not seem important, but it was still information that should be kept from prying eyes of any sort. He was torn as to whether he should return the briefcase to his car and lock it in the boot or hide it somewhere in his bedroom.

He frowned. Neither option was ideal but on balance, he thought it more likely his car might be stolen than that someone would break into his room in such a prestigious hotel as this. So far, the guests he'd seen had been elderly, wealthy and hardly likely to be enemy spies.

He put the papers under his pillow and remade the bed. He stood back and reviewed it and was satisfied nobody could see anything had been hidden there. He wondered what Clara had written to her friends and hoped she was as excited as he was to be planning their life together.

He was looking forward to tomorrow – it would be the first birthday that he'd spent with someone he loved and who returned his feelings. He didn't expect a present or a card – both were in short supply. It would be gift enough for him to be with Clara.

As he was locking his bedroom door, she stepped out of her own room. 'Did you get your work finished, Perry?'

'I did. Did you get your letters written?'

She handed him the key and then waved four envelopes at him. 'I only had two stamps so I'm hoping I can find a post office. Do you think one will still be open as it's almost five o'clock?'

'I doubt it, but I'm sure the concierge will have some,' he replied.

He could hear the murmur of voices and the rattle of

cups and cutlery coming from the dining room. 'Would you rather have tea than dinner or perhaps both?'

'Actually, I'd much prefer to have an afternoon tea as long as they've got freshly baked scones and so on. Do you think we're too late?'

They'd now arrived in the foyer and Perry slipped the keys in his pocket. If they weren't leaving the premises then they didn't need to hand them in.

The concierge greeted them with a smile.

'Good afternoon, Major Harrow and Corporal Felgate. Can I be of assistance?'

'I was hoping that you have stamps I could purchase and also that these letters go in your post for this evening?' Clara smiled and the elderly man positively glowed with pleasure.

Perry left her to charm the poor old chap and headed for the dining room. There were three empty tables and he could see that there was an old couple who still hadn't been served. This looked promising.

The head waiter hurried over to greet him. 'Have you reserved a table for afternoon tea, sir?'

'I haven't, but I see that you've got some tables free. My fiancée has decided that she'd rather have afternoon tea than dinner but only if you have freshly baked scones.'

The chap beamed. 'Indeed we do, Major, and also a delicious array of finger sandwiches, assorted savouries and today we have meringues and eclairs.'

Clara glided up to his side and had clearly overheard the conversation. 'That sounds absolutely perfect. I've not had a cream cake of any sort for years. I do hope you can fit us in as I can see that you're almost at the end of service.'

'It will be my pleasure to seat you both. Would you care to follow me?'

Perry was aware that their arrival in this room full of elderly guests was drawing attention; maybe coming to this particular hotel hadn't been such a good idea after all. Most of the residents were old enough to be his grandparents, let alone hers.

'I do love an afternoon tea, Perry, but I doubt that it will live up to prewar standards,' Clara said.

'I'm sure that it will, darling, if the price is anything to go by.' He regretted mentioning the cost as soon as he'd said it. But spending the equivalent of a working man's wage on afternoon tea for two didn't sit well with him.

She glanced at him and touched his hand. 'I agree it's somehow not right to be so extravagant when others are struggling to put food on the table for their families. Shall we forego this treat and donate the money to a local charity?'

How he loved her – he couldn't think of any other young lady who would immediately have picked up on his unease and made such a suggestion. 'No, I think that just occasionally, it's perfectly acceptable to be extravagant. It's my birthday tomorrow and it was your birthday last month, so this is by way of a birthday treat for both of us.'

The waiter had been hovering anxiously listening to this conversation and his look of relief was comical. Hastily, he pulled out a chair for Clara and was flapping her napkin onto her lap before he'd even sat down.

'We have a selection of teas, sir, madam; would you care to peruse the menu?'

Perry looked at her and she shook her head. 'No, thank you, just ordinary breakfast tea will suffice.'

As soon as they were alone, he reached across and took her hands which were resting on the pristine tablecloth. 'I think it's a good idea to find a local charity. Whatever the bill is at this hotel, I'll put the same amount into whatever box we find.'

'Goodness me, you don't have to be quite so generous.' She flushed and looked away, thinking that she'd upset him.

'I'm not your superior officer, my love; I'm your fiancé and you can say what you like without fear of offending me.'

She smiled. 'I'm not sure that's quite accurate as I think that I could easily annoy you if I wanted to.'

'Please don't do it deliberately. Being with you is relaxing, we share the same sense of humour and I'm hoping that you enjoy my company as much as I enjoy yours.'

She looked past him and laughed. 'Golly, there are three waiters heading this way with our tea. I think they're making sure we don't change our mind and slope off.'

When the waiters left, he could scarcely see her past the three-tier cake stand, the two-tier savoury one and the silver tea service.

'This looks absolutely scrumptious. Perry, it's real butter and cream as well as what looks like home-made strawberry jam to go on the scones.'

She moved the stand with the savouries closer to her so she could examine what was on each plate. The delicate finger sandwiches tasted as delicious as they looked and the various savouries were equally splendid.

By the time they'd cleared the table, they were the only ones left in the dining room.

'Thank you so much, Perry, that was the best tea I've ever had. I can't imagine how they managed to produce something like this when so much of it is rationed. I was told that the crusts they cut off from the sandwiches are made into breadcrumbs and used to coat the fish.'

He nodded. 'They have to do something with them as every scrap has to be used. Shall we go for a walk?'

'That would be an excellent idea if it wasn't raining.'

He hadn't noticed the weather had changed and frowned. He liked to stretch his legs after a big meal and the thought of being cooped up for the rest of the day didn't appeal.

'We could go for a drive?'

'No, we shouldn't waste petrol. You've only got some in your car because you're on official government business. I'm sure there's a cupboard somewhere full of boardgames and hopefully some books. We'll go in search of those, shall we?'

* * *

He was surprised to find a box of Monopoly in a cupboard in a small sitting room and they took it to a corner of the room and spent the remainder of the day happily playing this ridiculous but addictive game.

'I think we should declare this a draw or we'll be here till midnight,' Perry said and she nodded.

'It was such fun playing this with you. I expect you'll be surprised to know that I've never played it before. Can we have a rematch tomorrow?'

'About tomorrow, darling: I was thinking that maybe we should find somewhere a little less stuffy. I'm sure you've noticed that all the guests are ancient. There must be somewhere with a younger clientele – maybe even a place that has a small dance floor.'

'I wasn't going to suggest we moved but now you have, I can tell you I do feel a little out of place here. Not only are we the youngest by several decades but we're also the only ones in uniform. I'm sure we'll find somewhere else that's a little livelier.'

A waiter had come in to put some logs on the fire and overheard their conversation. 'There's the Castle Hotel; it'll be just the ticket for you two. It's not far from here.'

'That sound perfect. I'd forgotten they have a castle as well as the cathedral. Can we go and see that tomorrow?'

'That was my plan, my love.'

The waiter was hovering beside them and asked if they would like anything to eat or drink before the kitchen closed.

'I'd love some coffee and any savouries, cakes or sandwiches that might have been left over from afternoon tea,' Clara said.

'I'm sure we can find you something, madam. What about you, sir?'

'I'll have the same, thank you, and please add two glasses of cognac?'

* * *

Clara was glad he'd ordered some strong alcohol. She was going to need Dutch courage if she was going to carry out her plan. When their supper arrived, she was shocked to see that the balloon glasses were almost half full of amber liquid.

'Oh dear – I don't think I can drink all that. I was going to tip a little into my coffee as I don't really like it neat,' she said, viewing the glass with distaste.

'It's certainly a generous measure. It's one thing I don't know about you – does alcohol not agree with you?'

'I enjoy a glass of shandy in the summer and the occasional glass of wine but to be honest, I've had very little experience of social drinking. Remember that I joined the army as soon as I left school.'

'I can hardly believe that's true,' Perry said as he poured the coffee in the delicate porcelain cups, leaving room for him to tip in some of the brandy. 'I suppose being at boarding school from the age of seven taught you to be independent.'

'It certainly did. It also made basic training much easier as I was used to the lack of privacy, following orders, and sleeping in dormitories. I know that a lot of the girls found that really difficult.'

'Shall we forget about the past and concentrate on our future? We've not had the opportunity to raise a glass to our engagement. Shall I tip some of this into your coffee or have you changed your mind?'

'Yes, please do and then add a small amount of sugar, but no cream or milk, thank you.'

He tipped a more generous amount into his coffee but with no sugar. He looked at her in the special way that made her glow all over. After handing her a cup and saucer, he picked up his own.

'These look so fragile, I don't think we can clink them as we would a glass.' He raised the cup and tilted it towards her. She followed his lead. 'To us – wishing us a long and blissfully happy life together despite this bloody war.'

She snorted and slopped the precious liquid into the saucer. 'I'm sure you're not supposed to swear when you toast something.'

'Possibly not, my love, but you're definitely supposed to reciprocate and not criticise.'

She giggled, tipped the spilt coffee back into the cup and held it out. 'To us – knowing that we're going to be blissfully happy in the future, whatever it might hold.'

He swallowed his drink in one swallow and she thought she'd better do the same. It wasn't until the last mouthful that the potency of the brandy hit her.

She coughed and spluttered; it took a few moments to regain her breath. He'd remained where he was, hadn't offered to pat her on the back. In fact, he was watching her with amusement.

'If I didn't love you so much, you horrible man, I'd come round and punch you on the arm. I could have choked to death whilst you sat there laughing at me.'

Instead of answering or apologising, he grinned and poured another cup of coffee, this time with no alcohol in it. He dropped in a lump of sugar and stirred it before picking up the saucer and handing both to her.

'Have something to eat before you have any more brandy; it will soak up the alcohol.'

'I will. It would be a pity to waste this as they seem to have gone to a lot of trouble.'

She discovered she wasn't as hungry as she thought – maybe it was the thought of knocking on his bedroom door later that was spoiling her appetite. She filled the cup with coffee first and then added the brandy.

With some hesitancy, she took a sip. She drank it more slowly and enjoyed the warmth of the alcohol as it went down. She sighed and leaned back in the chair.

'That's better; you'll soon be a hardened drinker,' he said with an indulgent smile.

'You'd hate it if I were. Although I must admit, I'm really enjoying the floating sensation this brandy's giving me.' Before he could comment, she put her empty cup down, tipped the last of her glass into it and then added coffee. This time, she thought it might be more brandy than coffee, but it didn't matter.

His eyes narrowed. He was reaching out to take the cup from her but she pushed her chair back and prevented him from doing so. She drank it in three swallows and felt absolutely marvellous.

Admittedly, she was a bit woozy, but the sensation wasn't unpleasant. She finally understood what they meant by alcohol making you do things you might regret the next day. Instead of being nervous about her daring plan, she was now excited and more than ready to retire and get ready for this adventure.

'That wasn't a good idea, Clara; you'll have a shocking hangover in the morning,' Perry said but he sounded resigned rather than cross.

'I don't drink,' she giggled and continued. 'Or rather I should say I didn't drink because now I do.'

He drained his glass and stood up. 'Come along, I'd better get you upstairs before you pass out.'

As this was exactly what she wanted to do, she didn't argue. She held out her hands and he pulled her easily to her feet. For a second, her head spun but his grip tightened and he held her steady.

'Why don't we go to the other hotel so we can dance? I think I'd really enjoy dancing tonight.'

'And I think that dancing would be disastrous in your condition.'

She looked up at him and for some strange reason, the outline of his face was a little indistinct. 'Spoilsport.'

They'd spent so long in the small salon that the hotel was silent – all the other guests were safely in their bed. The grandfather clock that stood proudly in the central hallway struck the hour loudly, making her jump. She squinted at the face striking midnight.

She wriggled out of his grip and ran up the stairs ahead of him then had to wait for him to arrive and hand her the key.

'Goodnight, darling, I hope you don't regret your overindulgence.'

She ignored his words and rushed into the bedroom and closed the door. Her heart was hammering, her head somehow unconnected to her limbs, but that didn't matter. It was now Perry's birthday and she was about to give him his gift.

After a quick, cold shower, her head cleared and she believed she was more or less sober. She didn't have a filmy negligée to put on and wished that she had. Her flannelette pyjamas were hardly romantic but at least if she was seen, she'd be decently covered.

How long should she wait? Her hair was brushed and hanging in shiny tresses down her back, she'd removed all traces of lipstick and powder from her face, cleaned her teeth and drunk a glass of water from the jug that was standing by her bed.

She put her ear against the dividing wall and could hear him moving about. She waited until it was silent, thought she heard him switch off the bedside light. Should she go in to him now?

If she didn't do it immediately, her courage would fail and she knew that to knock on his door when he was already asleep wouldn't be wise. He'd told her to lock her door but didn't know if he did the same. Should she lock her door when she left the room? No – she might well lose the key and not be able to get back in again. There was nothing in here of any value anyway.

She really didn't want to be standing about in her pyjamas in full view of anyone who might emerge from their bedrooms for more than a minute or two. Leaving on one of the bedside lights – which was a frightful extravagance – Clara stepped out of her bedroom. She wasn't going to knock and give him the opportunity to ignore her. She would just walk in and wish him happy birthday.

He was an intelligent man and should immediately understand why she was there.

17

Perry didn't bother with pyjamas, although he always packed the trousers just in case the siren went off and he had to evacuate. After a quick wash, he cleaned his teeth and stripped off and folded his uniform onto the chair so it would be ready for him to put on the next morning.

He was about to remove his underpants and clamber into bed when the door opened and Clara walked in.

'Happy birthday, darling Perry. I'm your birthday gift.'

Before he could gather his wits and bundle her out of the room whilst he was still able to do so, she pushed the door shut and turned the key in the lock.

He'd never seen her with her hair loose. She was irresistible and if she didn't go immediately, he wouldn't be able to send her away.

She then launched into a rendition of 'Happy Birthday' – she sang beautifully and as she did so, she walked slowly towards him. Her feet were bare, the curve of her breasts apparent under the flannelette jacket.

'No. No, Clara, you shouldn't be here. Get out, get out now before I do something we both regret in the morning.'

Instead of being upset by his apparent rejection, she continued until she was inches away from him. It was taking every ounce of his self-control not to tumble her onto the bed and make love to her.

'I know you think it's because I'm a bit tiddly, but I decided this morning that I'd come to you tonight. The brandy has just made it easier for me to do so. I love you. We're going to be married in a few weeks. I don't want to wait.'

He groaned and stepped backwards, holding out his hands to keep her away. Her smile wasn't that of a shy, inexperienced girl but of an adult woman determined to share his bed. If he hadn't moved swiftly and put herself out of reach, she would have taken his hands and not been put off by his gesture.

He was now standing safely behind an armchair. He gripped the back, hoping the pressure would focus his mind on his fingers and not another part of his anatomy.

'Darling Clara, this is all but killing me. There's nothing I'd like more than to make love to you, but we can't tonight. Do you know what a prophylactic is?'

Her eyes widened slightly then closed and opened again; she nodded.

'Good, it's not something I thought I'd need. Gentlemen don't carry them around with them. If you're quite sure this is what you want to do then I'll have what we need by tomorrow night.'

'I see. I thought I couldn't get pregnant the first time.'

'That's a myth put about by unscrupulous men. I know we're getting married in a few weeks but I also know that you don't want a baby until the war's over. Now, for God's sake, go back to your bedroom before I change my mind.'

'I'm sorry, I didn't think this through. I love you and want to be your wife in everything but name. Tomorrow night can't come soon enough for me.'

'Go, we can talk about this tomorrow. Don't make a noise. If anybody sees you leaving my bedroom in your nightwear, your reputation will be gone.'

She was unlocking the door but before she opened it, she turned, smiled, and if he hadn't been safely behind the armchair, she wouldn't have left his room.

'And yours, my darling Perry, would have been enhanced. Things are so unfair to us women when it comes to matters of the heart.'

Then she was gone and in two strides, he was across the room and locked the door behind her just in case she changed her mind. If she returned, he'd not have the willpower to send her away a second time.

* * *

After a long, freezing shower, he'd recovered but was so cold, he dug out his pyjama bottoms and put them on. Like all military personnel, he'd learned how to fall asleep instantly and didn't wake until seven the following morning.

He rolled out of bed, rubbed the sleep from his eyes and headed for the bathroom. Another accomplishment he'd learned as a soldier was to be able to shave and be dressed in minutes.

He couldn't hear any movement from next door so Clara must still be asleep. He checked his appearance briefly in the long mirror on the back of the wardrobe door then, his suitcase in one hand and his briefcase under his arm, he unlocked the door and headed downstairs.

'Good morning, Major. You'll be pleased to know that it's no longer raining,' the cheerful concierge said.

'Thank you for the information. Would you please prepare my bill as my fiancée and I will be checking out after breakfast?' He didn't offer any explanation for their early departure and the elderly retainer didn't ask. They were far too well trained to question their guests.

'I'll have it done immediately. Corporal Felgate has been down for some time and has gone to look at the castle.'

Perry nodded his thanks and headed outside. After putting his belongings in the boot of his car, he went in search of her. He found her fussing a huge ginger tomcat which was sitting on a wall not far from the hotel.

He wasn't quite sure how she'd react to seeing him after their aborted tryst last night. He needn't have worried. When she saw him, she abandoned the cat and flew into his arms where she belonged. A highly satisfactory and enjoyable few minutes later, he gently held her away and examined her face.

'You don't look as if you have a hangover, darling. How do you feel?'

'Tickety-boo. I found the Castle Hotel; it's only a five-minute walk from here. I was tempted to go in and book two rooms but then reconsidered. If I turn my engagement ring around, it will look as if we're married already – it seems silly to book separate rooms when we intend to sleep together tonight and hopefully, the following night as well.'

His answer was to crush her against him. 'If you're quite sure then that's what I'll do.' His voice was gruff, his eyes damp. How had someone like him managed to have such a wonderful girl in love with him?

'Splendid. Shall we go and have breakfast? I've been for a long walk up and down the hill and am absolutely ravenous.'

Hand in hand, they strolled back to the hotel and after paying the eye-wateringly large bill, they were back in his car.

'I've got something for you. I didn't tell you that I'd bought this at the same time as your engagement ring as it might have seemed presumptuous – in fact, it was – but if you recall, I did ask you to marry me a few days after we met.'

He took her hand and gently removed her engagement ring and then slipped the wedding band over her knuckle first and replaced the diamond.

'You did indeed. I'm glad I didn't know you were serious then as I'd have run away. I wasn't ready to fall in love with you and I don't actually know when it happened. Some time during the past few weeks, I think; every time I received one of your wonderful letters, it made me realise how much I missed you.'

'God knows what we're going to do to fill the time. All I can think about is spending the night with you.'

'Why don't we tell them that we've just got married? They'll expect us to tumble into bed together, won't they?'

18

Clara had blithely suggested they masquerade as a married couple but as they approached the hotel, she began to have second thoughts. Perry glanced at her and squeezed her thigh.

'I'll park the car here, but I'll book by telephone. It will seem more genuine doing it that way.'

'All right. Let's hope they have a vacancy – do try and get one with a bathroom if you can.'

He nodded. 'I'll get a suite if they've got one. Why don't you go to the castle and wander around whilst I locate a telephone box.'

She was about to say that she wanted to come with him then remembered that he'd said he had to buy something so that they could be together without the risk of her getting pregnant. She didn't want to know where he was going to make this purchase and certainly didn't want to be with him when he did.

He glanced at his watch. 'Shall we meet by the entrance in an hour?'

'That makes sense. I wish I had a camera so I could take snaps.'

'If I can see one for sale, I'll buy it as a birthday gift for me. I'll probably not be nearly as long as an hour but don't worry, I'm sure I'll be able to find you if I'm there earlier.'

He kissed her and strode off. She watched him go down the hill and she wasn't the only one taking notice. He was tall, handsome and a senior officer – small wonder the ladies took note.

When he was out of sight, she headed for the castle. It was wonderfully preserved but she didn't really notice what she was walking past. She'd agreed to marry Perry, had committed herself to spending the rest of her life with him and she was beginning to have doubts about whether she was quite ready to do this. She'd always considered herself a decisive girl and yet where Perry was concerned, she was the reverse. Was it because he was older, authoritative and reminded her a little of her father?

She paused in her wandering and flopped onto a

convenient wooden bench that was dedicated to some local dignitary or other. She'd been walking for half an hour and had no clear idea exactly where she was but there was plenty of time to find a way back to the entrance.

Her stomach was churning and she was pretty sure it wasn't the brandy she'd consumed last night. She wasn't sure she wanted to pre-empt their wedding night after all, but he would already have booked the one room and told them that they were a honeymoon couple. She'd been the one to suggest that they made love so could hardly blame him for being eager to set things in motion.

Then she smiled. She was having pre-marital nerves, second thoughts, the way a bride did. After all, sleeping with him would mean they were as committed to each other as if they'd said their vows. He was a gentleman to the core and he would never change his mind.

She did love him, she did want to marry him one day, but maybe it wasn't sensible to share his bed tonight. She glowed all over at the idea and decided to see how things were tonight and not make a decision or get herself in a stew now.

She frowned. She'd told him that it had been the

fact that they were apart that had convinced her she was in love with him and that was so true. He was kind, loving and toe-curlingly attractive. Good girls didn't even think about such things and she was glad she wasn't one of them.

Brides were supposed to be nervous on their wedding night, not sure what to expect, not sure that they were making the right decision. As this was effectively the same as a wedding night, it was only natural that she was apprehensive.

She closed her eyes and enjoyed the autumn sun bathing her face. Somehow, she sensed him approaching but didn't react.

'What's wrong? Are you having second thoughts about tonight?' He was now sitting beside her.

She was about to deny this but then reconsidered and opened her eyes, turning to look at him. 'I'm so sorry, I think I got a bit carried away.'

'So did I. I love you and want to make love to you, show you in a physical way just how much you mean to me. But sleeping together now would be wrong.' His smile was tender and he put his arm around her waist and moved her closer. 'I booked separate rooms, not because I don't want to be with you but because we both know it wouldn't be right.'

She rested her head against his shoulder and felt the tension drain away. Should she tell him that she wasn't even sure she was ready to marry him, let alone sleep with him?

'I'm going to apply for a special licence so we can get married in December if you're ready, or next year or the year after if you're not. I'm prepared to wait as long as it takes for you to be sure.'

'I am sure that I love you but I'm not sure that I want to marry in December – next summer seems a better idea. I really want to serve abroad before settling down. It's not because I don't love you; I do.'

'I guessed that might be the case. You have a very revealing face and you look like a woman who's having second thoughts. Absolutely no pressure from me – as long as we remain engaged, I know that one day, when you're ready, you will be my wife.' He reached out and slipped the engagement ring from her finger and then removed the wedding band and replaced the diamond solitaire.

'I'm going to be honest with you: I really don't like historical buildings. I look to the future and dwelling on the past isn't good for anyone in my opinion,' he said.

'Not even cathedrals?'

'Especially cathedrals – that said, I'm happy to

spend all day walking around here or the castle if that's what you want to do today.'

'What I'd like to do is check into the hotel, see what they have to offer by way of entertainment, and then find a park where we can commune with nature instead of old buildings.' She tilted her head and pursed her lips. 'That's if you don't object to parks as well as historical buildings.'

'I'm famous for my devotion to ornithology, you know.'

'I challenge you to name five birds, either from a sighting or from their song.' She nodded solemnly. 'In fact, I'll be delighted to borrow your binoculars, which must be in your car. A keen bird watcher would always have those to hand, wouldn't he?'

His rich, deep laugh turned several heads in their direction and made her pulse race. He was attractive, dangerously so.

'I don't know a sparrow from a magpie, my love, so it will be you identifying birds, not me.'

'You know the names, which is a start.' She pointed at a pair of pigeons cooing on the wall just ahead. 'If you don't know those, I'll eat my hat.'

'I'm tempted to pretend I don't recognise a pheasant but that would be unfair.'

For a second, she believed him, then they both

laughed. 'I've told you several times, Major Harrow, you are a nitwit. Now, let's go in search of the country-side. Checking in can wait until this afternoon.'

'Fine. By the way, it's a suite with a sitting room and bedrooms at either end. Sadly, there's no dancing tonight; it's only on Saturday nights.'

'As long as there's Monopoly or something simi-lar, I'll be happy. We could always listen to the evening concert. There should be a wireless some-where, I should think.'

'I didn't ask, but you're probably right.'

* * *

They found a delightful country hotel that served lunch and afterwards, they meandered through the extensive wooded grounds where Clara introduced Perry to half a dozen birds that were new to him.

When they eventually checked into the hotel, she was impressed. 'It's not as grand as the White Hart and it has a more relaxed atmosphere.'

'Definitely. There are a couple of RAF chaps in the bar, and the guests are nearer our age.'

'The lift looks a bit rickety. I'm going to use the stairs,' she told him after hearing it creaking and rat-tling as it ascended.

'Wise choice, my love. The suite's on the first floor, far end, overlooking the castle.' There was only one key, which he dangled from his hand. 'I've reserved a table for dinner at seven. Is that too early for you?'

'No, perfect.'

The suite was even better than she'd expected. If she didn't know he was wealthy then she'd have been embarrassed by him having to pay so much. The rooms were identical and she took the one on the left, he the one on the right. As she'd nothing to unpack, she just used the bathroom to restore her lipstick, tidy her hair and then returned, intending to explore the spacious, well-appointed sitting room.

He was lounging on a sofa, totally relaxed, jacket and tie off and shirt sleeves rolled up. He patted the space next to him.

'Join me, darling; we've got an hour or so until dinner.'

This was a reasonable request so why did it make her heart pound and prickles of unease flicker from her toes to her crown?

* * *

Perry saw Clara's hesitation – fear in her expression – and sat up, removing his arms from the back of the sofa, not sure what he'd done to cause this reaction.

'You don't have to sit with me, darling, if you don't want to. Don't you trust me to keep my word?'

She remained stationary, her face pinched, making it abundantly clear something was drastically wrong.

'I do trust you, Perry, but I don't trust myself. I think getting a suite of rooms was a very bad idea; it would have been much better to have separate rooms like last time – preferably at the opposite ends of the hotel.'

'Use the bolt on your door. I intend to use mine.' He hadn't intended to bark at her.

'Yes, sir, I'll do that.' She saluted and he smiled, thinking this was a joke, then to his horror, she smartly about turned and marched out of the room, leaving him stunned.

He snatched up his jacket, didn't bother to unroll his sleeves and was still doing the knot on his tie as he exited the room at speed. What had possessed him to revert to barking at her as if she was his subordinate rather than his future wife?

He was halfway down the stairs when he realised he hadn't got the key, hadn't locked the door, and he thundered back to collect it. He threw it on the shiny mahogany counter, startling the girl standing behind it, and ran across the foyer and out of the door.

He looked in both directions but there was no sign of Clara. Where the hell was she? She couldn't have got far in the few minutes since she'd rushed off, but he didn't know in which direction she'd gone.

An elderly gent walking a retriever of some sort was approaching from the right. 'Excuse me, sir, has an ATS girl run past you just now?'

'No, Major, she didn't come this way.'

Perry walked fast, not quite running, but covering the ground satisfactorily. He got to the end of the road and was faced by three small lanes, all of which led down to the town centre. He couldn't see her hurrying down any of them and if she'd come this way, he should have been able to.

Frowning, he strode back and was about to walk past the hotel and head in the opposite direction but paused by the front door. Possibly she'd not come out of the hotel at all, was somewhere inside and he'd not thought to look there first.

It took him fifteen minutes to explore every nook and cranny but he was confident she wasn't inside. There was only the car park and a small, terraced area outside and she certainly wasn't there.

There wasn't much else he could do but wait and he might as well do that in the comfort of his own very expensive accommodation. The girl who'd been behind the desk was no longer there and the concierge was back.

'Your fiancée collected the key, Major, so your suite will be unlocked.'

Perry nodded his thanks and bounded up the stairs. He didn't expect to find her sitting calmly in the sitting room and he was right – the door to her bedroom was firmly closed when before it had been open. No doubt she'd done as he'd suggested and pushed the bolt across.

Banging on the door, asking her to let him in, would be a pointless exercise. Eventually, she'd recover her composure and come out and he just had to wait patiently until she did. Clara's reaction reinforced his initial concern that she was too young to be engaged and certainly far too young to embark on a physical relationship with him.

He returned to the sofa but before he sat down, he noticed there was indeed a wireless on the mantel shelf above the cheerfully burning fire. He fiddled with the knobs and stopped when he heard band music. He'd have preferred an orchestra playing something classical, but this would do.

There were three newspapers in a wooden rack by the door and he pulled out the *Manchester Guardian*. Not one he'd usually read but the alternatives were even worse.

He read it from cover to cover, the afternoon concert finished and was replaced by a silly programme – a cast of unbelievable characters doing ridiculous things – and he got up and switched the wireless off.

'Oh, please leave it on. I really like *It's That Man Again.*'

He didn't turn to face her as he did as she asked. This gave him the necessary seconds to arrange his expression so he didn't show her how relieved and delighted he was that she'd finally emerged and sounded her usual happy self.

'*ITMA* isn't something I enjoy but if you want to listen then I suppose I'll have to sit here in silence and suffer whilst you do.' His tone was light and he prayed she didn't take his remark seriously, which was a risk considering what had happened earlier.

'I'm not sure which is going to be more amusing, Tommy Handley and his friends or you trying to remain silent.' She nodded, not smiling, but her eyes were warm when she walked across the room. 'I suppose if you're going to be silent then I'll have to order a pot of tea.'

He put his finger on his lips and sat down, gesturing towards the telephone. She giggled as he'd hoped she would and after requesting the tea, she joined him on the sofa.

'I think I rather overreacted. I know young men of my age have died fighting for this country, that the brave fighter pilots and bomber crews are probably younger than me, but for some reason, you make me feel gauche and inadequate.'

He was about to reassure her, tell her how much he loved her and apologise for barking at her like a sergeant major, but she shook her head.

'You said you were going to remain silent. I shall continue to talk and you will listen.' This time, her smile was flirtatious. This was going to be a very difficult afternoon.

'I think on balance, it would be better if you'd allowed me to stay last night, then you wouldn't have treated me like a child and I wouldn't have reacted like one.'

He reached out, lifted her and cradled her on his lap. He wasn't allowed to speak but he was going to show her how much he loved her and pray to God that he'd be able to keep things under control.

Several passionate and heady minutes later, the tea arrived and she scrambled from his lap, cheeks flushed and her lips slightly swollen, and rushed across to the door.

The time it took for her to tip the tea through the silver strainer, add the milk and pass him the delicate porcelain cup and saucer had given them both the chance to recover.

The idiots on the wireless were still wittering away but he ignored them.

'All right, you can speak now, but only if you don't snarl at me,' she said as she took a sip and peeked at him over the rim of her cup.

'Would you mind very much, darling, if I turn this rubbish off as neither of us are listening?' He grinned as he turned the knob and peace descended on the room. He wasn't quite sure how to answer her previous inflammatory statement but knew he had to address this now or it would create difficulties later.

'You're entitled to change your mind – it's a woman's prerogative, after all. I don't think that us sleeping together is going to solve this problem. I didn't mean to revert to being an officer and I'm quite sure you didn't intend to react like a child.' This wasn't quite what he'd meant to say and he knew at once that he shouldn't have called her a child. He hardly dared look at her, fearing she'd either be furious or tearful, and maybe rush off again as she had before.

She hadn't spoken and he risked a glance in her direction. Her smile was anything but childish and his eyes darkened. With slow deliberation, she put down her cup and saucer and stood up.

'I have twin beds in my bedroom – does yours have a double?'

19

Clara stretched like a contented cat, her bare legs entwined with Perry's and her head resting on his chest. He had one arm around her shoulders and he was slowly running his fingers through her hair.

'If I'd known how wonderful this making love is then I'd never have hesitated,' she murmured. 'I can understand now why men and women create scandals in order to do it.'

'I love you, my darling, and...' He sat up suddenly, taking her with him. 'Bloody hell, we've missed dinner.'

'Oh dear, now they'll know what we've been doing. I do hope they didn't send someone up to find us. We certainly didn't hear them.'

His laughter made his chest vibrate and she just snuggled closer. She was hoping they could repeat the amazing experience soon and food was the last thing on her mind.

'This is a major disaster, and you don't care.' He gazed down at her and she reached up and pulled his head closer.

'Care what strangers think of us? No, I don't, all I care about is you,' she whispered as she kissed him.

With what sounded like a groan, he tightened his hold and the kiss deepened.

* * *

The room was dark when Clara woke up and she could hear him breathing softly next to her. She slipped from the bed and felt her way to his bathroom. She needed a shower.

The water was hot, and halfway through, she remembered she'd not tied her hair up and this would now be as wet as she was. She looked around for shampoo, a scarce commodity now, and found none.

As she stepped out, Perry strolled in unashamedly naked and enveloped her in a bath towel. 'I hope you've left some hot water for me, darling,' he said as he held her close.

'Get in and see. A cold one would probably be more suitable in the circumstances.' She slid out of his arms and ran into the bedroom, laughing.

The bed was wrecked and she'd no intention of returning to it. Perry had switched on a bedside lamp which meant she was able to recover her watch from the pile of clothing on the floor. It was ten o'clock. Her stomach rumbled. No chance of ordering room service so late.

Hastily, she stepped into her voluminous and decidedly unflattering drawers and was just fastening her equally dire bra when he wandered out, this time with a towel wrapped around his waist.

His eyes widened and he grinned. 'Good God, what a dreadful set of undergarments.' His smile was wicked as he walked purposefully towards her. 'Allow me to remove them for you.'

'Certainly not, I'm starving and I need to eat. Get dressed and we'll see what we can find.'

He stopped and shrugged. 'If you insist. I'm pretty sure it's too late for room service.'

'I thought we might raid the kitchen. After all, you'll have to pay for the meal we missed, won't you?'

'Absolutely no kitchen raid – we'd be arrested. I'll see if the night manager will make us a sandwich and some coffee.'

She dressed and found enough hairpins to twist her wet hair into a pleat and pin it out of the way. By the time she'd done this, he was immaculate, tie straight, jacket on. Then she glanced at his feet.

'You've forgotten your socks and shoes, darling Perry; you can't go down like that.'

He smiled. 'Can't find them. God knows where I threw them earlier.'

'In the sitting room perhaps?'

He nodded. 'Yes, quite possibly.' He frowned at the dishevelled bed. 'We'll sleep in your room, darling; this one is ruined.'

The thought of being in a single bed with him made her quiver with anticipation. She tried to hide her expression but too late. He pounced.

'Let's not bother with food, darling; let's go back to bed.'

She pushed firmly on his chest and he released her. 'You're insatiable, Major Harrow. I intend to have something to eat and drink before resuming our premature honeymoon.'

'If you insist, my love, then I'll go in search of sustenance for us both.'

He headed for the door whilst she stared at the bed and wondered if she should strip it, make it, or leave it. Whatever she did, the chambermaid would be only too well aware of what had taken place.

'Clara darling, come and see this.'

She rushed into the sitting room and her mouth dropped open. 'Where did all this come from?'

The table from under the window had been laid up with brilliant white napery and crystal, there was a bottle of champagne in a silver bucket and several covered dishes in the centre.

'Gosh, how super.' She rushed over to lift each lid and exclaimed at the delicious array of tasty morsels displayed there. Then her smile faded and she clutched the edge of the table. 'They must have come in and set his up when we were, when we...' She couldn't continue. Knowing that the waiters must have overheard what had been going on next door made her feel sick.

'Darling, it doesn't matter. We'll check out tomorrow and never return.'

She swallowed with difficulty. 'It's not because we're not married. I would be mortified even if we were actually on our honeymoon. It's humiliating thinking someone was listening.'

He was about to speak but she shook her head. 'I think this was an invasion of our privacy, unforgivable. We didn't order this and didn't give them permission to come in here. How dare they do this?'

He tried the door and it was locked. 'They used a pass key to enter. My initial reaction was that it was kind of them but now I agree with you.' He was no longer smiling, looked formidable, and Clara wished she'd not been so vehement.

'It would be shame not to eat this even though we're both furious that they thought it was okay to come in uninvited and do this.'

'There's still some ice in this bucket. So it hasn't been here more than an hour.'

A wave of relief washed over her. 'Thank goodness. An hour ago, we were both asleep.'

His easy smile made things seem a little less embarrassing. 'Then it seems a shame to let this go to waste.'

He expertly popped the champagne cork and half-filled her glass. 'It really doesn't matter if I drink as I'm already a fallen woman,' she said gaily and drained it, then held her empty glass out. With some reluctance, he filled it almost to the brim.

'It's not you getting drunk that worries me; it's you having a horrendous hangover tomorrow morning. I don't want you to feel unwell.'

'I won't have more than this. I just noticed there's

a large thermos flask on the sideboard – do you think it might contain coffee?'

As he was on his feet, he went across to investigate. She couldn't help noticing that his toes were long and straight – that even his feet appeared muscular compared to hers.

'Yes, coffee and it's still piping hot. It will finish off this not quite a midnight feast perfectly.'

Despite being hungry, they didn't eat everything on the table, but they did drink all the coffee and the champagne. At least, he finished the champagne; she was satisfied with her glass and a half.

'I'm going to put this lot outside the door and make it abundantly obvious that we don't want them to come in,' he said as he began to stack everything on the two trays they'd found discreetly hidden under the long tablecloth.

The room was clear, the wireless playing a piano concerto she didn't recognise, and they settled down together on the sofa.

'Do you think that I might be pregnant?'

'I think it's quite possible. I wish now that I'd bought what we needed to prevent an unwanted conception.' His expression was serious as he continued. 'I'll arrange things so that we can be married as soon as possible. If you're carrying my child, it won't show for some months.'

'It's strange how things have changed in just a day. Now I don't really care if I never drive an ambulance on foreign soil – I just want to marry you and for you to stay safe until the end of this beastly war.' She frowned. 'Do you think by saying that I'm being disloyal to my country?'

'Of course not. It's changed me too. I think the possibility of a baby makes things different. I've only got three more barracks to visit and then I'm done. After that, it's just the paperwork and report to do. I'll be free at the beginning of December and I'll use my position at the War Office to pull a few strings so you can be free too.'

'I wrote to my friends and told them that we were going to be married so it won't seem as if we've rushed into this. Do you really have to go to Africa? Could you remain in England and continue doing whatever it is you do for your general?'

She'd asked this not expecting him to agree but he did.

'I've been desperate to get back to my regiment, fight on the front line, put my life at risk for king and country. Now I honestly think that knowing that most of the quartermasters are short of socks for the men and a whole variety of other essentials is actually going to be of far more benefit when we invade than me actually being there.'

* * *

Perry hadn't thought of himself as a sentimental sort of chap, he'd considered himself a soldier to the core, king and country first always, but he'd just said something that contradicted this.

Clara was staring at him as if he'd taken leave of his senses and he thought perhaps he had. 'Darling Perry, I can't believe you've just said you want to stay in England with me. If you do, can we find a house and live together, have a normal married life?'

'I've no idea whether I can do that as I don't know any married officers. I do know that married RAF can live off base as long as they're no more than a couple of minutes away by bicycle.'

'You already live in a hotel. That's the same thing really as living in a house or flat.'

'Technically it is, if we're within walking distance of my desk then I can't see my general objecting.'

'I suppose I could move into your room in the hotel but I'd rather not – I don't think the old gentlemen would approve of us.'

He chuckled. 'I'm sure they wouldn't. Look, leave it with me. I know the general I work for will be delighted that I want to stay, which means I can certainly remain in London until things hot up.'

'You'll have to go when the invasion starts, whenever that is; I fully understand that every able-bodied man and possibly woman will be needed to finish this war.'

'I'm pretty sure that nothing's going to happen until next year,' Perry said, confident this was true.

Her eyes shone and he knew he'd made the right decision. He'd do his duty when the time came but, unlike thousands of other poor sods, it looked as if he was going to get at least twelve months living a relatively normal married life in the company of this wonderful girl.

They relaxed and listened to the wireless until it shut down after the midnight news bulletin. The newscaster had informed his listeners that Montgomery had attacked the German and Italian armies in North Africa and was now pursuing them across the desert.

They stood to attention for the national anthem but neither of them joined in.

They decided they would definitely check out of the hotel and that he'd drive her back to her base and then he'd return and complete his mission as rapidly as he could.

'I'll use my bathroom, darling; I'll join you shortly.'

'It's going to be a bit of a squash in one of those beds – do you think we can put them together and make a larger one?'

Perry nodded. Her suggestion made perfect sense as he was far too big to sleep in such a small bed without at some point during the night inadvertently squashing her.

'Let's do it immediately,' Clara said.

Putting the beds together wasn't difficult but neither the sheets nor the blankets were now any use on the six-foot bed.

'You could put them widthwise, but then your feet will stick out of the bottom.'

'What about using the blankets from the other room?' He deliberately didn't suggest using the sheets.

'That would work just about. I'll put the sheets sideways whilst you fetch them.'

Eventually, she was satisfied the bed would do and he trotted off to use his own bathroom. He'd been happy to tumble her into bed half an hour ago – in fact was desperate to do so – then decided he'd have a cold shower as he didn't want to rush things. This was going to be the last night they spent together before they were married and he wanted to make the most of it.

* * *

The following morning, Perry dressed in the other room, giving Clara the privacy she seemed to need. He was sad she wasn't comfortable being naked with him unless they were under the sheets.

He showered quickly and was dressed, his suitcase closed and ready to head downstairs to make clear his displeasure about the intrusion of the hotel staff last night. They were also going to check out. He left his case on the chair so when Clara came out, she'd know he was coming back.

As he strode towards the reception desk, the bespectacled young man standing behind it blanched, dropped his pen and vanished. Perry smiled grimly and stood ramrod straight in front of the desk. He'd calculated roughly how much their stay would have cost and then deducted a considerable amount as compensation.

A man he hadn't seen before, in tailcoat and bowtie, arrived at the desk. Perry put down the cheque he'd written and fixed the trembling man with a steely gaze.

'My fiancée and I are leaving. We don't require breakfast and we certainly won't be staying here again.' He pushed the cheque across the shiny surface with one finger. 'This will fully settle our account.'

The man looked down and wasn't impressed. Before he could comment, Perry continued, his tone positively arctic.

'Your invasion of our privacy last night was unconscionable, unforgivable, and I was tempted to pay you nothing so you're fortunate to have what I've given you.'

The matter hung in the balance for a moment and then the manager nodded, picked up the cheque and vanished from whence he'd come.

Smiling to himself, Perry returned to the suite and was pleased to see Clara ready to leave.

'I'm afraid we can't have breakfast here but I'm sure we can find somewhere equally good and half the price.'

'Thank goodness for that. I was dreading being sneered and smirked at by the staff when we went into the dining room. I won't ask what you said to them. I'm assuming that as you look pleased with yourself, things went the way you hoped.'

He grinned. 'I worked out roughly what we should be paying and reduced it by roughly half. I handed the chap a cheque and with some reluctance, he took it.'

'I feel a bit guilty as we ate quite a lot of the food they brought up but I'm glad that you made it clear how upset we were. It's no more than half an hour from here to my base and I'm pretty sure we won't find a café or restaurant between Lincoln and it.'

'I thought the same. We'll find somewhere to park in the city centre and look for some breakfast there.'

* * *

The marketplace was heaving with stores and eager housewives possibly hoping to find an onion or two on one of the stalls. These were, like a lot of things, in short supply although not actually rationed.

There were two cafés doing a roaring trade and they were fortunate to grab a table as one became vacant. They had a huge pot of tea, two slices of toast each and more toast with poached eggs on top.

'That was delicious, Perry, nothing fancy but perfectly cooked and exactly what I wanted.'

They strolled hand in hand back to the car and when they were settled inside, before he pulled away, he swivelled in his seat to look at her. 'You've still got twenty-four hours before you have to report back. I'd really like to spend the rest of the day with you and take you back this evening.'

'I was hoping you'd suggest that. What are we going to do? It's barely nine o'clock. How do you suggest that we fill the time?'

He leaned across and whispered some very improper suggestions into her ear and she laughed. 'Behave yourself, Major Harrow, nothing is going to happen between us until our wedding night.'

He nibbled her ear, tilted her face, kissed her hard and then with a deliberately loud sigh of resignation checked there was nothing coming and pulled smoothly into the road. They decided to return to the place they'd had lunch yesterday and were welcomed like old friends.

In the afternoon, they went for a long walk through the grounds and found a fallen tree trunk they could sit on to talk.

'Why don't we book separate rooms, stay here tonight? We don't know how long it will be before we're together again.'

'I'd rather not if you don't mind. Darling Perry, I

really want you to get to London and set things in motion for our wedding. I'm still worried that we won't be able to coordinate our time off, or be able to arrange to be married, and what if I find myself in a very difficult situation?'

'I give you my absolute word that you'll never find yourself in any situation that is difficult or compromising. It occurs to me that I could almost certainly ask the padre at the next barracks I go to to marry us. When service people are being posted overseas, they only get a week or two's notice – I'm pretty sure that waiting three weeks after applying for a licence is often ignored since the war started.'

She didn't seem as delighted by his suggestion as he'd hoped. 'We could do that, but I'd much rather have my friends there and then a small celebration together.'

He was somewhat exasperated by her seemingly contradictory wishes. 'Look, darling, either you want to be sure you're married before you find out if you're carrying my child or you don't. You can't have it both ways.'

Her eyes filled and he felt a brute for making her cry. 'I know I'm being silly. You're right – if we can get married immediately then I suppose it makes perfect sense. Then maybe we could have a blessing like my friend Grace did.'

'There's definitely some sort of chapel adjacent to the War Office. I'm sure we can arrange to have it done there. What about having our wedding breakfast there as well? It does decent food and there's certainly plenty of room in December.'

'Then that's what we'll do.'

He grinned. 'Why wait? No time like the present, my love. We might be able to get married today or tomorrow.'

They returned to the car and drove away.

20

Clara should have been ecstatic at the thought of marrying the man she loved but she wasn't. What was wrong with her? They wouldn't be in this situation if she hadn't instigated what happened last night.

Why wasn't she smiling, humming to herself like Perry was?

She risked a sideways glance at him. She did love him, and suddenly things fell into place.

'Perry, can you pull over? We need to talk.'

He didn't argue, indicated, and drove into the entrance to a field where they were safely off the road.

'I was expecting this. You don't want to marry me today, do you?'

'No, I want a relaxed wedding with friends there to witness it. In London, as you suggested. If I am expecting a baby, that doesn't matter either.'

He grinned, apparently not at all upset. 'Marry in haste and repent at leisure, they say, don't they? Don't look so apprehensive, my darling; to be honest, I'd rather do this properly too.'

'I've always thought of myself as decisive, but since I met you, I seem to be flip-flopping from one conclusion to another. I wonder why that is, Major Harrow?'

His smile melted the last reservations that lingered. She leaned forward for his kiss. It wasn't passionate, hard like the last time, but gentle and tender.

'I expect, my darling, that you're in awe of my commanding presence and want to practise being an obedient and docile little wife.'

He waggled his eyebrows and she reached up and pulled his hair, making him yelp.

'It's a good thing I don't have a large frying pan to hand, otherwise I might well have done you some serious damage.' She giggled and settled back in her seat. 'I really hope you won't become a bullied husband once we're married as I do seem to have a tendency to attack you when annoyed.'

'I'm a lot bigger than you, my love. Aren't you

afraid that I'll put you across my knee and spank some obedience into you?'

'I know you wouldn't do that. You're not the kind of man who would raise a hand to any woman or child.' She stuck her tongue out at him and he laughed.

Perry checked there was no traffic and they resumed their journey. This time not to a barracks to be married but to her depot, where her first job would be to speak to her commanding officer and get permission to get married.

'Actually, when you're angry and look at me in that horrid, icy way, I am terrified. I'll have to practise looking equally unpleasant if I don't want to be tiptoeing around you.'

'You don't have to do that, my love; just shed a few tears and you'll be forgiven even if you have hit me on the head with a frying pan.'

* * *

As they grew closer to her base, the banter slowly faded. Saying goodbye even for a few weeks was going to be difficult – he was no longer a stranger but her lover and the man she was going to marry.

'Do you want me to take your engagement ring, darling, and keep it safe for you?'

'No, I'm going to thread it on the chain of the locket you gave me. It'll be perfectly safe there.'

'Dammit! I was going to buy a camera and take my own photo of you as I haven't got one that I took.' He smiled. 'I don't think the one I've got does you justice.'

'I'm pretty sure that one of the girls has a little Box Brownie camera she was given for her twenty-first birthday. Shall I ask her to take some more pictures of me so I can send them to you?'

'That's good. I take it you're going to speak to your officer immediately?'

Clara nodded. 'I am. I'm sure she'll agree. Can you telephone tonight and I'll make sure whoever answers the phone has the information you need? I gave you the number in my last letter – do you still have it?'

'I do – it's engraved on my heart.' His smile made her eyes fill.

He stopped a hundred yards from the entrance to her accommodation and looked across at her.

'Would you prefer it if I stayed in the car?'

'You're my fiancé; I'm happy for anyone to see us

together even if you're a very superior person and way above my touch.'

Hastily, she opened the door and hopped out before he could do anything reprehensible. It was all very well exchanging a chaste kiss in public, but a passionate embrace was definitely not going to happen.

'Am I allowed to kiss you goodbye?'

Willingly, she stepped into his arms. She rested her face against his rough khaki jacket and inhaled his unique scent.

'I love you, darling Perry, and I can't wait until we see each other again and can get married.'

'I'm going to count the days until we're together. I never thought to fall in love but you changed everything for me. I love you, my darling. It's been a spectacularly wonderful two days.'

She looked up and his kiss was gentle. 'Drive carefully, Perry. I think you go too fast in that car of yours.'

He grinned. 'Pot and kettle come to mind, Clara, as your speeding on a motorbike is far more dangerous.'

'I promise to be careful if you do the same. Goodbye, darling. I'll see you in a few weeks.'

She hurried away, didn't look back as she didn't want him to see her tears. Goodness knows how she was going to cope when he was actually sent overseas to fight. It brought home to her how lucky they were when so many men and women were separated, sometimes by thousands of miles.

She didn't have to show her papers as the old rectory was outside the perimeter of the base. She marched in and then went straight to the room she shared with Freda Simpson, also a corporal, to leave her haversack and change into a clean shirt and collar.

Her mind kept returning to other couples who were apart because of this beastly war. It must be unimaginable pain for those whose husbands were incarcerated in prisoner of war camps somewhere. Perhaps their families considered these men the lucky ones as they were less likely to be killed by enemy fire than those on the frontline.

She put aside these gloomy thoughts and turned her mind to happy ones – she was about to ask permission to get married and arrange to have the remainder of her leave and she could hardly speak to the commanding officer looking miserable.

Clara walked into the main administrative

building and the clerk behind the desk screeched. 'I can't believe you're back early. Absolute pandemonium here – are you back to work?'

'Yes, I'm only too happy to help. What's going on, Private?'

The officer on duty rushed out. 'Corporal Felgate, we've got four drivers down with chickenpox. Get changed, immediately report to the garage. I fear you're going to be working well into the night. I've had non-stop complaints on the telephone all day from very senior people needing a dispatch rider to collect or deliver something.'

* * *

Driving in the dark wasn't something Clara enjoyed but as the roads were relatively free of traffic and pedestrians it wasn't too hazardous. When she was finally able to park her motorbike, she belatedly remembered that Perry had been going to call.

There was nothing she could do about it now but first thing tomorrow, she'd speak to whichever officer was on duty and hopefully, because of her willingness to give up a day's leave and work so many hours without a break, they might consider her request more favourably.

The other bed in her room remained unoccupied and she guessed that poor Freda must be one of the drivers who'd caught this unpleasant childhood illness. Gritty eyed and half-asleep, Clara headed for the bathroom – a quick wash would hopefully revive her. As they were living in a house, they didn't have use a nasty cold ablutions block or latrines. Here they had a bathroom and WC on the first floor and a scullery and washroom and another WC on the ground floor – luxury indeed.

'Morning, Corp, thought you weren't back until tonight.' The speaker was Mary Wilshire, an older woman but perfectly pleasant. She was busy at the kitchen sink filling the kettle.

'I came back early and it's a good thing I did. Excuse me, I haven't eaten since yesterday lunchtime and I'm absolutely famished.'

'I could do you some toast and dripping and a nice cuppa if you can wait.'

'Thanks, but I'm on duty soon.'

She was first at the counter in the NAAFI. Clara had no intention of being late and she'd been told to report at seven o'clock.

After a substantial breakfast and three mugs of tea, Clara was ready for another busy day. She glanced at her watch; she'd fifteen minutes which would hopefully be time enough to speak to whichever officer was in charge today.

Senior Subaltern Jenkins was already at her desk and waved her in with a friendly smile. 'Thank you for your sterling work yesterday, Corporal, much appreciated. Major Harrow rang up yesterday expecting to get a message and was somewhat put out to discover that his fiancée was back at work a day early.'

'He must have been a bit cross. To be honest, I completely forgot about him telephoning until I got home just after midnight last night.'

'I told him that I would give you permission to get married in December and that you would be given a seven-day pass. Congratulations, Corporal Felgate, we'll be sorry to lose you.'

Clara was about to say that she didn't intend to ask for a different posting but then refrained. Probably better to leave things as they were as she might be pregnant and then would have to leave whether she wanted to or not.

'I can't believe that he actually asked for permission on my behalf.'

'Of course he did, Corporal; he outranks me, and I was only too happy give him the news he wanted. He said he will write to you with the dates and so on.' Jenkins straightened, once more an officer in charge.

'I'm sorry to tell you that you're going to be even busier today, but you must make sure you do take a break as I know that you didn't yesterday.'

* * *

Perry finished his tour of the barracks in record time and was pleased with his findings. Not socks but boots were missing.

Lieutenant Samuel Winchester was the young man assigned to guide him around and take notes. It should have been an officer of equal rank but Perry was too eager to get it done and move on to complain. 'I'm delighted to inform you, Winchester, that I know where your errant boots are. When I get back to my temporary office here, I'll give you the details and leave your quartermaster to do the rest.'

'Yes, sir, thank you, sir. Is there anywhere else you want to see?' the young man stammered; obviously, Perry hadn't been as relaxed and friendly as he'd thought.

'No, I'm finished. Thank you for your assistance; you made things much easier for me.'

This wasn't true as Winchester had been all but useless but he was newly promoted, fresh out of

Sandhurst, and was finding his unexpected role as guide to a senior officer terrifying.

All Perry had to do before he left was complete his paperwork in duplicate and submit it to the CO. Then tomorrow, he'd head back towards the capital and visit the places that hadn't wanted him prowling around when he'd started.

After talking to General Pickering, it had been clear there was nothing suspicious about their reluctance to have him there. One had been sending a regiment to Africa and the one they were replacing would be coming to them. One of the others had just had a flood, the third had a major influenza outbreak.

Perry telephoned Pickering and was put though at once. After giving his verbal report on this barracks, he told his CO that he wanted a week's leave to get married in December.

'Of course, my dear boy, congratulations to you. You can put in for leave when you've got a definite date.'

'Yes, sir, thank you. Now, you might be surprised at my next request.'

The old man chuckled. 'Not much surprises me, Harrow. You don't want an overseas posting. Want to remain here if possible?'

'Yes, exactly that. It means I can find somewhere

for us to live together. I'll start looking as soon as I'm back in Town. I'm aware I'll be attached to a regiment when the invasion takes place but until then, I'd be grateful if I can continue in my present role.'

'Best news I've had all year. We work well together and the PM thinks highly of you. Yes, you'll remain attached to the War Office until things heat up.'

Thoughtfully, Perry replaced the receiver in the cradle. He was pretty sure the PM had never heard of him but it was kind of Pickering to say that Churchill approved. All that needed doing now was for him to get back to London, book a padre or a registry office, make arrangements for a wedding breakfast, compile a list of guests with Clara and find somewhere to live. He smiled. Not much then.

He was somewhat premature in thinking they'd live together as the only way that would happen was if she was actually pregnant – she couldn't leave her job and couldn't ask to be posted somewhere just because it was convenient.

Tonight, he'd write to her, give her the good news, but first he had to endure a tedious formal dinner in the officers' mess. He'd much prefer to eat in the NAAFI but had no choice as it was expected of him as a visiting senior officer.

* * *

Some cretin who was supposed to be repairing a
large pothole in the road outside the mess managed
to put his spade through the water main so there was
no water available and dinner was cancelled, much to
Perry's delight.

Fortunately, he hadn't changed into his number
two dress uniform – this had to be worn at a formal
meal – when he heard the good news from his temporary orderly.

'I should nip along to the NAAFI, sir, before
everybody else does. It'll be chaos in there in a bit.'

'I'm on my way. Thank you for bringing me the
information so speedily. I'll be leaving immediately
after breakfast. Thank you for taking care of me.'

He tossed the private half a crown, which was
generous as he'd only been there two nights. There
was no queue and Perry was able to collect a decent
plate of food from the cheerful server behind the
counter – it was a stew; Perry wasn't sure exactly what
it was but it smelt appetising – and a large china mug
of freshly made tea.

He was halfway through his meal when the officers started pouring in. He hadn't been first but certainly ahead of the bulk of the men. It annoyed him

that ATS officers weren't allowed in the men's mess – if they were supposed to be an integral part of the army then they should be treated with more respect.

Before he'd met Clara, it wouldn't have occurred to him that ATS officers were being treated unfairly. He returned the tray to the counter, received a smile of thanks from the busy women, and then marched to the room he'd been using and wrote his letter.

My darling Clara,

I've the best possible news as not only can I stay in Blighty for the foreseeable but can also take leave for our wedding whatever date it is in December.

I've only two more places to visit and they are on the way back to London so I'll be there at the end of next week hopefully.

When I have made the arrangements, I'll write to you again, although I'd much rather speak to you on the telephone if that's possible.

Would you ring me at the hotel two weeks from today? Seven o'clock would be perfect.

I love you, I can't wait for you to be my wife and for us to start a life together.

He scrawled his name underneath, blotted the paper, and rammed it into the envelope. With any luck, if he took it to the postal department now, it would leave tonight and possibly be delivered tomorrow.

21

Perry completed the final inspections and returned to London satisfied that he'd done a damn good job. Pickering wasn't expecting him for another two days so he headed for the hotel where he was billeted.

He emptied his suitcase, hung up his dress uniform then dropped the dirty laundry into the bag provided and draped it on the doorknob outside the room. He had today to complete the list of things that needed doing before he and Clara could get married. Although he wasn't expected for forty-eight hours, he'd definitely be pushing his luck if he remained away from his desk for more than today.

First, he had to track down the chaplain he'd often seen lurking at the War Office and find out if he was prepared to marry them in the small chapel next door.

The best place to start his search, he decided, was the chapel itself and he was lucky as the Reverend Theobald was actually there, pottering about with a duster in his hand.

'Excuse me, sir, could you spare me a few minutes?'

'Of course, Major, I don't have to be anywhere for an hour which is why I'm doing some housekeeping in here.'

Perry quickly explained and the genial old gentleman nodded enthusiastically. 'I should be absolutely delighted to marry you and your fiancée. Let me check my diary. I am free between 14 and 18 December. Which of those days would be suitable?'

Perry did a rapid mental calculation and thought that the 18th was a Friday. 'The Friday would be best as I think it more likely that our guests would be able to get a pass. Do I have to apply for a licence?'

'No, give me your future wife's details and your own and I'll take care of that. What time would suit you best?'

'It'll be dark by late afternoon so midday would be ideal.'

This was agreed and Perry handed over the necessary information which he'd had the foresight to write down and have ready in his pocket.

'Excellent, that's the most important thing arranged. I now need to find a venue for the small wedding breakfast and somewhere for the honeymoon.'

'If you don't want anything elaborate, Major, why don't you have the meal in my church hall? My ladies will be only too happy to rustle up some sort of buffet. I'm afraid you will have to provide any alcohol – but we have sufficient crockery, cutlery and glasses for the maximum allowed to attend a wedding celebration.'

'Is your church far from here, sir?'

'No more than a hundred yards. Well, what do you think?'

'I think it's very kind of you and I accept your offer. Do I give you the money to pay for the food now or after the event?' Perry wasn't quite sure how extra food could be obtained when rationing was so strict.

'It's more than six weeks, ample time for me to speak to my ladies and find out how they want to do this.'

'I'm attached to General Pickering so perhaps you could drop in and see me when you've got some information.'

They shook hands and Perry strode out, delighted the two most important parts of his long list had been accomplished so easily. He could afford to book them the honeymoon suite – if there was such a thing – at the Ritz or the Savoy but thought that neither he nor Clara would enjoy the formality.

He recalled that someone in another office had mentioned a hotel called the Catherine Wheel at Henley-on-Thames as being the perfect place for a honeymoon. Not too far away from Town but still romantic and relatively rural.

It would be easier to make this reservation from his desk and not from a public call box, so he postponed this until he was back at work. Finding suitable accommodation for both of them, if Clara was to join him, was going to be more difficult.

So many buildings had been demolished or bomb damaged and were now boarded up and unsafe to be occupied. He wasn't optimistic that he'd be able to find anything good enough within walking distance of work.

Instead of heading to the canteen in the War Office, which was closest, he returned to his hotel as they served a decent lunch. He rarely came back in the middle of the day to eat and was rather surprised to find it as busy as it was in the evening.

Lunchtime there was no choice so those eating gathered in the bar until the gong was sounded. Perry recognised most of the men and thought they might be just the people to give him the information he needed. He approached a captain – he should know his name but didn't – who was drinking alone.

'Getting married, old bean? Good for you, I've just got engaged but with no plans to tie the knot this year,' the lanky, redheaded captain said jovially.

'Congratulations. I'm hoping to find somewhere more permanent to live; I can't bring my wife back here when she's on leave.'

'There's not much available but I do know of a house just the other side of the bridge that would be perfect.' The captain looked around as if worried about someone overhearing what he was going to say next. 'The place belongs to my great-aunt, but she relocated to America at the start of this bloody war. She's refused to sell or rent the place and it's my unfortunate duty to keep an eye on it for her.'

Perry immediately understood. He could rent the place as long as it was unofficial but as the war wasn't likely to be over for another couple of years at least, that was more than enough for him.

'I'll take it. I assume it's fully furnished and so on?'

'Not only that, old bean, it's got a housekeeper and two resident maids. At the moment, I'm having to pay their wages as well as their board and lodging. If you don't mind being there somewhat unofficially and are prepared to foot the bills, you'll be doing me a huge favour.'

'And you'll be doing the same for me.'

'I've got a couple of hours free this afternoon and if you have the time, we'll trot along and I'll introduce you to the staff.'

Barney Bairstow, which was the captain's name, shared a table with him for lunch. Over the meal, Perry was told exactly what this house was going to cost him, and he was pleasantly surprised. It was a prestigious address; the houses were grand. Then Barney explained.

'The side of the street my great-aunt is in is untouched but there are only two on the opposite side of the road still habitable and three have gone altogether. Does that bother you?'

'Not at all. Can I get my car down the street still?'

'They cleared a path so fire engines and ambulances could get down, but I doubt your little sports jobbie would enjoy the potholes.'

'I should have put it on blocks for the duration,

but I'll do that now. I can use a staff car and driver in future.'

Perry didn't ask if a perambulator could be wheeled safely but this was also important. 'What about the pavement? Does mail and milk get delivered to the house?'

'Good God, old bean, of course it does. Those living there would be creating merry hell if they didn't. Walking's no problem.'

'Then I'm going to take it. I know it's too big but better for the place to be occupied and the staff taken care off. My future wife, like myself, comes from a wealthy family and will enjoy living in comparative luxury after army billets.'

They shook hands on it and Perry devoured every morsel of his rabbit casserole and apple pie with custard.

'I'll visit my bank this afternoon and get something set up,' Perry said. 'I just need your details.'

Barney couldn't have been happier. 'Are you quite sure? You've not even perused the house. But I was there a couple of weeks ago and it was all tickety-boo. No damp, everything clean and well cared for and the two bathrooms and WCs fully functioning, if a bit antiquated.'

'What about a garden?'

'Not huge, but more than adequate. That's an expense I didn't mention: an old boy toddles along occasionally to keep it in order, cuts the grass and so on. There's a decent terrace outside the drawing room where you can sit.'

The more Perry heard about this house, the better he liked it. He'd never have known about it if he hadn't returned for lunch.

'I hope you and your fiancée will come to my wedding. It's in the chapel next to the War Office on the 18th of next month.'

'Be delighted to. Jenny loves a wedding. Wish we could set a date for ours.'

* * *

Clara scarcely had time to think about her forthcoming marriage or to worry about the possibility that she might be expecting a child. Her monthly courses had always been somewhat erratic so there was little point in worrying about whether she might be late.

Coincidentally, the first day that they were back to full strength as far as dispatch riders were concerned was the day that she was going to ring Perry. She'd received his letter and put it with the others and occasionally, when she wasn't too tired in the evening, had got them all out and read them for the umpteenth time.

The dozen dispatch riders were living fairly comfortably in this old rectory – a great improvement on Nissen huts or wooden sheds – but it was a brisk half-mile walk from there to her workplace. It was strictly forbidden to take their motorbikes home with them, which seemed a shame in the circumstances.

There was a telephone where she lived but it only received incoming calls; they couldn't make them. Therefore, armed with a pocketful of pennies, she headed for the village telephone kiosk.

There was a definite chill in the air which was hardly surprising as it was officially winter. A housewife was chatting away, nodding and shaking her head at intervals, and although Clara couldn't hear what she was saying, she did catch the occasional word.

Eventually, the woman emerged. 'Sorry, love, didn't know you were waiting. Should have knocked on the door and I'd have hung up.' The woman's metal curlers rattled beneath her headscarf as she vanished into the darkness.

In the wavering beam of her torch, Clara set up three piles of pennies ready to drop into the slot when the operator answered. Her intention was to talk to Perry for as long as possible and three shillings' worth of pennies should be more than adequate.

The operator connected her to the hotel and Clara pushed button A and immediately asked the man who answered if she could speak to Perry. Instantly, he was on the other end of the line – he must have been standing next to the telephone.

'My darling, I'm so happy to speak to you. I love you and I've got the most amazing news for you. First, are you well?'

She knew at once to what he was referring. 'As far as I know, I'm perfectly fine. I love you too. Now what's this amazing news?'

She'd put in half her stack of coins by the time he'd finished explaining about the house. 'Even if I'm not living there, darling Perry, you'll be far more comfortable than living in one room in a hotel. I can't believe our good fortune.'

'I don't have many people I want to invite to the wedding, General Pickering and his wife obviously, and Barney and his fiancée and that's about it. I didn't realise I had so few close friends until I sat down to make a list.'

'I've got my four friends and their boyfriends,

husbands or fiancés, plus the girl that I share with now. I'm sure you could ask some of the people you work with to make up the numbers. I think if we've got twenty including ourselves, that would be perfect.'

'Do we need to get printed invitations, wedding service sheets and so on?'

'Good heavens, no, we don't need any of that. This is a small, informal affair; verbal invitations are sufficient at your end and I'll write to my friends tonight.'

Someone rapped on the glass and made Clara jump. There were now two people waiting to use the telephone so she'd have to cut her call short.

'I'm sorry, there's a queue outside the box; I've got to go. I'm going to ask for my leave to start on the 17th so that we have a day to iron out any problems that might have arisen. Will you have the key to the house by then?'

'I've got it now. I'll have everything ready for you. I was wondering if I should cancel the reservation for Henley now we've got the house?'

'Yes, do that. It'll be like going away and we can visit the theatre, the cinema, somewhere smart for dinner or even to a nightclub if we want. I can't wait to see you again and to be your wife.'

She replaced the receiver and pressed button B.

Six pennies dropped out into the little metal cup. The young man who was next, the one who'd knocked on the window, opened it for her and grinned.

'Sorry to rush you, love, but I'm on duty in twenty minutes.'

She smiled but didn't answer as there wasn't much she could say. There were two children, dressed in hand-me-downs with chapped faces and a pinched look hanging about as well. Surely they weren't waiting to use the telephone themselves?

Then she guessed they were probably hoping someone might leave a few pennies behind which they could retrieve for themselves. 'Here, I think there's just over a shilling – I didn't need to use it all. Why don't you buy yourself something nice at the village shop?'

Two grubby hands came out and she carefully divided the money between them. She was rather disappointed and shocked when they ran off without thanking her. She hoped they weren't going to buy cigarettes with the money.

After negotiating the complicated blackout arrangements at the front door of the old rectory, Clara shone her torch on the wall looking for the light switch. She clicked it down, but nothing happened. She clicked it up and down several times.

The fuse must've gone – again – and it didn't sound as if anybody else was at home to see to it. She turned her torch so the beam was pointing up at her and carefully peeled off the tape so she had the full beam. She'd never had to do this herself, but she was a trained mechanic so putting a bit of fuse wire across the fuse should be well within her capabilities.

This modern electrical setup had been put in by the army when they requisitioned this house for use as accommodation for the female drivers. Unfortunately, if one light bulb went out then all the others on the same circuit went out as well. She recalled being told that when the metal element inside the glass bulb broke, it sent a surge of power back to the fuse and this melted the wire.

Maybe it would be sensible to light the two oil lamps and wait for somebody who'd done this before. Lighting lamps was straightforward – everybody knew how to do that and she rather liked the amber glow they made.

There was no gas in this house – but the old range worked well enough as long as someone remembered to riddle it and fill it with coke twice a day. Clara put the two lamps on the table and put the kettle on to boil. There wasn't much food kept here as they ate on the base where the food was free – if they cooked it here, they'd have to buy the ingredients and their ration books were already held by the army.

However, they did have tea leaves, a box of broken biscuits and usually some fresh milk. Putting it on the slate shelf in the pantry kept it cool, especially now that the weather was cold.

There was no heating in this house apart from the kitchen range and none of the fireplaces were used. There was no fuel available for fires – another reason those that lived here preferred to remain on the base and use the rec room, which was always lovely and warm.

It had been enjoyable living here initially but now it felt damp and unwelcoming in the unused rooms. Thankfully, the range provided ample hot water for their needs as long as they took it in turns to have a bath.

Whilst she waited for the whistle, Clara dashed upstairs and grabbed her stationery wallet. She was back before the kettle went and had time to set out her pad of paper and the matching envelopes.

When the others returned, she'd finished writing the invitations and had them ready to drop in the army post box the next morning.

'I've just topped up the teapot, ladies; does anyone want a cuppa?'

Everyone did and Clara found herself inviting all of them to her wedding if they could get a twenty-four-hour pass to attend.

Freda followed her up to bed. 'It was nice of you to invite everybody.'

'If they all came, it would be a bit tricky, but we can't be off duty at the same time. I hope you can wangle the time off; I'd really like you to be there.'

'I've already booked Christmas week, so I'm sorry, I can't come. My mum's poorly and this will be her last Christmas; it's important that all the family that can be there come.'

'I'm so sorry, I didn't know that.' Clara didn't offer to hug Freda as they didn't go in for that sort of thing.

As Clara was drifting off, images of her beloved Perry filled her head and she realised that deep down, she was perhaps hoping she was pregnant. Was driving overseas no longer her dream? Would she now be satisfied with domesticity, with being just a loving wife and mother?

She smiled. There were plenty of things she could do to help the war even if she wasn't in the ATS. She could join the WI, WVS, maybe become an ARP.

No longer half-asleep, Clara opened her eyes in the darkness, listening to Freda's slow, steady breathing. It didn't seem credible that almost overnight, she'd changed her mind. She smoothed her hand over her flat stomach. Was there a baby inside sending messages to her brain, telling her that she had someone else to think about?

This might be nature's way of protecting unborn children; she didn't know much about human reproduction. Biology at school had been firmly about rabbits. What she did know was that if she hadn't had her monthly by December, she would be expecting. However, if she had then she'd insist Perry used these prophylactics that he'd mentioned and continue with her push to be posted overseas.

22

Perry settled his account at the hotel and was on his way out, eager to start his new life in the grand house in Belvedere Crescent. Barney waylaid him as he was leaving. He only had an hour before he was due at his desk so couldn't hang around chatting.

'There's something I should have told you, old bean. You've probably been wondering why I didn't take up residence myself.' He frowned. 'The staff would report back to my parents and that would be a disaster.'

'I say, old chap, whatever do you have to hide?'

'I'm marrying someone they'd not approve of. She comes from a working-class family, salt of the earth. I prefer them to my own parents, but there's going to be hell to pay when they find out. They don't know I'm engaged.'

'You're of age; why can't you marry whoever you want?'

'They'll cut me off, no doubt about it; they already have a girl in mind for me. I'm saving every penny so when I finally marry against their wishes, I've got a bit put by.'

Perry nodded. 'It makes sense now. You'll keep the money you get for the upkeep of the place as I'll be footing the bills. Won't the staff report this?'

Barney grinned. 'No, I explained they'll be far better off, the house will be warmer, that you'll likely entertain, and this was enough to convince them. My great-aunt isn't generous and has been transferring the barest minimum. You must have noticed how pleased they were to meet you?'

'I must admit I was surprised at the enthusiastic welcome. I'm glad we can help each other. Even your great-aunt should be content her home's being used.'

'Good God, if she knew you were paying the bills, I'd not get another penny.'

They shook hands and Perry strode off, sad that this young man didn't appear to love his fiancée enough to stand up to his parents. He knew that he'd always put Clara first.

* * *

There was no telephone at his new home, which was hardly surprising considering the age of the previous resident. Fortunately, the position he held with the general meant he'd never be called in at short notice. They had his address, and it was no more than a brisk ten-minute walk so they could send someone if there was an emergency.

Perry marched up the short flight of front steps that led to the impressive front door with a shiny brass knocker. The door opened as he arrived on the top step.

'Welcome, Major Harrow, to your new abode. Will you be requiring luncheon today?' The elderly housekeeper, Mrs Beavis, reached out, intending to take his two suitcases.

He shook his head and smiled. 'I can manage these myself, thank you, Mrs Beavis. I'll be at my desk all day. I'll be dining in tonight if that's convenient.'

He'd already handed over his ration book and a significant amount to cover the next few weeks' housekeeping expenses. The three women working here had obviously not been eating properly if their pale and somewhat emaciated appearance was anything to go by. Whilst he was in charge of the household finances, he'd make sure they were comfortable and well fed.

'At what time do you wish to dine, Major?'

'Seven o'clock.' He looked around the spacious entrance hall – not a thing out of place, not a cobweb, not a speck of dust. 'I don't want to eat in solitary splendour in the main dining room. I prefer to eat in the kitchen with you – it'll be warmer and the food will be hotter.'

If he'd suggested that he preferred to eat in his underpants, the old lady couldn't have been more shocked. 'Oh, no, sir, that will never do. We're here to take care of you...'

'It wasn't a suggestion, Mrs Beavis; it was an order. I will eat in the kitchen and you, Mary and Sarah will eat with me. Is that understood?' He'd used his sternest voice, issued the statement as if he was directing recalcitrant troops. It did the trick. Poor old thing wilted and nodded.

'Yes, sir, food will be served in the kitchen.' She looked so wretched at the thought that he took pity on her.

'Naturally, if I have guests or my fiancée is here, we will use the dining room. We've decided to spend our honeymoon here.'

Mrs Beavis smiled. 'Then, naturally, sir, you'll require what could be referred to as room service. How exciting – we've never had a married couple here to take care of. The mistress never married as her fiancé died at the Somme.'

Perry dumped his cases on the acre of Axminster carpet in the main bedroom and gazed around. The fire was laid but not lit but the room didn't feel cold and damp. He thought they must have been lighting a fire in here every day since he'd agreed to take on the place.

This house was ridiculously large for just two people – possibly only one most of the time – but he revelled in the space, the lovely antique furniture and the general feeling of opulence and comfort. The furniture was old and somewhat faded but perfect for this Georgian, terraced house. Being here, one could forget there was a war on and that things were hard.

He'd not explored everywhere but intended to when he next got a few hours free. The housekeeper had told him there was a library-cum-study at the rear of the house as well as the main reception rooms – the drawing room, dining room and music room. This latter was misnamed as there wasn't even a piano in there, but maybe in grander times there had been.

There were four main bedrooms, all far bigger

than was comfortable in this weather and no doubt a host of smaller rooms for the servants on the basement floor. He'd been relieved when Mrs Beavis had said she and the two maids had their accommodation downstairs – it would be freezing in the attics under the roof.

What he hadn't enquired about was the whereabouts of the air-raid shelter – not that one was really needed at present, but this might change. Occasionally, a lone fighter bomber would tear up the Thames and drop their loads on the docks. The big cities in the north were still getting bombed but again not as regularly or as heavily as they had last year.

The only disadvantage, as far as he could see, with living here was that he could no longer communicate with Clara by telephone. He wasn't sure how he'd survive the next few weeks without being able to hear her voice.

* * *

Perry's first week living in Belvedere Crescent had worked out even better than he'd expected. After their initial shock at having the master of the house coming down to the basement to eat, the three ladies were now relaxed in his company and accepted that his suggestion made sense for all of them.

They'd compromised and for breakfast put a pretty floral cloth on the table and for dinner a crisp white linen one. He enjoyed their company, liked listening to their stories of life below stairs and knew that Clara would be just as happy here as he was.

'I want the three of you to come to my wedding and the reception afterwards. I'll not take no for an answer.'

Instead of being shocked as he'd expected, they exchanged happy smiles and all nodded. 'We've not been to a wedding for a decade at least, Major; we'd be delighted to accept your kind invitation.'

Mrs Beavis exchanged a telling look with the two maids. 'If your fiancée is staying here before the wedding then you will be moving back to the hotel, won't you? You can't both be under the same roof before you're married.'

This was the first time anything they'd said to him had annoyed him. However, they were his employees and had no right to criticise or comment on his actions.

'Please don't take offence but the fact that I prefer to eat down here where it's warm and the food I get served is palatable and hot doesn't give you the right to question anything I do.'

He looked at each of them in turn and they each flushed and looked away. Sadly, he stood up, knowing that from now on, he'd have to eat in the chilly dining room as he wouldn't be welcome in the kitchen any longer. He'd had no choice; he wasn't going to be told how to behave by these old ladies.

As he returned to his domain, the one he really shouldn't have left, he grinned. They were going to be horribly shocked when they discovered Clara would be sleeping in his room from the day she arrived. Whether they still attended his wedding after that was debatable, but he hoped they would. Despite their thinking they had the right to comment on his behaviour, he rather liked the three of them. He'd smooth things over later. He didn't want them to be upset.

* * *

Clara was ticking off the days until she left for London. She was still unsure if she was pregnant, but she thought it must be six or more weeks since she'd had her courses. If only she'd thought to note down the actual date of the last one.

There was no one to ask about the signs of pregnancy as all the ATS at her depot were either single or childless. She overheard two women standing in a queue at the post office discussing this subject. They'd called it being in the family way, which she rather liked.

One of them was heavily pregnant, while the other didn't show. The larger one had told her friend to expect to feel sick, to be constantly in the loo, and to have sore breasts. Hearing such intimate things being talked about so openly had shocked Clara but now she was glad that she'd inadvertently overheard.

She couldn't be expecting as she'd none of these symptoms. Much as she'd love to have Perry's baby and make a home with him, she was a valuable member of a team and as the Allied troops got ready to invade Normandy, her role would be even more crucial.

Clara tried to be relieved but knew she was disappointed. She had to be strong, put her personal feelings aside and continue to put her duty to her king and country first and Perry second.

She was up early and had a pot of tea made when the others drifted in. 'Good morning, ladies. It's bitter today. Good thing we've got a greatcoat,' Clara greeted them.

'It's blooming cold in here, not just outside, Corp,' Daph said. She went to the range to warm her hands. 'There's ice on the inside of my bedroom window.'

'On all of them, I'm afraid. I just hope the pipes don't freeze,' Clara said.

'Them what sleep in huts have a big iron stove in the middle of the room; we ain't got nothing apart from this range,' Jenny chimed in.

'Stop moaning, you two,' Freda said. 'Some poor folks haven't even got a roof to call their own.'

Clara poured the tea and they helped themselves to the last biscuits in the tin. 'Whose turn is it to fill this up?'

'I'll nip down the shop later and see if they've got any,' Freda said.

'I'll ask at the NAAFI,' Clara offered. 'They sometimes have broken biscuits but usually, the men get there first.'

As they were all around the table, it was the ideal time to see who was coming to the wedding in two weeks' time. Nobody could make it. She thought it was too far and too expensive for them to travel just for a few sausage rolls and a glass of sherry. This was a relief really as it was a small wedding and all the guests were very close friends, which these weren't.

Clara had heard from all her friends and they'd be attending. She couldn't wait to catch up with them all. Minnie was now a sergeant and the only one not bringing someone with her. Grace had completed her officer training after marrying her handsome squadron leader and returned to Clacton.

Ruth was engaged to her sergeant and hoping to get married in the New Year and was on a Royal Artillery battery in Regent's Park. Eileen was waiting to have her divorce finalised and then she too would be marrying the handsome officer she'd got involved with when they were doing basic training.

'You thinking about your wedding night, Corp, because you're not listening to us. We're having a bit of a knees up on the Wednesday before you go; it's all arranged at the NAAFI,' Freda told her with a smile.

'Golly, how kind of you. Thank you for thinking of me.' She took her mug to the scullery, rinsed it and the others followed suit. They always marched to the base, arms swinging, heads held high, proud to be dispatch riders and pleased that others would see them looking smart.

They'd only gone a few yards when Freda, who was leading the girls today, stepped on a patch of ice and her boots flew from under her. She fell backwards. The two behind her tried to catch her but in the confusion, they went down too. Before Clara could yell halt, there was a tangle of girls, arms waving wildly as they skidded in all directions, half ending up on their backsides like the first three. She and two other girls who'd been at the rear of the column were able to avoid the melee.

She was laughing so much, she couldn't speak. The more those on the ground attempted to stand, the funnier it was. Eventually, she was able to regain control of her voice.

'All of you, just sit still and stop floundering about.' She waited until they did as she asked. 'Excellent. Is anybody hurt? I don't mean bruised behinds or banged elbows but something sprained or broken.'

Those on the pavement were laughing helplessly but all of them gave her a thumbs up.

'Right, you two,' Clara said to the girls giggling beside her. 'It only seems to be the pavement that's so slippery. If we make our way carefully along the road then I think we can help them get up.'

The racket they'd been making had, despite the earliness of the hour, brought several locals out of their homes.

A woman in a dressing gown, slippers and a mass

of metal curlers looked over the hedge and sniggered. 'What a palaver! My Billy went flying and landed on his bum last night and I meant to put a bit of sand on it. Some silly bugger must've dropped something and then tried to wash it off with a bucket of water.'

'If you've got that sand handy, ma'am, we'll put it down so nobody else slips over on the ice,' Clara said to her.

'Just a tick, my Billy's bringing it out now. Ever so sorry, ladies, never meant for no one to get hurt.'

As she was speaking, the last of the fallen gingerly regained their feet with the help of those standing more securely in the road.

Billy turned out to be a boy of no more than ten or eleven and he handed the bucket of sand over the hedge. 'Here you are, Corp, this'll do the trick. Mum asked me to do it last night, but I never did.'

Daphne was closest and took the bucket and then carefully sprinkled it over the dangerous part of the pavement. Satisfied they'd done all they could to make it safe, the ATS squad brushed themselves down and continued towards the base – this time, they marched in single file on the road.

They arrived at the ATS canteen just as it opened. After the excitement, everybody was more than ready for another cup of tea and whatever hot breakfast was being served that morning.

Before sitting, they removed their yellow gauntlets, helmets and heavy greatcoats. Far too hot inside to keep those on. Clara spoke to each girl in turn, checking that they were fit to ride their motorbikes. Even a sprained wrist could prove problematic when the weather was so poor. A dispatch rider needed both hands to be safe on a motorbike when the roads were icy.

It was the jolliest breakfast she'd had since joining this depot – they were in such high spirits that several other ATS came over to ask why they were so merry so early in the morning. Clara was sure that this amusing incident would be the talk of the base by lunchtime.

Before she could go out on her first dispatch, she was obliged to fill in a report because even though nobody had been injured, any incident of this sort had to be recorded and handed in. No doubt nobody else would read it but at least she knew she'd done what she was supposed to do.

* * *

Two days later, her monthly courses appeared but the loss was light and only lasted a day. Now the uncertainty was over, she threw herself wholeheartedly into her work and the days passed much quicker than she'd thought they would.

The weather was vile, freezing sleet and a bitter wind which made delivering messages and documents more dangerous. The day of the event that was being held to celebrate her wedding, she had a long run and was worried she might be late for her own party.

Three times she skidded but, being an expert on her motorbike nowadays, was able to correct the machine and regain control easily. Daphne had had a nasty spill and would be out of action for a week at least. Clara thought she should feel guilty about abandoning her post, leaving so much extra work for the others, but she'd had no time off since she and Perry had been together and was entitled to leave like everybody else.

That night, she was offered drinks but refused, not wanting to have a hangover the next day. Although she thoroughly enjoyed the event, laughed and danced as expected, all she could think about was being with Perry tomorrow night.

In his last letter, he'd told her about the three old

ladies who looked after him and how horrified they were going to be but that didn't deter her. She was going to enjoy every second that she was with the man she loved, the man she was going to marry in three days' time.

She slipped away early, but the party continued in her absence. This time, she was taking her kitbag; she was going to be gone for just over a week and couldn't possibly take everything she needed in her haversack.

For the first time, she regretted not having a wedding gown to wear on the day, nor some enticing silk nightwear for her wedding night – khaki was such an unflattering colour. She would wear her number two dress uniform, still khaki and still not fitting her the way her civilian clothes had.

* * *

Clara crept out of the shared bedroom the next morning not wishing to wake Freda, and downstairs, she riddled the range, made sure it was burning properly before leaving. Even with her long greatcoat on she was cold, far colder than she would have been in her jodhpurs and battledress.

There was an early bus that left from the stop

outside the base at just after seven and this was the one she was going to catch. Then she'd travel up to London with the businessmen in their pinstriped suits and bowler hats. It didn't matter if she had to use her kitbag for a seat – any discomfort was worth it in order to be reunited with her beloved Perry.

23

Perry didn't want the main rooms of the large house to be heated just so he could dine in comfort. Therefore, he asked Barney if he'd help him move furniture around.

'Be happy to, old bean, as I have an obligation to check the empty properties either side of yours once a month. See there're no burst pipes, burglars and so on.'

'How about tonight?' Perry smiled. 'I've already told Mrs Beavis that you'll be dining with me.'

'Then you're in luck as I'm not meeting Jenny as she's on nights. Did I tell you she's a nurse?'

'You didn't, but this makes it even stranger that your parents won't accept her into the family. Nurses are an essential part of beating the Nazis, surely they understand that?'

'I'm not prepared to take the risk. I'll be in a position to marry next year and I'll introduce her then because it won't make any difference if they cut me off as I'll already have a nest egg put by.'

They met that evening outside the hotel where Perry had lived, and Barney accompanied him on the walk home; on the way, he explained why furniture had to be moved.

'It's not on, heating the main reception rooms just for me. The so-called music room's a reasonable size and I intend, with your help, to turn it into our living and dining space.'

'Makes perfect sense to me. To be honest, I don't blame those that lived there for abandoning their houses. Safer and more comfortable in the country, or America in my great-aunt's case.'

'I think all empty buildings like these should be used to rehome those poor sods bombed out. Shocking that the government doesn't make the wealthy do that.'

They were approaching the house when Perry stopped. 'Look, did you see a light flash behind the curtain in the upstairs room of the empty house on the left?'

They stood in the darkness, both instinctively holding the thin beam of their own torches against their palms. They didn't speak, both staring at the window where Perry was certain he'd seen a flash of light. The young man whispered.

'I've got the keys in my pocket. Better to go in through the basement. If there's someone inside, they're less likely to hear us.'

'Lead the way.'

In order to reach the rear of the terrace of five Georgian houses, one would have to walk to one end or the other where there was a path wide enough for a carriage to have travelled along. There was stabling and a coach house at the end of the path to the left of the house that Perry lived in but obviously, this was no longer in use. They were closer to the other end so made their way there and managed to reach the back gate to the house in question without mishap.

Barney pushed the gate and it opened. Either someone else had a key or the lock had been broken. Perry moved closer and whispered directly into his ear. 'This isn't good. God knows what villains have broken in and there could be more than one. Do you think we should retreat and contact the constabulary?'

'We're soldiers, old bean; we don't retreat in the face of an enemy.'

Perry thought this might be a better motto if either of them was armed but he could hardly let Barney go in on his own, whatever his reservations. His motives were entirely selfish as he didn't want to risk being injured the day before Clara arrived.

It was a good thing his companion was familiar with the layout at the rear of these houses as after the gate, they had to negotiate some outbuildings and then trek through the garden which was identical to the one behind his temporary home.

Barney stopped and pointed to the back door. 'I just saw a flicker of light in the boot room. Someone might be coming out.'

They stood beside the door and waited. Perry's heart was thumping. He wished he had some sort of weapon as fists wouldn't be much use against a gun. Then he grinned and his hands unclenched.

'Come on out, we won't hurt you,' he called.

There was a slight sound of scuffling feet and then the door slowly opened. Barney was rigid beside him, probably thinking Perry had lost his mind. But he had excellent hearing – he'd heard one of the intruders speaking and knew they were children.

Two scruffy urchins stepped cautiously around the door, probably expecting to be arrested.

'Blimey, it ain't the bleedin' rozzers. It's a couple of Tommies,' one of them said, completely unbothered at being caught breaking and entering.

Perry gripped Barney's elbow, indicating that he was in charge of this. He noticed they were empty-handed, which was strange. 'What the devil are you two doing creeping around in there?'

'We wasn't doing nothing,' the smaller one whined.

'You obviously were doing something you shouldn't. As you don't appear to have any ill-gotten gains about your persons, I'm assuming you weren't robbing the place.'

'I ain't no thief. Ma's lost her bleeding cat – a scruffy black bugger. She reckons it's hiding in one of these empty houses.'

Now Barney laughed. 'Actually, son, it's living in the lap of luxury next door. I don't think it'll want to come home with you.'

Then Perry remembered seeing a black cat curled up on a cushion by the range in the kitchen. 'He's right, I've seen it myself. Mrs Beavis has adopted it.'

'It ain't hers to keep. Ma wants it back. That tom's the best mouser down our road.'

This articulate boy was correct, but it wouldn't be fair on the cat to hand him over now he'd found a good home. 'You know very well, young man, looking for a cat by breaking into somebody's house is no excuse. I'm sure your mother would much prefer that you came home safe than that you were in trouble with the law.'

'We'll get a tanning if we don't go back with that bleeding cat, mister,' the smaller boy said tearfully.

Perry smiled. 'Do you think your mother would still be angry if you returned with a ten-shilling note in payment for the cat?'

The boy's eyes bulged and he rubbed his face dry with his sleeve. The older brother beamed.

'Mangy old thing ain't worth more than a tanner, but I'll take ten bob if that's what you're offering.'

Perry handed over the note and they held it up, examining it carefully in the light of their torch. He thought that they'd never seen one before.

'I'm getting married in two days' time and am feeling generous. However, I promise you that I won't be so lenient if I catch you anywhere near these houses again.' He'd deliberately sounded stern, and it did the trick.

'Ta, mister, we won't be round no more. You're welcome to the smelly thing. I don't reckon there's any mice or rats for him to catch somewhere posh like this.'

The boys dodged past them and were gone, leaving an unsolved mystery – how had the boys opened the doors?

'Is there any chance, Barney, that you forgot to lock this place up last time you went in?'

'Probably my fault. In fact, definitely my fault. I'll do a quick tour of inspection, Perry. If I give you the keys to the other place, would you please do the same in the other one?'

* * *

Mrs Beavis and the maids were waiting in the hall when they came in. 'We thought it would be quicker if we gave you a hand, sir, then you and the captain could eat in the new room and not in the freezing cold dining room.'

'Thank you, Mrs Beavis, I appreciate your offer. The captain and I can manage the heavy lifting but I'd be grateful for any help with moving smaller items, and generally setting things out as they should be.'

Barney greeted the staff with a smile. The music

room was warm; the fire had obviously been lit earlier in the day, which Perry appreciated.

He'd already selected the items of furniture he wanted and the two of them began the removal by collecting the large rug that had been languishing in one of the spare bedrooms.

'This needs to go down first, obviously, and I think it's the most awkward and heaviest of the items. None of the other things involve coming down a flight of stairs,' Perry said apologetically as they staggered, breathless and red-faced, into the music room.

'If you put it down, Major, we'll spread it out for you so when you bring in the other items, you can put them straight down,' the housekeeper said.

'Good show, then we'll get on with it,' he replied.

An hour later, it was done and Perry thought the room looked even better than he'd expected.

'This is just the ticket,' Barney said enthusiastically. 'It will be far more comfortable remaining in here. The house is too big and being so old, it's draughty and cold.' He held up his grimy hands. 'Crikey, we can't sit down like this. The old dears wouldn't approve.'

The two of them eventually collapsed into the armchairs that had been placed on either side of the roaring fire. 'I'm not as fit as I thought I was, Barney; I need to do some sort of regular exercise, otherwise I'm going to be no use to whatever regiment I join when we invade.'

'Officers don't do PT – I think we should. That said, old bean, I'm not sure when we're going to have time as we're kept at our desks from eight in the morning until six o'clock at night.'

'There must be a gym somewhere close enough that we could use. I used to box for my school and that's one form of exercise I enjoy.'

'As long as you're not the one punching me, I'm game. You're several inches taller and broader and probably a stone or two heavier than me.'

Perry laughed. 'Good God, we won't be punching each other, just using the punch bags, dumbbells and skipping ropes. I'll make enquiries when I get back from leave.'

The two elderly maids had been pottering about at the dining table at the door end of the room and Perry glanced over his shoulder. The table had been laid for two, a ridiculous array of silver cutlery and several glasses put out as well as crisp white napkins folded into the shape of a fan.

'If you would care to be seated, sirs, we'll bring in your first course,' one of the maids said.

'Thank you, after all that physical effort, we're both ravenous.'

After taking his seat, Barney flipped open his napkin across his knees. 'I've never dined here; I used to come for afternoon tea when I was still in short pants, but my great-aunt didn't entertain, even family.'

'I've been well looked after but this is the first time they've done this.' Perry gestured to the sparkling crystal and shining silver. 'God knows why they've put all this out – but if you say your great-aunt never had guests, this might be the first time in a decade that they've had the opportunity to lay up so extravagantly. Let's hope the food is of a similar standard tonight.'

Perry picked up the cut-glass decanter and sniffed appreciatively. 'This is an excellent claret. I think they must have raided the wine cellar, too.'

Almost two hours later, Perry and Barney finally left the table. A large silver jug of real coffee was waiting on one of the side tables by the long sofa for them to serve themselves.

'That was a truly magnificent dinner, old bean, as

good as anything I've eaten at the Ritz or the Savoy. I didn't know the old dears had it in them. I'll not be able to move for an hour at least.'

The housekeeper had come in whilst he was speaking and had overheard his compliments. 'Thank you, Captain, I'm glad you both enjoyed it. It was an absolute treat to be able to cook a real dinner with several courses.'

Perry stood up. 'I think it was one of the best meals I've ever eaten. Forgive me for asking, where in heaven's name did you manage to get hold of all this?'

'You can get anything you want if you're prepared to pay for it. Fortnum & Mason's and Harrods can always find luxury items if you know who to ask.' She smiled warmly. 'Your very generous housekeeping meant I was in that fortunate position. I'm so glad you enjoyed your dinner and if you don't require anything else tonight, gentlemen, we're going to eat ours now.'

'Goodnight, ma'am, and thank you again for everything you've done for me.' When he'd moved in a couple of weeks ago, he'd insisted that those that looked after him had exactly the same food that he did. He smiled as he resumed his seat, knowing the ladies' evening was going to be as good as theirs had been.

* * *

Barney staggered to his feet, intending to return to the hotel. He'd drunk most of the claret as well as several glasses of a crisp, dry white wine which had been served with the fish course. He was inebriated and walked into two pieces of furniture.

'Stay here tonight, Barney; you're in no fit state to walk back.'

'It'll be bloody cold in a spare room, so thanks for the offer but I'd rather toddle off to my nice warm room at the hotel.'

'Sleep in here. You can use the sofa – I'll find a couple of blankets and a pillow.'

'If you don't mind me doing that, then I'll take up your kind offer.'

After settling his unexpected guest, Perry made his way through the silent house by the light of his torch to his bedroom. He carefully folded his clothes over the wooden rack, tucked his rolled socks into his shoes and flipped back the blankets. Tomorrow night, he'd not be alone in this bed. He fell asleep smiling.

* * *

Clara was bubbling inside, not sure if this was excitement or nerves. How much worse it would be if she was also a virgin and worried about her wedding night. She'd managed to find a seat and was squashed between a bad-tempered businessman and a stylish woman in mink. Neither of them wanted to chat, which was a relief.

The train steamed into King's Cross and Clara was on her feet first and with her kitbag held in front of her, she rushed to the nearest exit. A young man in RAF uniform, not a pilot as he had no wings, was there first and had opened the door. She jumped out after him and wove her way through the press of early-morning businessmen and lady shoppers heading for the barrier.

Perry didn't know which train she was arriving on, just that she'd be at his new address by lunchtime. As she elbowed her way out, a hand reached over her shoulder and removed her kitbag.

'I'll carry that for you, my darling, so don't argue,' Perry said from right behind her.

She couldn't keep back her squeal of joy. Ignoring the crowd who were trying to get to the Underground or the streets, she flung her arms around his neck. His free arm encircled her waist and she was airborne. He somehow evaded the throng and didn't put her down until they were in a quiet corner of the station.

Her precious bag was dumped unceremoniously on the ground and his mouth covered hers. She returned the kiss with equal passion and her head was spinning when he eventually released her.

'Darling, darling Perry, how did you know I'd be on that train?'

'It's the first one from Lincoln and I was just going to wait by the barrier until you appeared.'

'I was happy just to be in London but now I'm ecstatic.' She smiled up at him. 'Actually, I'm also relieved I don't have to try and find my way to your Belvedere Crescent.'

His smile made her toes curl. 'It's your home too, my love. It's one of five in a lovely Georgian terrace but it's old-fashioned and cold. I do hope you love it.'

'I don't care if it's a basement with damp walls and no windows as long as we're together.'

'Shall we go? I've just got to make a quick call to my office at that telephone box. I've got a staff car at my disposal for the next two days: a wedding gift from my CO.'

They only had to stand outside the station for ten minutes before the car arrived. An ATS driver got out, saluted, and put the bag in the boot.

Clara sat close to him and he put his arm around her, holding her safe, ensuring she didn't slide off the seat. She closed her eyes and enjoyed the drive. Then she remembered the thing she knew she should have told him first.

'I'm so sorry, darling Perry, but my friends are coming to the house sometime this afternoon, possibly with their partners as well.'

'Why are you apologising for that? Of course they'd come to us; it's the easiest place for us all to meet. They can stay overnight; there's ample room.'

'Won't your Mrs Beavis be cross at us giving her such short notice? We can eat out somewhere; I don't expect her to cater for so many.'

He kissed her and she forgot all about her friends.

24

Perry didn't care if Clara's entire squad turned up as long as she was there too. He hoped none of them wanted to remain up too late. He shifted uncomfortably. Tried to turn his mind away from making love but it was hard when she was in his arms.

The car pulled up at the corner of the crescent as access was limited. 'Stay where you are; we'll let ourselves out,' he told the driver.

'Yes, sir. I'll be here at eleven tomorrow to collect you both.'

He grabbed Clara's bag and took her hand in his, slinging the bag over his shoulder. As they approached what was to be their shared home, a watery winter sun came out, bathing the houses in yellow light. This had to be a good omen.

'It's the middle house, darling. What do you think?'

'It's very grand. Frighteningly like the Town house my parents used to have in Hanover Square.'

'I didn't realise you were from that sort of family. Any titles?'

She pulled a face. 'My grandmother on my mother's side is a lady, the daughter of an earl, but I never cared enough to find out who that was.'

'My parents have no titles on either side of their family, but I believe our bloodline goes back to William the Conqueror – or so my father was over fond of telling everyone.'

'It's going to be a little bit strange not having any family there, especially as my parents and your father are still alive. Will you tell him that you're married?'

'My solicitor will inform him. Do you wish him to do the same for yours?'

She thought for a moment and then shook her head. 'No, they made it very clear I was no longer a member of the family. You're my family now.' She supposed she should tell him she wasn't in the family way after all and that she didn't want to conceive yet.

'From your expression, I guess that you want to

tell me that you're not having a baby. Honestly, I'm not sure if I'm disappointed or relieved. More importantly, my love, how do you feel about the situation?'

'I feel exactly the same. I do want to have your children but not right now. I hope you got some of those things that you told me about.'

'I have, don't worry, everything's in hand. The main drawback to you not being pregnant is that I'll be rattling about in this house on my own until I rejoin a regiment probably next year. I don't suppose you'd allow me to pull a few strings and get you posted to London?'

'Please tug those strings as hard as you can – I don't mind what I drive as I'm qualified from motorbikes to lorries and can drive in any conditions and at any time of the day.'

'I can't guarantee I'll be successful but believe me, I'll do my absolute best.'

He didn't need to knock as the door opened when they arrived on the top step and Mrs Beavis was there to greet them.

'Welcome to your new home, madam. I hope you'll be very comfortable here.'

'I'm sure that I shall, Mrs Beavis.' The old lady stepped back and Clara walked past her and was looking around with interest. Perry watched her. The hall was definitely cold, not much better than the outside temperature, but everywhere was spotless, the furniture highly polished and not a speck of dust to be seen.

Perry put his hand on the small of her back and guided her to the door on the left at the far end of the spacious hall.

'If you go in there, darling; I'll take this up for you.'

The stairs were on the right of the hall, highly polished and with a dark-green carpet running up the middle.

'I'll come with you later; I want to see everywhere.'

He dumped the kitbag on the bottom stair and followed her.

'This was the music room, but the major had it turned into your living space. Very sensible and we can keep it lovely and warm for you both,' the house-keeper said proudly.

'It's perfect. I know I'm going to love it here. Rather bad news for you, Mrs Beavis, I have four of my close friends plus their partners descending on the house sometime this afternoon. Perry has said that they can stay here but if it's not convenient...'

'My word, madam, we are here to take care of you

and the major and any friends that you might care to have visit. I'll have all the bedrooms made up and a fire lit in each of them. I can supply light refreshments when they arrive, but it would be easier for me if you dined out tonight.'

'We'd already decided to do that; thank you for being so understanding.'

The old lady hurried off smiling and Perry wondered if she'd still be as happy when she discovered that he and Clara would be sharing a bed tonight.

'What do you think? This is a lot better than a damp basement or a hotel,' he said.

'It certainly is. My friends will be impressed that you found us somewhere so splendid to live at such short notice. There'll be nine of us wanting to eat – where do you suggest?'

'I'll give the Ritz a ring and see if we can book there. Don't look so horrified – I've drawn out a substantial sum to cover any expenses during our honeymoon. It's a once-in-a-lifetime occasion, my darling, and I want it to be memorable.'

'That just seems so extravagant but I'm sure my friends will enjoy being spoilt this once. My knowledge of London's somewhat limited as you know. Is it a comfortable walking distance?'

'Cross the bridge, down Whitehall, through the

Haymarket and we're there in Piccadilly. Twenty minutes' brisk walking. I can't think of anywhere else closer.'

'What about your hotel? You said the food is good and it's not quite so grand. I'll sit here and enjoy the fire whilst you go and speak to them, shall I?'

'Actually, I think that's a much better idea. And you're right, it'll be quicker to go in person than go in search of a telephone box. Why don't you come with me? We can grab something to eat. I'm sure you didn't have breakfast and I certainly haven't.'

'Even better. Good thing we haven't taken off our coats.'

* * *

The hotel manager greeted him like a long-lost friend and sent them to a small salon with comfortable seating and a decent fire.

'I'll bring you a jug of coffee, and whatever's available currently in the kitchen. Breakfast service is over and it's too early for lunch but I'm sure they'll find you something tasty.'

'Thank you,' Perry said. 'Before you go, is there any chance that you can fit in a table for nine early this evening?'

'Yes, I'll put you in the breakfast room where you'll be undisturbed by the other guests and can celebrate in peace.'

* * *

Things couldn't be going any better, Perry thought, he hadn't yet told Clara things had also come together for the reception tomorrow. They were grateful for their thick greatcoats as the wind had picked up and the skies were grey and ominous.

'I hope it's not as bad as this tomorrow, Perry; getting married with a runny nose and scarlet cheeks from the cold would be awful.'

'You'd look absolutely beautiful even with a paper bag on your head, my love,' he said as they fell into step and marched briskly across the bridge and back to their home.

The maid was waiting to take their coats as they stepped in. 'I'll have these lovely and dry by this afternoon, sir,' she said as she draped them over her arm.

'I've not seen upstairs yet, and I need to unpack my things. I don't want what I'm wearing tomorrow to be creased.'

Perry wasn't sure that them being alone in their

bedroom would be sensible. Then she said something that astonished him.

'I've decided we shouldn't sleep together tonight. I don't want anyone to know that we've pre-empted our wedding vows. I'll share a room with Minnie.'

He noticed that the kitbag had vanished from where he'd left it at the bottom of the stairs. 'When did you decide that?'

'As we were walking back – until then, I was so looking forward to being with you tonight. But then I remembered that brides are not supposed to see their future husbands before the wedding. I think it might be bad luck if we share the same bed.'

'I'd forgotten about that old saying. How are you going to manage the something borrowed, something blue?'

'I've no idea but I'm sure one of my friends will come up with a solution. Let's go upstairs and see where your housekeeper has actually put my belongings.'

He grinned. 'You can be very sure it won't be in my room. Good God, I now understand why she was so pleased to have your friends staying here tonight.'

Clara frowned then laughed. 'She's from another generation so I suppose she thought it wouldn't be seemly – I think that's the correct word – for an unmarried girl to stay under the same roof as an unmar-ried man.'

'That's it exactly. I'm assuming that your friends won't expect to stay here tomorrow night as well.'

She blushed, knowing exactly what he meant. 'Of course they won't; I think they've got to be back at their posts by tomorrow night.'

As expected, Clara's kitbag was in the bedroom as far away from his as was possible. They were both surprised to find the bag was empty, that every item of clothing had been carefully put away.

'Goodness, I'm not sure I want so much attention from your staff. I certainly don't want them coming into our bedroom whilst I'm here.'

'Then I won't tell you what they suggested.'

She scowled at him, and he grinned and told her. 'Mrs Beavis offered to serve our meals on a tray in our room.'

'Golly, I really don't want that. I suppose if they left it outside, it would be all right. Where do they sleep?'

'They've got their rooms in the basement level where the kitchen and scullery are situated.'

'Then we need to put a table for the trays to be placed on outside our room.'

* * *

Clara didn't entirely trust him not to do something he shouldn't if they remained in a bedroom alone for any longer. Luckily, the problem was solved when there was a loud knock on the front door.

'Gosh, I didn't expect any of my friends to arrive so soon. I suppose we have to wait for one of the ladies to open the door.'

'You could always hang over the banister and listen. It might be a postman.'

'Well, it certainly wouldn't be a tradesperson delivering as they go round the back.'

She did as he suggested and hovered in the wide upstairs passageway, hoping to hear who it was at the door.

'Come in, Sergeant. The major and Corporal Felgate are upstairs.'

Ignoring Perry, Clara flew down the stairs and embraced Minnie. 'I can't tell you how good it is to see you again, Minnie, and you look absolutely splendid.'

'Blimey, this is a bit grand. I'll need to mind my Ps and Qs whilst I'm here.'

'I'm Perry, Clara's future husband. I'm so pleased

to meet you.' He didn't offer his hand but stepped in and kissed Minnie's cheek.

'I've never been kissed by an officer before but must say I enjoyed the experience.'

'We're sharing. I'll show you where we are so you can dump your bag,' Clara said.

They thundered up the stairs and Clara glanced back to see Perry laughing. She couldn't believe she was marrying this wonderful man tomorrow and all her very favourite people would be there to see it.

Once they were in the room, she had time to look at her friend more closely. Minnie seemed different somehow, even sounded different, but Clara couldn't quite work out what it was.

'I reckon we've done all right for ourselves, haven't we, Clara? I like your bloke: not only handsome but charming too.'

'You sound different; your speech has changed.'

Her friend grinned. 'I don't swear as much, that's for sure. Mixing with officers all the time, you can't help but pick up some of their ways. I love being a sergeant, being in charge of a hundred girls, and the extra that I get really helps my family.'

'You didn't bring a boyfriend – I hope you won't feel a bit of a gooseberry on your own.'

'Boys aren't my thing, if you get my meaning, and

whilst I'm in the army, it's better I don't get involved with someone who is my taste.'

Clara hugged her friend. 'As long as you're happy, I don't care what your preferences are for a partner. So much has changed for all of us in the past six months. I want to hear everything, but it'll have to wait until tonight when we're alone in here. We can't really leave Perry by himself.'

'I didn't know I'd be staying here. Are the others going to as well?'

'Yes, it makes sense. Tonight's for us girls to catch up – the men will just have to talk amongst themselves. Now that Ruth's fiancé is no longer a sergeant in the army, he shouldn't feel awkward being with two officers.'

'I don't reckon your bloke or Grace's husband would treat him any differently even if he was still a sergeant. I haven't met Ruth yet as she missed Grace's wedding.'

'Sam will be the only one not in uniform but as he might still be on crutches after breaking his leg, no one will think he's not doing his duty.'

'I can't tell you how pleased I was to get your invitation. It'll be ever so nice catching up with you all. Do you remember the train journey when we met?'

'I certainly do. Grace was different then – in fact, we all were.'

* * *

'There you are, I was resigning myself to being ignored the remainder of the day so am delighted that you deigned to join me,' Perry drawled as they came in. He was lounging on the long sofa, looking very much at home – which was hardly surprising as it was his home and hers too after tomorrow.

'Today's my last day as Clara Felgate and I want to spend every minute with my friends. I don't think I've got time for you today.'

Minnie was standing behind her and didn't see her wink at Perry and waggle her eyebrows, making him laugh.

'I absolutely forbid you to spend a minute with anyone but me. Come and sit next to me immediately.' He tried to sound genuinely angry but failed dismally and Minnie laughed.

'I'll hide behind that armchair, shall I, sir? I'm only a tiddler and you'll hardly know I'm here.'

Perry sat up and Clara dropped down beside him. 'That might not be a good idea, Sergeant, as you might hear things that would shock you.'

Clara punched him playfully on the arm and he flinched dramatically. 'Major Harrow, I've no idea why I'm marrying you because you're quite impossible.'

He smiled that special smile of his and for a second, she forgot they weren't alone and leaned towards him.

'Now I've seen everything. I think striking an officer's a hanging offence, Corporal, and as I outrank you, I might be tempted to write you up. I reckon I can be persuaded to forget what I saw if I could have a nice cup of tea. I'm absolutely parched.'

Perry refused to ring the bell that sounded in the basement so wandered off to collect the tea in person.

As soon as the door closed behind him, her friend clapped as if she'd just witnessed a stirring performance. 'He's a bit of all right, perfect for you. A bit long in the tooth but I approve of your choice.'

'Thank you. Strangely, Perry fell in love with me before I realised I had feelings for him. He didn't pressure me, stepped away when I asked him to, and left me to make up my own mind.' For some reason, she wanted to confide in Minnie, even though she'd indicated she had absolutely no experience with men. 'We've already slept together a few weeks ago. Are you horribly shocked?'

'Don't blame you. Why wait when you're getting married anyway? Next year or the year after, our army will be on the move with the Yanks so make the most of the time you've got is what I say.'

'I'm hoping to go with the army either as a dispatch rider or ambulance driver. He doesn't want me to but won't stand in my way.'

'Then he bloody well ought to. Why risk your life if you don't have to? We do our bit, get paid half what the men get for doing the same job; let them take the risk as they take everything else.'

Clara stared at Minnie. She was even more outspoken than she'd been before. What she said made sense, but the sentiments jarred a little – probably spending so much time at Putney barracks had made her somewhat jaundiced about things.

'To be honest, I'm not even sure that I want to go any more. Perry's going to try and have me posted to London so we can spend more time together.'

'Good for him. He's got his head screwed on properly, won't take unnecessary risks, and he'll come back to you in one piece if he possibly can.'

They were chatting companionably about their different lives when he came back carrying the tray.

'Coffee for us, my love, tea and cake for you, Minnie. We've had breakfast and from what I saw going on in the kitchen just now, it's going to be a substantial lunch.'

Not long afterwards, Eileen Ruffel turned up but without her handsome fiancé, Captain Ben Sawyer.

After introductions, Eileen apologised. 'Ben will be here tomorrow; he couldn't get more than a twenty-four-hour pass.'

'I'm surprised he's able to come at all,' Clara said. 'I thought he'd be overseas with his regiment.'

Eileen shook her head. 'He joined them in Libya but had only been there a couple of months when the regiment was brought back and another one replaced them. They'd suffered heavy losses over the past year and need to recover and replace those lost or who are no longer able to fight.'

'That's good news for both of you,' Clara said. 'Can you set a date for your own wedding?' She didn't like to talk about Eileen's divorce from her abusive husband as she hadn't told Perry about this.

'March, we've set the date and I hope you'll be able to come. Ben's saving his leave so we can have a week away somewhere.' Eileen turned to Perry, who was listening carefully. 'I know I shouldn't really ask you this, but as you work at the War Office, can you tell me if you think the invasion will be next year or the year after?'

'Not the coming year but I think early in 1944. You'll be able to marry next spring, I'm sure of it.'

'Grace is already married, I shall be tomorrow, and you in March. I had a letter from Ruth not long ago and she's intending to be married to Sam very soon.'

She settled next to Perry and smiled. Life just couldn't be better.

25

Perry enjoyed the company of Clara's friends but was relieved when the last two girls arrived with their partners in tow. He was introduced to the squadron leader and the civilian chap and immediately liked both of them.

Coats were disposed of, belongings taken up to the respective bedrooms, and by the time that was sorted out, the housekeeper informed him that luncheon was served in the main dining room. This made sense as getting eight people around the much smaller table in the living room would be impossible.

Clara clapped her hands and the racket stopped for a moment. Perry exchanged a wry smile with the other two men as she herded her friends from the living room into the dining room.

'Goodness me, the table's amazing. Perry's told me about Mrs Beavis; I knew she'd be able to produce a good meal for us with very little notice,' she said, and Perry agreed.

He took Clara's hand and walked to the far end of the table which, thank God, hadn't been pulled out to its full extent or they'd have been shouting down its length in order to hold a conversation.

'I'm assuming that we're expected to sit here, darling, as we're the hosts.' He smiled at their guests. 'Sit wherever you like – there's a spare chair as Eileen's captain can't make it today.'

In here, there was no rug, just highly polished parquet flooring, and he waited to hear the screech of chair legs but every one of them lifted their chairs to move them – even Minnie, which surprised him.

There were baskets of freshly baked rolls on the table, actual butter in the butter dishes, but no sign of any other food.

'We've got soup spoons, Perry, but I can't see or smell any soup,' Clara said.

'Crikey, we've got to serve ourselves,' Minnie said and pointed to the long sideboard. 'There's a big pot of something with a lid on and soup bowls next to it.'

Grace and Clara were on their feet immediately. 'We'll serve, you stay where you are; it'll be simpler that way,' Clara said, and nobody argued.

The soup, leek and potato, was delicious and there wasn't a drop left in the tureen by the time they'd finished.

They were then served bubble and squeak – a delicious combination of mashed potato and cabbage – accompanied by a slice of rabbit pie and rich brown gravy. Simple fare, but expertly cooked and as good as anything you'd get in an expensive hotel. Dessert was baked apples and custard which was equally splendid.

No alcohol had been served but nobody complained. It was washed down with mugs of tea.

'Wherever did Mrs Beavis get mugs?' Clara asked him. 'I don't believe anything as plebeian as these has ever appeared on this table before.'

'She's a resourceful woman and worth every penny. I'm going to suggest that you girls take the sofas and chairs and we chaps can sit round the table and have a game of cards.'

'Why don't we play board games? We all like Monopoly and we could play in pairs.'

He laughed. 'If you can find that game anywhere, I'll eat my hat. I've got a pack of cards upstairs as I doubt you'll even find any of those here. This house has been occupied for decades by a spinster living on her own.'

Eileen had overheard this conversation and like a conjurer producing a rabbit from a black top hat, she delved under her chair and handed Clara a parcel wrapped in brown paper and fastened by string.

'This is from Ben and me; he won't mind if I give it to you without him being here.'

Perry sat back and allowed Clara to neatly untie the string and fold back the paper. Nobody wasted anything nowadays.

'Monopoly. Look, it's the ideal wedding present. How perfect is that?'

Chris chuckled. 'Really? I think they might well be spending their evenings doing something a little more interesting than playing Monopoly.'

His wife, Grace, frowned. 'We might have been thinking that, but you certainly shouldn't have said it out loud.'

Fortunately, the awkward moment was defused by Sam. 'I'm not being banker – anyone else volunteering?'

* * *

The remainder of the afternoon was spent playing the ridiculous game and Eileen and Minnie eventually bankrupted everybody and were declared the winners. At times, they'd been crying with laughter, and Perry had enjoyed himself as much as everyone else, which had surprised him.

'We have to be at the hotel by six; it's not far but we need to allow fifteen minutes. This evening, of course, is my treat.' Perry was looking forward to spending the remainder of the day with Clara's friends but he'd hoped to be spending it quite differently and with no one but his beloved girl.

They automatically divided into their pairs, so he was able to walk with Clara in the dark, freezing December evening.

'I can't think of a better way to have spent today, darling Perry; it was so good to catch up with everyone. You outrank all of us, don't you?'

'Chris is the equivalent rank to me. We've got a lot in common as he's no longer flying and is permanently based at Bentley Priory.'

'But you'll be back on the front line at some point and he won't.'

She sounded so wretched, he regretted having mentioned it. 'Someone of my rank won't be leading from the front, my love; I'll possibly be in the field but not at the front.'

'I'm not sure I believe you, but I don't want to think about what could happen as it's not going to be for at least a year.'

So hard for the women left behind as they waited and worried about their sons, brothers, fathers, husbands, and lovers. War was 90 per cent boredom and 10 per cent terror but being a civilian on the home front was worry, rationing and hardship.

There was a shout behind them and he stopped and shone his torch back. Sam was on the ground and Ruth wasn't helping him up but leaning against a lamppost laughing.

The others also stopped and as the combined beams of the torches puddled around the fallen man, Chris offered to assist. Sam was laughing and making no attempt to get up.

'My bloody stick got stuck in the pavement and tripped me up. I broke it as I fell.'

Chris leaned down and heaved Sam to his feet. 'I'm not hurt, thanks for asking,' Sam said and his sarcasm made Ruth laugh even more.

'I'm sorry, but it was so funny. Only your dignity suffered.'

'And my stick,' Sam said sadly as he waved the two pieces about.

Perry moved closer. 'Can you manage without it? There's an elephant's foot full of them back at the house. I can fetch one if you need it.'

'I was told by the quack to use one but really I don't need it. My ankle's fine and the bloody stick's more trouble than it's worth.'

'In which case, shall we continue? We don't want to be late,' Clara said from the darkness ahead.

The head waiter was waiting for them and conducted them to the beautifully presented breakfast room.

'This looks lovely,' Clara said and squeezed Perry's hand. 'They've gone to so much trouble to make this a celebration meal. Silver candelabra, silver cutlery, crystal...'

'And too many blooming knives and forks,' Minnie said, laughing. 'Don't worry, I've learned which is what, and won't use a fish knife to butter the bread.'

Without being told they were one less, the waiter quickly removed what wasn't wanted from the table.

Their coats and so on were taken from them and as soon as they were seated, the waiter was beside him.

'Tonight, we have egg mayonnaise, sole meuniere followed by chicken chasseur and for dessert, a gateau especially made to celebrate this wonderful occasion.'

'Thank you. I'll leave the choice of wines to you. Champagne with the dessert, if possible,' Perry said.

'Already on ice, sir. Coffee, brandy and petits fours to end the meal.'

Clara's smile was bright. 'That sounds perfect, thank you so much for arranging this for us.'

The head chap nodded, beamed and stepped aside so the waiters could serve the first course. Everything was delicious, and nothing was rushed.

It was nine o'clock when they were eventually relaxing over coffee and brandy.

'That cake was scrumptious,' Grace said, and the other guests agreed. 'Real cream, glacé fruit and chocolate to decorate the top, such a treat.'

'I'm glad you enjoyed tonight as tomorrow's reception will be much simpler. Expect sandwiches, sausage rolls and maybe, if we're lucky, cheese straws.'

'It doesn't matter, nobody will care; they've come to see us get married, not to eat a sumptuous buffet. Will there be any alcohol? That always help things along.'

'Barney – it's his great-aunt's house that we live in – gave me permission to raid the wine cellar so there'll be a glass of something decent for the toast. Mrs Beavis said I could take a dozen bottles as a wedding present. Not really hers to give but I wasn't going to argue. Don't look so disapproving, darling; I'm a very generous tenant.'

They were talking quietly to each other, as were the other couples. Chris tapped his glass with his spoon and got to his feet. 'I'd like to make a toast to the happy couple. To Perry and Clara: may they be as happy as Grace and I are.'

They clinked glasses and repeated the toast. Then Chris remained on his feet and looked directly at Clara. 'I know you don't have any family coming tomorrow, I know you've only just met me, but if you'd like me to escort you down the aisle tomorrow, it would be my absolute honour.'

Perry's pleasure in the occasion sank to his boots. Why the hell hadn't he thought of this?

'That would be so kind of you. I was rather dreading walking down on my own tomorrow.'

'That's settled then.' Chris sat down, and his lovely wife kissed him. It was obviously her idea.

'If you don't have a best man, Perry, I'd be happy

to stand with you, even though I'll be the only one in mufti,' Sam offered.

Perry banged his head on the table, making everybody laugh. He sat up smiling. 'I appear to have forgotten two of the most important aspects our wedding. You must think I'm an absolute idiot, Clara.'

'I think I'm as much to blame as you, as I really should have thought about who was going to walk me down the aisle and mentioned it weeks ago. I suppose because we're marrying in uniform, no family coming, just friends, it's hardly surprising we forgot some of the formalities.'

Nobody had room for the petits fours but the hotel kindly packed them in a small box so that they could take them away with them. Whilst Perry went to settle the bill, the others got into their outdoor garments. He was pleasantly surprised at the amount and thought it was worth every penny and happily added a generous tip.

As they made their way back through the blackout, their voices were loud and their laughter even louder and he couldn't have been happier.

'I'm not sharing with Minnie as she wants to be with Eileen. They used to be best friends but haven't seen each other for a while and are desperate to catch up.'

Perry caught his breath. 'Does that mean that you'll be on your own tonight?'

'I will, and I intend to remain that way. We've got the rest of our lives to be together and this is one tradition I want to respect.'

* * *

Clara had a sudden urge to drink cocoa despite being full to bursting. As soon as they were all inside, she asked the others. Everybody said yes.

'You girls take a pew,' Perry said. 'We chaps will venture downstairs and return triumphant.'

Eileen and Minnie sat at the table talking quietly, Ruth wandered off, which left Clara and Grace to sink into the comfortable sofa.

'I'm having a baby next summer and you're the first person I've told,' Grace said.

'How wonderful. Have you resigned your commission?'

'Yes, I leave after Christmas and can live with Chris.'

Clara decided to tell Grace about her and Perry. Her friend wasn't shocked. 'Do you think you could be expecting too?'

'I'm not sure. I went two months then had a day

and nothing since. I did wonder if I might have got it wrong. But I don't have any of the symptoms.'

Grace laughed. 'I bet you are. Wouldn't it be lovely for our children to grow up together?'

There was no time for further conversation as Ruth rejoined them and a few minutes later, the cocoa arrived.

* * *

Clara retired immediately after the cocoa had been consumed, said a brief goodnight to the guests and firmly locked the door just in case Perry ignored her request. If he actually came into her bedroom then she wouldn't be able to send him away, so far better to prevent this happening.

Her smart uniform was hanging in the wardrobe and tomorrow, she'd be wearing silk stockings and French cami-knickers: a gift from Grace. Eileen had given her a delicious silk nightdress and matching dressing gown that clung in all the right places.

She glowed all over at the thought of how little time she'd actually be wearing this garment to-morrow night. She would technically be improperly dressed without her hideous lisle stockings, giant bra and knee-length bloomers but she was quite sure nobody was going to check her undergarments on her wedding day apart from her new husband.

She giggled and wasn't sure if it was excitement or the two glasses of wine that she'd had with her meal. As she sat down, her head spun. She'd obviously had more to drink than she thought. She'd be more careful tomorrow as she didn't want to miss a moment of her wedding night.

After a few hours, she woke up and slipped out of her bedroom and made her way to the bathroom wearing her new nightwear. The house was silent. Clara stood for a few moments breathing in the atmosphere, hardly able to believe that this was going to be her home for the next year at least.

As she reached out to open her door, there was a scuffling noise and something shot through her legs. She screamed. The sound echoed in the quiet house and inevitably, doors flew open and her guests, in various stages of undress, burst into the passageway.

Chris and Sam were in their underwear and both holding torches. The girls had dragged on their greatcoats but didn't have their torches. Perry was stark naked. He'd obviously forgotten there were others sleeping in the house tonight.

She shone her torch away from him but was pretty sure everybody had seen that he was in his birthday suit even though no one commented. 'I'm fine, something startled me. I'm really sorry to have woken you all up. I'm pretty sure it was the cat but I'd forgotten we had one for a second.'

There was a chorus of goodnights and the doors closed. She shone her torch at Perry's room at the far end of the corridor; his door was still open. He reappeared decently covered in his pants with an apologetic smile.

'I'm so sorry, I didn't think. When I heard you scream...'

'It's fortunate that all our friends are broadminded and that the old ladies sleep in the basement as I doubt they'd ever recover. The cat went into my room.'

'Don't you like cats?'

'I love them but I can think of only one reason he went in like a rocket and that's because he was chasing a mouse, or even worse, a rat. I'm absolutely not going in there until I know it's rodent free.'

The light in his bedroom was on and she saw his wicked smile. 'As we've already broken the rule that brides and grooms shouldn't see each other on their wedding day until the ceremony, why don't you come in with me?'

She was about to firmly refuse when she heard

squeaking and crashing somewhere in her bedroom and shuddered. 'I don't have a choice.' She shivered and this time, it was anticipation, not disgust at the thought of mice roaming about where she might tread on them.

In two strides, he was close, picked her up and almost ran back to his room – which would also be hers from now on.

She reached over his shoulder and pushed the door shut, not at all embarrassed that her friends would know where she was sleeping. They were adults and understood things like this happened when you were as desperately in love as she and Perry were.

He didn't toss her on the bed as some men might have done but gently put her on her feet. Then he ran his hand down her arm. 'I absolutely adore your negligée. Do you mind if I remove it?'

She looked up at him, trying not to laugh. 'I don't mind at all. It seems a shame to get it creased when it's new.'

'We sound ridiculous, don't we? I'm trying not to overwhelm you – it's been weeks since we made love and I've thought of little else these past days.'

'Then I'll make it easier for you. I'll take them off myself.'

She moved a short distance away from him and deliberately, slowly, removed the outer garment which puddled around her feet in a shimmering mass of blue silk. Then she pushed the straps of the nightdress down her arms, keeping her eyes fixed firmly on his face as she did so.

His eyes were dark, the tell-tale flush of desire across his cheekbones. He was tense. His hands clenched. She loved that just watching her undress had such a powerful effect on him.

As the item slithered down her overheated body, he growled – at least that's what it sounded like. She closed the short distance between them and expected him to tumble her between the sheets but for some inexplicable and disappointing reason, he remained where he was.

He was looking at her differently, his eyes still dark but he was less tense.

Slowly, he stood up, reached out and cupped her breasts. 'These have changed. In fact, you look different. Are you quite sure you're not pregnant?'

This was the last thing she'd expected him to say. 'I didn't think so, but Grace made me wonder.'

He laughed and tenderly drew her down to sit next to him on the bed. 'When is your next one due?'

'I've no idea; I can go anything from four to six

weeks between them. I think it's probably three months since I had a normal one.'

'I'm not an expert, but I've been doing some reading about the subject, and I think – no, I'm sure – that we're having a baby.'

Clara looked down at herself and for the first time, she noticed that her nipples were darker, larger somehow and her breasts were definitely bigger and they were more sensitive.

'That means I can live here with you; I can leave the ATS and we can be a family until you have to go.'

Her hair was still in its night-time braid and he slowly released it. 'Imagine it, my darling, next summer there'll be three of us. Are you as happy as I am?'

'I am. I'll be even happier if you stop talking and kiss me.'

EPILOGUE

Perry stood beside his beloved Clara in the freezing chapel waiting to exchange their vows and it was he that was shaking, not her. She glanced up at him, her smile radiant.

'I love you, my darling, and can't wait to be your wife.'

'Then let's get on with it.' He nodded to the ancient vicar and the service began. He scarcely knew what he was saying and then he was sliding the ring over his wife's finger.

He pulled her into his arms and was about to kiss her when she whispered, 'Please can we go now?' She shifted uncomfortably and he grinned as he guessed her predicament.

'We certainly can.' He kissed her lightly and then, hand in hand, they ran down the chapel and burst out into the weak December sunshine. No confetti, no rose petals, certainly no rice, so no need to hang about.

'Next door will be quickest,' he said and laughing they raced up the steps and raised several eyebrows in the War Office as they skidded to a halt outside the ladies'.

Less than ten minutes after abandoning their guests, they rejoined them milling about outside the chapel.

'Come on, follow me, the church hall is just around the corner,' Perry called out. Surrounded by their friends, he and Clara dashed for the warmth of the hall. They stepped into a small vestibule and then into the main room itself.

'Look at that,' Clara gasped. 'Flowers, balloons, streamers, even a cardboard wedding cake. This is the most perfect wedding ever.'

He pulled her close and kissed her tenderly. 'And you are the most perfect bride and I'm the happiest man in the world.'

BIBLIOGRAPHY

Girls in Khaki by Barbara Green

Sergeant Elsie by M. Crossley

Sisters in Arms by Vee Robinson

Army Girls by Tessa Dunlop

Farming, Fighting and Family by Miranda McCormick

The Girls Who Went to War by Duncan Barrett and Nuala Green

Wartime Women by Dorothy Sheridan

The Girls Behind the Guns by Dorothy Brewer Kent

The Women's Royal Army Corps by Shelford Bidwell

A to Z Atlas Guide to London by Alexander Gross FRGS

Wartime Britain 1939–1945 by Juliet Gardiner

How We Lived Then by Norman Longmate

The War Illustrated News edited by Sir John Hammerton

BBC History Archives

It's a Long Way to Tooting Broadway by Reginald Cambridge

The War Diaries of Colin Dunford Wood edited by James Dunford Wood

An Englishman at War: The Wartime Diaries of Stanley Christopher DSO, MC, TD, 1939–45 edited by James Holland

Oxford Dictionary of Slang by John Ayto

ACKNOWLEDGEMENTS

I've enjoyed writing this four-book series about the Army Girls and hope you've enjoyed reading about them. The ATS were the biggest service and at one point, there were over 400,000 women and girls serving. Princess Elizabeth, a driver, and Mary Churchill, behind the guns, were the most famous. We owe a lot to these brave women.

ABOUT THE AUTHOR

Fenella J. Miller is the bestselling writer of over eighteen historical sagas. She also has a passion for Regency romantic adventures and has published over fifty to great acclaim. Her father was a Yorkshireman and her mother the daughter of a Rajah. She lives in a small village in Essex with her British Shorthair cat.

Sign up to Fenella J. Miller's mailing list for news, competitions and updates on future books.

Visit Fenella's website: www.fenellajmiller.co.uk

Follow Fenella on social media here:

facebook.com/fenella.miller
x.com/fenellawriter

ALSO BY FENELLA J. MILLER

Goodwill House Series

The War Girls of Goodwill House

New Recruits at Goodwill House

Duty Calls at Goodwill House

The Land Girls of Goodwill House

A Wartime Reunion at Goodwill House

Wedding Bells at Goodwill House

A Christmas Baby at Goodwill House

The Army Girls Series

Army Girls Reporting For Duty

Army Girls: Heartbreak and Hope

Army Girls: Behind the Guns

Army Girls: Operation Winter Wedding

The Pilot's Girl Series

The Pilot's Girl

A Wedding for the Pilot's Girl

A Dilemma for the Pilot's Girl

A Second Chance for the Pilot's Girl

The Nightingale Family Series

A Pocketful of Pennies

A Capful of Courage

A Basket Full of Babies

A Home Full of Hope

Standalone

The Land Girl's Secret

Sixpence Stories

Introducing Sixpence Stories!

Discover page-turning historical novels from your favourite authors, meet new friends and be transported back in time.

Join our book club Facebook group

https://bit.ly/SixpenceGroup

Sign up to our newsletter

https://bit.ly/SixpenceNews

Boldwood

Boldwood Books is an award-winning fiction publishing company seeking out the best stories from around the world.

Find out more at www.boldwoodbooks.com

Join our reader community for brilliant books, competitions and offers!

Follow us
@BoldwoodBooks
@TheBoldBookClub

Sign up to our weekly deals newsletter

https://bit.ly/BoldwoodBNewsletter

www.ingramcontent.com/pod-product-compliance
Lightning Source LLC
Chambersburg PA
CBHW010659100726
47900CB00010B/2727

* 9 7 8 1 8 0 5 4 9 2 8 1 8 *